THIS BOOK BELONGS TO

_____

THE DOOR BY THE STAIRCASE

THE DOOR BY THE STAIRCASE

KATHERINE MARSH

WITH ILLUSTRATIONS BY
KELLY MURPHY

Disney • Hyperion

LOS ANGELES NEW YORK

First Edition, January 2016
10 9 8 7 6 5 4 3 2 1
FAC-020093-15196

Printed in the United States of America

Library of Congress Cataloging-in-Publication Data
Marsh, Katherine.
The door by the staircase / Katherine Marsh.—First edition.
pages cm
Summary: Happy to be adopted at last, twelve-year-old orphan
Mary Hayes soon learns a terrifying secret about her new mother,
the mysterious Madame Z.
ISBN 978-1-4231-3499-2—ISBN 1-4231-3499-0
1. Baba Yaga (Legendary character)—Juvenile fiction. [1. Baba Yaga
(Legendary character)—Fiction. 2. Witches—Fiction. 3. Adoption—
Fiction. 4. Orphans—Fiction.] I. Title.
PZ7.M353235Do 2015

Reinforced binding
Visit www.DisneyBooks.com

THIS LABEL APPLIES TO TEXT STOCK

FOR JULIAN, SASHA,
AND NATALIA—*MOYA SEMYA*

FOR LYDA—*MOYA PADROOGA*

ONE

JUST AFTER MIDNIGHT, Mary Hayes crept into the kitchen of the Buffalo Asylum for Young Ladies and opened a small door on the side of the enormous cast-iron stove. Then she took a deep breath and shoved herself inside.

A chilly October wind blew across Lake Erie, but the stove was not fired up. Mrs. Boot was always telling Mary and the other orphans that cold was good for them—that it toughened them up. But Mary had recently learned from one of the older girls that Mrs. Boot did not keep the stove lit at night so that she could pocket the money she saved on fuel. It was this seemingly dismal bit of news that had given Mary an idea.

Even for a skinny twelve-year-old, the clean-out door was

a tight fit. But the worst part wasn't squeezing herself through it, or even the pitch-blackness when she closed the door behind her. It was the smoky carbon smell. For a moment, Mary found herself thinking about her brother, Caleb. He had been just thirteen months older, and her best friend. It was he who had taught her to read and who had given her *Grimm's Household Tales*, the book she had sneaked out of the bedroom they shared on the night of the fire. It was this book that had saved her life.

The *Household Tales* lay inside her shoulder bag, tucked snugly against her. The book was her most cherished possession now that Caleb and her mother were gone. But it was a poor substitute for a family. The acrid smell of soot made her eyes sting. Or was it the memory of her mother, an arm around each of them before bed, calling one her heart, the other her soul? Mary was never quite sure which one she was, only that there was a power in their being three. She murmured her mother's words—*my heart, my soul*—but they just made her feel worse. Her forehead slid onto her knees. At least the dark stove seemed the right place to mourn, curled into a fetal ball in its cast-iron belly of ashes.

It was tempting to stay like this forever; but Mary knew it was only a matter of time before Mrs. Boot realized she was missing and went looking for her. So after a few minutes she sat up, wiped away her tears, and began to hunt in the dark, feeling blindly along the crusty sides of the stove until she found what she was looking for—the pipe that led up into the chimney.

The opening of the pipe was narrow and round. She pushed her bag, with her copy of *Household Tales*, up through the pipe, then stuck in her head. But she had to press the soles of her boots against the sides of the stove to wedge her shoulders through. After an uncomfortably tight squeeze, she popped into the flue. She wriggled all the way out of the pipe and began to shimmy her way up, using her elbows and knees. But as the smell of soot grew stronger, she felt a stab of breathless panic. She had read stories in the newspaper about chimney sweeps, boy apprentices even smaller than she, who had suffocated trying to clean inside the tight flues. Her palms felt sweaty and slick against the brick, and her heart pounded as she imagined a similar fate. The stove would start to smoke and Mrs. Boot would complain that something—a dead animal, perhaps—was blocking the chimney. Eventually, they would find her blackened body. Mary's breath came in ragged gasps, and she struggled to control her trembling, which for once wasn't from the cold or the threat of Mrs. Boot's switch.

But turning back wasn't an option. For the first four years after the fire, she had lived at an orphanage for younger girls, where she had been kept warm and decently fed in the hope that one of the wealthy couples who sometimes came through would adopt her. But the few girls who were adopted were cheerful and eager to please. Even their straight, tightly braided hair seemed obedient. Mary had wild brown curls and clung to a battered copy of Grimm's fairy tales—she seemed too bookish, too sly. And here, among the older girls, there was no such hope. No one ever came to adopt. If the girls were lucky enough to survive the cold and the meager portions, Mrs. Boot might find them a job at a textile factory. But Mary wasn't going to be one of the lucky ones—Mrs. Boot had taken an instant disliking to her. Within weeks of arriving, Mary had realized that her only chance at a better life was to flee, preferably before winter.

Counting silently to distract herself, Mary climbed farther up the flue. Her knees and elbows scraped against the blackened brick as she shoved herself upward. Once, a patch of hardened creosote gave way, and she nearly fell before catching herself by jamming her knees and elbows out to stop her. She was certain she was bleeding, but she dared not look. As the flue narrowed, her shoulder bag wedged against her. Her head began to feel thick and heavy from the smell of soot. How far, she wondered, could the chimney cap be?

At just that moment, the crown of Mary's head smashed against something hard. She worked one arm up and felt a small steel square. She tried to shove it open, but it wouldn't give. "Come on," she whispered. She banged on it with her fist. Her heart began to race as she realized that after all this way, she was locked in, trapped. In a moment of terror, she butted the cap with her head.

It popped open. Mary stifled a cry of relief as cold, fresh air flooded her lungs. The moonlight was so bright it made her blink. She scrambled out of the chimney and gave herself a quick once-over. Her dress was torn at the elbows, and the exposed skin was scraped and bloody. She had left her coat behind, afraid she couldn't fit through the chimney with the extra layer of clothing. But now, shivering on the roof in the chilly October night, Mary regretted leaving it behind. Her knees, like her elbows, glistened darkly with blood where she had skinned them. Her hands and dress were blackened by soot, and she could feel a layer of it on her face as well. But this Mary did not mind. It would help camouflage her during the next, dangerous step.

She sprinted to the edge of the roof. A drainpipe ran down the side of the building, right by Mrs. Boot's bedroom window. Mary quietly lowered herself, until she was clinging to it with her hands and knees. The drainpipe creaked, and her pulse quickened as she wondered if it would bear her weight. When the pipe didn't pull away, she took a breath and slowly, inch by inch, slid down it. Just before she reached Mrs. Boot's window, she stopped. The shade was drawn and the light was off. As silently as possible, Mary slid past, allowing herself to pick up speed—until a few feet from the ground, she let go and jumped. She landed, catlike, on her feet.

Mary pressed herself flat against the wall of the orphanage, looking for lights or witnesses. But it was past midnight, and the normally busy city street was deserted. She looked up one last time at the Buffalo Asylum for Young Ladies to make sure all the windows were dark.

Just then a whistling, whirring sound filled the air. Mary swung around. Down the street, the wind was gathering into a funnel, swirling up leaves and bits of trash. Mary had spent her entire life in Buffalo. She knew the icy winds and the heavy autumn snows, but she had never seen anything like this. Her breath quickened, and she could feel the blood drain out of her fingers as she watched the funnel grow. When it was as tall as a two-story building, it began to blow toward her down the center of the street. She willed herself to run, but she was paralyzed, her legs frozen and her eyes fixed on the advancing twister. There was something almost human about how it undulated from side to side, like a giant shifting its weight. She could feel her curls flying around her face, her thin dress twisting around her legs, as the wind drew near. She instinctively flattened herself against the brick wall of the asylum and closed her eyes.

And then, suddenly, the whistling, whirring noise grew quieter, changing to a low hum. Mary opened her eyes. The whirlwind was only a few feet away from her. It spun in place. The top of its funnel bent down as if it were studying her. Mary kept as still as she could, her every muscle tense. She knew she had to do something.

She stared up at the funnel. "Go on, then."

From inside the whirlwind, she thought she heard a robust laugh. Then the whistling noise started up and the whirlwind backed away from her.

But just as she took a step, the whirlwind picked up speed and hurled itself against Mrs. Boot's window. A light turned on, and the matron's head emerged.

"Mary, you little witch!"

Mary tried to run, but the whirlwind pinned her against the wall with its furious gusts like a pair of strong hands. A minute later, the door opened and Mrs. Boot charged out like a small, angry bull and seized her by the arm.

"The wind!" Mary shouted, although she would have been quite happy if Mrs. Boot were swept away forever.

But the moment Mary said it, she realized the wind was already gone. There was no funnel, no driving gust, just a light and invisible breeze.

With her free hand, Mrs. Boot walloped Mary over the head. "Don't try to trick me."

Mrs. Boot marched her inside, wrenching her arm painfully as she dragged her up the stairs. But instead of taking Mary back to bed, Mrs. Boot shoved her into a storage room that housed mops, brooms, washboards, and buckets.

"Tomorrow I'll chain the clean-out door of the stove closed," she said, jabbing a fat finger into Mary's sooty face. "And then I'll whip you in front of the others."

She slammed the door and locked it behind her. Mary ran to the storage room's single window, but it had been welded shut. Although she could see the street a story below, there was no way to reach it.

"I hate you!" she shouted to the whirlwind, not at all caring if Mrs. Boot thought Mary was talking to her. She threw a punch into the air, imagining she could strike the funnel. Then she curled up on the floor, resting her head on top of her shoulder bag and the copy of *Household Tales* inside it, and cried herself to sleep.

TWO

MARY WAS AWAKENED by sunlight streaming through the window. The events of the previous night came rushing back. Stiffly, she stood up and looked outside. The street was once again crowded with factory workers, migrants, boatmen, stevedores, and peddlers. But there was one curious sight. A gig was parked directly in front of the Asylum for Young Ladies, and an enormous golden-brown horse stomped impatiently in front of it and shook its mane. Mary wondered whom it belonged to. She hoped it wasn't an undertaker and that one of the girls hadn't perished during the night. But before she could think more about it, she heard the click of the lock, and the door swung open.

"Mary Hayes!"

At the sound of Mrs. Boot's shrill voice, Mary covered her backside as she remembered the whipping the matron had promised.

"She has no family at all, poor *devochka*?" said a woman's voice in a thick foreign accent.

It was only then that Mary realized someone else had joined them. The woman was wrinkled and hunched, with a long nose and big ears that had clearly continued to grow while the rest of her had shriveled. She wore her silver hair braided and coiled into a bun. One gnarled hand clutched a simple birch cane. Yet despite her obvious age and frailty, her wide-set gray eyes were keen. They flashed at Mary above a pair of sharp cheekbones.

"Her father died before she was born," Mrs. Boot said. "Her mother and brother died in a fire. The naughty imp sneaked out of bed to read. Otherwise, she'd be with them."

Mary winced at the memory. They had lived in a boarding-house—her mother was a seamstress, and a single room was all she could afford. Another lodger had given Caleb the *Household Tales*, and he had used the simplest stories, such as "The Nail," to teach Mary to read. Knowing how to turn letters into words had seemed a wonderful kind of power . . . until that horrible September night. She had sneaked out to the porch to read the tale of the straw, the coal, and the bean that escaped a fire. She didn't remember falling asleep, only being awakened by the smell of smoke. Dashing inside, she had found a wall of flames blocking the single staircase. She would never forget those powerless moments of shouting Caleb's and her mother's names, pleading for others to help. But there had been no way to save them.

"She is completely alone, then," the old woman said, shaking her head ruefully.

"Yes," Mrs. Boot said, affecting a businesslike tone. "And I am happy to get rid of her. But if you want an older girl, I have plenty of other, more obedient ones."

Mary snapped out of the terrible memory of that night as she realized what was happening. The old woman meant to adopt her. Mary had no idea who she was, but she realized the miraculous opportunity before her. She wasn't going to allow this last, precious chance to slip away.

"No!" Mary said. "Take me! It's me you want."

The old woman grinned, seemingly amused by Mary's enthusiasm. "The child is quite certain," she said.

But Mrs. Boot seemed not to hear her. "She is an idle one, too. She lazes about, reading. Fairy tales. Nonsense. Believe me, I'd love to get rid of her, but you'll end up returning her in days. I have a girl who can clean and cook for you—"

Mary ran to the old woman. "I can clean and cook!"

"Of course you can, *devochka*," the old woman said. Her gray eyes fell on Mary's scraped-up elbows. "But you are thin, aren't you?"

A flicker of hesitation crossed the old woman's face. Mary was determined not to let her change her mind. "Thin but strong! And I am clever, too."

"Clever enough to escape," Mrs. Boot said. "She will run away, just like she did last night, and then you'll be back looking for another girl—"

"I *won't* run away," Mary said, adding under her breath, "as long as I am well treated."

"Impertinent, too!" Mrs. Boot said. "Look, madam, a woman your age cannot go chasing after a runaway in the middle of the night. I have a simple girl, strong as an ox, perfect to help with your infirmities."

The old woman inhaled deeply through a pair of large nostrils as if she were summoning the patience to deal with Mrs. Boot. "No, *nyet*, my dear lady. I want *this* one." She beckoned to Mary. "Come, child, I'm taking you home." Then she turned and hobbled toward the door, tapping her birch cane in front of her.

Mary could hardly believe her ears. *Home.* For four years, she had longed to hear this word. She didn't even care what kind of home it was—rich or poor, large or small. Before Mrs. Boot could stop her, she slung her shoulder bag over her head and raced after her new guardian, past the curious faces of the other girls. She didn't even stop to get her coat—afraid any delay might change her fortune—but stayed close by the old woman's heels, following her out the door.

On the street, the wind sent men's hats flying. Mary half-feared it might blow away the old woman, too, but she appeared no more bent in the strong wind than she had inside. In fact, she seemed less feeble now, holding up her cane and scuttling toward the gig as if she feared Mrs. Boot might yet chase after her and again try to change her mind. She unhitched the golden-brown horse, who thrust up his head, stared at Mary, and snorted a hot, steamy cloud.

"His name is Sivka," the old woman said, "after his color.

And I am Madame Zolotaya. But you, *devochka*, may call me Madame Z."

"I am Mary," Mary said, unsure whether Madame Z knew her name. "You sound as if you're from someplace far away."

"I am from a land that was once next to Russia, *devochka*. But I live in America now, in a small yet interesting town. It's not so far."

Madame Z stepped up into the gig and patted the seat beside her. Mary climbed in, and when she sat down, she noticed that Madame Z had produced a fur wrap, which she proceeded to drape over Mary. "It will do for now," she said.

It would more than do. Mary's coat had been threadbare and too short. The fur wrap was toasty and warm. "Thank you," she said.

At the sound of a piercing whistle from Madame Z, Sivka trotted off. Mary's stomach rumbled, and she realized she had not eaten anything since the previous day.

Although the noise was very soft, Madame Z seemed to hear it. She pulled an entire loaf of black bread and two hard-boiled eggs from beneath the bench and handed them to Mary.

"But I couldn't possibly eat all this," Mary lied. "Would you like some?"

She held out an egg. Madame Z stared down at it. Mary thought she looked a bit hungry, but she shook her head. "All yours, *devochka*. I'd rather save up my appetite for later."

Mary couldn't believe her new guardian's generosity. She wolfed down the bread and eggs, enjoying the unfamiliar feeling of a full stomach. By this time, her birthplace—with its

mansions and breweries, canal and railroads—was behind her. The gig raced along a post road that wended past orchards, pumpkin fields, stone farmhouses, and rolling hills carpeted with orange and yellow leaves. Madame Z began to sing. Her voice was high and raspy, and Mary could only assume the nonsensical words were some language close to Russian. Before long, the old woman's voice combined with the wind and the warmth of the throw to put her to sleep.

When Mary awoke, the sun was low in the sky, and Madame Z was no longer singing. She held the reins loosely as Sivka, who seemed to know the way, pulled the gig into a town. Mary wondered if they had reached Madame Z's home. She fluttered her eyelids as if she were still asleep, possibly dreaming, but in fact she meant to take a secret look around.

The little town consisted mostly of colorful cottages with spindlework porches, balconies, and gabled roofs, packed tightly together. Men and women, dressed as elegantly as those in the finest neighborhoods of Buffalo, drifted in and out of them. Mary wondered if her new home was some vacation colony for the rich—perhaps a spa town where they went to bathe in healing waters. Her mother had heard of such places from the servants of wealthy households who brought their masters' clothes to her to mend.

Mary spotted a sign hanging outside one of the cottages, rocking gently in the chilly wind: **AURA THE EYE, SHE SEES THE FUTURE**. Next to it was an eye inside a triangle. There were fortune-tellers in Buffalo, too, so at first this did not surprise her. But then she noticed another sign, in front of a cottage with a wand in the window, that read **THE GREAT DEBOSCO, BEHOLD TO BELIEVE!** A magician, right next to a fortune-teller?

While Sivka stopped to let a group of women pass, Mary gazed across the street to see the town's other proprietors. An awning over a black house with red trim advertised **MADAME PETITSA, THE FIRE-EATER**. This one gave her a shiver, not only because she was still deathly afraid of fires but because there was clearly something odd about the town she had awakened in. She forgot all about pretending to be asleep and sat up to study her surroundings. Save for a handful of ordinary establishments such as a hotel and a bank, the town was filled with storefronts that advertised the occult—from mind reading to magic to communicating with the dead.

"Where are we?" Mary asked.

"Iris," Madame Z said with affection. "A town of con artists, fakes, and charlatans."

Although Mary was too old to believe in magic, she somehow felt disappointed. She caught Madame Z looking at her with a grin, as if she knew.

"I didn't think it was real," Mary said.

"Of course you didn't, *devochka*," said Madame Z agreeably. "But many less sensible people do. They believe magic and the occult flourish in Iris, rather than just swindlers and frauds."

"Why do you live here?" Mary asked.

"I don't," Madame Z said. "I live outside town."

She pointed a crooked finger past the last cottage—RUSALINA, SPIRIT GUIDE—to where the road curved toward the setting sun. Mary didn't feel this exactly answered her question, but she decided not to press Madame Z until she knew her a little better. Perhaps she had been one of these fakes herself.

Sivka trotted swiftly out of town. Mary paid careful attention to the route, which was simple; the gig never turned but stayed on the same road, past farms and fields, heading west. After a couple of miles, they reached a white wooden fence. Madame Z scrambled down to open a gate, and they continued until the road dead-ended at the edge of a forest.

Dusk had fallen, and in the fading light, Mary could see a small house set at the edge of flame-colored trees. It had wooden lace shingles, two chimneys—one small and the other large— and an enchanting tower topped by a dome. Rosebushes, still covered with blue-tinged white roses, curled up the railing of a wraparound porch. The forest surrounded the house on the other three sides; it was so close to the house that the tall trees—oaks and pines—seemed to bend over its eaves.

The gig rolled to a stop in front of the house, and an old man emerged from the woods, waving wildly. He was tall and gaunt, with a long, scraggly gray beard and craggy gray eyebrows that hung over pale blue eyes.

"Is that your husband?" Mary asked as the man loped over to them.

"Husband?" Madame Z laughed. "I have no husband, *devochka*. This is Koshchey. He takes care of Sivka for me and lives in a hut in the woods."

"Ah, there she is!" Koshchey cried, enveloping Mary's hands in his own long ones and giving them a squeeze. "The mistress said she was going to find a child to adopt, and I can see she has found the perfect one!"

Mary, who was unaccustomed to flattery, felt herself blush.

"Leave the girl alone," Madame Z said with a tinge of irritation. "Sivka is thirsty."

Koshchey unclasped Mary's hands and bowed toward Madame Z. Then he winked at Mary and ran to unhitch Sivka.

"He overdoes it," Madame Z muttered, stepping down from the gig.

Mary watched Koshchey lead Sivka into the darkening forest. "Where's the stable?" she asked.

"Behind the house," Madame Z said vaguely. "But there will be plenty of time for you to explore later. Come, *devochka*. You must be hungry."

Mary reluctantly shrugged off the toasty fur throw, slung her shoulder bag over her sooty dress, and hopped down to the ground. She followed Madame Z up the stairs and onto the wide porch that encircled her new home like a skirt. There were several chairs fashioned out of knotty boughs, and a tinkling wind chime that Mary guessed was made of ivory. It seemed a pleasant spot, but the autumn chill was growing as night fell. Mary, lacking a coat, was glad when Madame Z opened the front door—which was carved with figures of birds and leaves—and led her inside.

"Welcome, welcome," Madame Z said.

Mary followed her into a candlelit foyer. Enormous silver urns stood as sentries.

"Samovars," Madame Z explained, noticing her gaze. "Native to my land. They heat water for *chai*—tea."

She picked up a bowl lying on the floor and filled it with steaming water, then produced a soft cloth, which she dipped in the water and wrung out. "Wash your hands and face, *devochka*."

Mary obediently cleaned herself, enjoying the feel of the warm cloth, which quickly turned black with soot.

Madame Z gave a little sniff, then nodded. "Better. We will take care of the rest of you later."

After setting the dirty cloth and bowl of water on a side table, she led Mary into another room. As Madame Z scurried about lighting kerosene lamps and starting a fire in the hearth, Mary could see they were in some sort of parlor. The walls were covered in dark, patterned wallpaper of flowers and vines. Dried orange flowers that resembled tiny lanterns poked out of tall vases. Spiders, flies, and other insects encased in honey-colored gobs of amber sat on display on the side tables. A small writing desk with slender, coltish legs, a chair tucked beneath it, occupied one corner. In another corner was a small round dining table. In the front of the room, next to a plain wooden bench, stood a primitive-looking loom as tall as Mary herself.

She was about to reach out and touch it when she sensed a shadow behind her. She turned around to find a gray cat stretching himself in front of the fire. The cat began to wash his paws, then stopped to stare at Mary with gooseberry-green eyes. Mary remembered how Caleb had befriended and fed a stray in the alley behind the boardinghouse. Just as she remembered Caleb doing, she crouched down and held out a hand to the cat, which he sniffed with a regal air.

"What do you think, Yulik?" Madame Z asked him playfully. "Do you like her?"

Yulik meowed in response. Mary, who had never heard a cat meow on command before, applauded.

Madame Z laughed. "Spoken like a true creature of instinct." She pointed Mary toward a sofa. "Let's get you more to eat."

Madame Z disappeared through a doorway that presumably led to the kitchen. A few minutes later, she reappeared with a wooden tray laden with two enormous bowls of stew and an entire loaf of bread. Mary felt her mouth water at the sight of it.

"I regret that this is all I have for tonight," Madame Z said, setting the bowls down at the small round table.

Mary couldn't believe Madame Z was apologizing. She was used to portions a tenth of the size, if not smaller. Even when her mother and Caleb were alive, they had eaten thin soups on many a night. She slipped into a chair across from Madame Z, picked up a large wooden spoon, and devoured the meal. The stew consisted entirely of mushrooms, but it was as rich as any meat dish Mary had ever eaten. She followed Madame Z's lead and used the bread to sop up every drop of the thick brown gravy. Madame Z smiled warmly at her clean bowl.

"Now," she said, "what about a hot bath?"

Mary nodded. The idea was heavenly. Baths had been an ordeal at the Buffalo Asylum for Young Ladies. Mrs. Boot allowed them only once every two weeks, five minutes per girl. The water had always been lukewarm and gray by the time Mary, naked and ashamed in front of the others, had her turn.

Madame Z led her out of the parlor, up the stairs that bisected the foyer, and into a large bathroom. In the center of it was a claw-foot tub filled nearly to the brim with steaming water.

"But when did you have time to fill it?" Mary asked.

"Busy hands never rest," Madame Z said with a smile. She

dipped her own bony one into the water and clucked, seemingly pleased with its temperature.

"Stay as long as you wish, *devochka*," she said. She handed Mary a thick towel and then left, closing the door behind her.

Mary yanked off her soot-stained and torn orphanage dress and, with a deep sigh, stepped into the tub. The water was so hot that, as she lowered herself, it turned her skin pink and tingly. She took the rough cloth and the bar of rosemary-scented soap by the edge of the tub and scrubbed away the last remnants of soot from her scalp and neck. Then she submerged herself completely. Beneath the water, she could feel a welling in her chest, and when she came back up for air, she realized she was crying. She bit her lip so that Madame Z wouldn't hear—it seemed even more embarrassing to cry out of happiness and relief than out of loneliness and fear.

By the time she was out of tears, her fingers were puckered and the water had grown lukewarm. Taking a deep breath, Mary stepped from the tub and dried herself with the thick towel. She was thinking about how it seemed a shame to put her dirty dress back on, when she noticed that Madame Z had left her a flannel nightgown. It was slightly long, as if fashioned for a taller girl. Mary briefly wondered who had worn it before. But when she slipped it over her head, it was so soft and comfortable, its history hardly seemed to matter. She yawned, exhausted to the bone.

When Mary stepped into the hall, Madame Z studied her in the nightgown, then sniffed deeply, as if to check that she was truly clean.

"Better?" Mary asked.

Madame Z squeezed her arm. "Still too thin, but at least you smell like a child now and not a piece of kindling."

She led Mary up a narrow spiral staircase to a small circular room in the cupola. Mary loved it immediately. She had never had a room to herself, having shared a barracks-like space with the other orphans, and before that a single bed with her mother and Caleb. Here, a round window looked out on the forest, and a curved bed reminded Mary of a crescent moon. On top of the bed was a stack of crocheted blankets and another fur throw. She would never be cold.

"Do you need anything else?" Madame Z asked.

"No," Mary said. It thrilled her even to hear such a question. "Thank you."

Yulik darted into the room and leaped up onto the bed.

"The little devil wants to sleep with you," Madame Z said, shaking her head. "That is a first."

Mary scratched the cat under his chin. "I don't mind."

"Good night, *devochka*."

Mary stretched out on the curved bed and stroked Yulik, who purred contentedly. A few minutes later, a door closed on the second floor and the house grew quiet. But Mary couldn't sleep. Part of her feared that if she did, she would wake up back at the Buffalo Asylum for Young Ladies, Madame Z and Iris and the cottage in the woods having all been a dream.

Slipping out of bed, Mary grabbed her shoulder bag and took out the battered copy of *Grimm's Household Tales*. But before she could open it, a light flashed in the forest outside. Mary pressed her nose to the circular window. An orange orb, like a lost sun, was dancing among the branches of the trees. It soared and dove like a firework, flickering, then bursting into flame. Was it someone's lantern, a distant fire, a falling star? Mary watched the light until her lids grew heavy. Tomorrow she would ask Madame Z what it was—there was probably some logical explanation. But tonight she would let it be her own little bit of magic, a sign that she had finally found a home.

Clutching the *Household Tales* tightly to her, she crawled back under the covers of her crescent-shaped bed and fell fast asleep.

THREE

WHEN MARY AWOKE THE NEXT MORNING, her bed, mounded high with blankets, was as warm as an oven. With no Mrs. Boot shouting at her to dress and line up for chores, she allowed herself to luxuriate, yawning, and opening and closing her eyes. At last, she rolled out of bed. Folded neatly on a chair by the window was her dress. Mary picked it up. It had been laundered, and the elbows were patched so carefully that she couldn't even see the seams.

Not even her mother had been able to sew this well, although she felt a little guilty thinking it. But even more wondrous than the quality of the repair was the simple fact that Madame Z had taken the time to do it. Not since Mary's mother died had anyone truly cared how she looked; the people at the orphanage for younger children had tended to her appearance only when they knew someone was coming by who might adopt. Mary put on the patched dress and even tried to pin up her wild hair. Then, humming a bit of the tune she remembered Madame Z singing in the gig, she went downstairs. The foyer looked different in the morning light—the samovars had been moved, and the carved front door was open.

"*Devochka!*" came a voice from outside. "We're on the porch."

Mary found her new guardian sitting in one of the rough-hewn chairs, Yulik stretched out at her feet in the sunlight. The morning was crisp and pleasant. A round table had been positioned in front of the chairs, and one of the stout samovars sat on top of it. Beside it were teacups decorated with birds, a jar of blackberry jam, and a loaf of bread half-covered by a cloth.

"Hungry?" Madame Z asked with a smile.

"Very!" Mary admitted.

She could barely believe it. Her breakfast at the orphanage had been a thin gruel. On Sundays, the girls were each given a piece of stale bread, but there had never been any jam. At home with her mother, their landlady always gave the highest-paying tenants—mostly workingmen from the docks—the largest portions. Her mother had usually split her own piece of bread in two to give to Mary and Caleb.

"*Sadis*, sit," Madame Z said, pointing to the other chair.

As Mary sat down, Madame Z lifted a teacup, filled it from the samovar, and handed it to Mary.

Mary took a sip. The tea had a musty, almost rotten flavor, and her first instinct was to spit it out. But she did not want to be rude, and so she forced herself to swallow it. The flavor seemed to change as it traveled down her throat—mellowing, tasting more like roots and damp earth. With her second sip, the taste grew more varied, as if she were drinking fallen leaves and raindrops and damp bark. By the third sip, she could almost say she liked it.

As Mary drank, Madame Z picked up a silver knife and cut thick slices of bread, which she piled on a plate painted with a picture of a red bird. She put a large spoon into the jam jar and placed it on the plate in front of Mary.

"Go ahead," she said, waving Mary on.

Mary picked up a slice of bread. It was warm, clearly baked that morning. She spread the blackberry jam over it, first in a thin layer and then, with the encouragement of Madame Z, in heaping spoonfuls. The sweetness of the jam complemented the bitter taste of the tea. The pale wind chimes tinkled softly. Madame Z wrapped a black woolen shawl around Mary's shoulders.

"After breakfast, we shall go into Iris," she said. "You need a coat."

Madame Z was giving her all the jam with bread she wanted. Madame Z was going to buy her a coat. Mary felt a welling in her throat.

"Thank you," she said gratefully. "And for washing and mending my dress. I don't know when you found the time."

"Busy hands never rest," Madame Z said. The old woman appeared to like this saying.

A half hour later, they were in the gig, rattling along the rutted road toward town. Madame Z had once again wrapped the fur throw around Mary. Sivka's steamy breath rose in the cool air, and he swished his tail, seeming to enjoy the clear autumn morning as much as Mary did. A tree with leaves so vibrantly orange they seemed on fire made Mary remember what she'd wanted to ask Madame Z.

"Last night I saw something out my window," she said.

Madame Z gave her a sideways glance. "Oh?"

"An orange light."

"Perhaps Koshchey's lantern."

"I don't think so," Mary said. "It was up in the trees."

Madame Z chuckled. "You must have been dreaming, *devochka*."

Mary knew she hadn't been, but Madame Z seemed to be a very rational woman, not one who believed in unexplainable sights. Mary decided not to press her. She would let the orange light remain her own little mystery.

Soon, Iris came into view. The town looked sleepier than it had when she'd seen it at dusk. Some of the cottage storefronts were closed—their all-seeing eyes turned inward—shades pulled down in the living quarters above.

"Atmospherics," said Madame Z, cocking her head at the CLOSED signs. "Magic is supposed to occur only at night. What nonsense."

"You seem to know a lot about it," Mary said. She was beginning to feel more comfortable with Madame Z, as if she could speak freely. "Did you work here once?"

Madame Z just laughed. "No, *devochka*."

"How did you end up here, then? Did you have family here?"

"I have no family," Madame Z said.

Mary studied the old woman's wrinkled face; it betrayed no sadness over this fact. Mary envied her. She seemed perfectly at peace with being alone. But this made Mary wonder why Madame Z had adopted her.

"Why did you adopt me?" Mary asked.

"I've always liked children," Madame Z said with a gleaming smile. "And here no one cares if an old woman like me brings one home. An unusual town, Iris—small yet accepting."

As they pulled up in front of a midnight-blue cottage on a street adjacent to the main one, Mary thought this was undoubtedly true. There were so many odd people in Iris that probably no one blinked an eye at Madame Z's exotic accent or her living with an orphan in the woods. Still, she didn't quite believe Madame Z's reason for adopting her. Mary wondered if the old woman had some other use for a child—perhaps here in town.

Mary looked at the sign hanging from the porch eaves of the midnight-blue cottage: MAGIC AND CURIOSITY SHOP, it read. It seemed a strange place to come for a coat. But Madame Z jumped down from the gig and, after hitching up Sivka, waved for Mary to follow her up the porch stairs and through the door.

The instant she stepped into the shop, Mary's hope for a new coat faded. The front room was like someone's cluttered attic, filled with old and odd objects of every size and kind. There were Indian headdresses, rings of rusty keys, tables laden with wishing stones and wands, musky-smelling animal pelts, anatomical charts, and piles of Oriental rugs. A stuffed bear loomed on its haunches in a corner, its head nearly touching the ceiling. But Mary quickly reminded herself that even a used coat—she was sure there had to be one hidden in all this bric-a-brac—would be better than no coat at all. Plus, it was important to be grateful, especially since Madame Z did not seem especially wealthy.

"Mr. Less," Madame Z called.

There was a rustling sound, and a moment later a man with a bushy beard and striking green eyes emerged from behind a counter.

"Madame Z!" Mr. Less said. "And—?"

"Mary," Mary said.

"I have just adopted her," Madame Z said, beaming proudly. "Her parents, alas, are dead."

Mr. Less shook his head. "The worst sort of parents."

Mary was taken aback. But there was a twinkle in Mr. Less's green eyes.

"She needs a coat," Madame Z said. "Something warm. Pleated and perhaps blue."

"Presentation is important to you," Mr. Less said with a proprietor's knowing nod. "I should be able to find something."

Mr. Less opened a door in the back of his storeroom and disappeared.

"He seems to have everything," Mary said.

"Less is all-purpose," Madame Z said, picking up a white stone egg that rested on a wooden stand and inspecting it. "Moonstone. Very nice."

Mary scanned the tables and counters, which were piled high with scarves, lacquer stacking boxes, old dolls, chess sets, wooden flutes, and other objects, for something that caught her fancy. But what drew her attention was a worn leather boot. She felt a pang of sadness for it—alone, without its mate, its tongue twisted and laces frayed. Who would ever buy a single boot? Just as she was thinking this, the toe of the boot lifted up off the table and tapped twice in an impatient manner. Mary blinked and looked again. The boot was still. But before she could say anything, Mr. Less came bounding through the door of his storeroom with something blue draped over his arms.

Stopping before Mary, he unfurled a double-breasted wool coat that appeared to be in perfect condition—no patches or moth holes, missing buttons or stains. In fact, if Mary hadn't seen the condition of the other objects in Mr. Less's shop, she would have assumed it was new. The coat was her favorite color—a bluish lavender—and the collar was trimmed with soft brown fur.

"Let's see if it fits," Madame Z said. "Try it on, *devochka*."

Mr. Less held it up so that Mary could slip her arms inside. Her fingers brushed against a silky lining, then popped out of the sleeves, which ended just past her wrists. Mary looked down. The coat had a pleated bottom that fell right above her knees. She buttoned it up. It was snug but not too tight, as if the coat had been made just for her.

"It fits perfectly!" she said in amazement.

"So it does," Madame Z said. "Mr. Less, you have done it again. What do I owe you?"

But Mr. Less was not finished. He waded through the bric-a-brac until he reached a large wooden oval affixed to a frame. He flipped it over to reveal a mirror.

"Go ahead, *devochka*," Madame Z said. "Take a look."

Mary ran to the mirror and surveyed herself. Madame Z was right—the blue suited her dark curly hair. But more important than that, she looked cared for and neat, like a girl who had a home. The girl in the mirror looked as though she might cry.

"You are a magician, aren't you?" she said, turning to Mr. Less.

But the proprietor just laughed. "Children need so little to believe," he said, shaking his head.

"It's what makes them so sweet," Madame Z said. "Put this on my tab, Mr. Less."

"Thank you," Mary said to both of them. "Truly."

"It's nothing, *devochka*. *Pora*, let's go."

With a businesslike nod at Mr. Less, Madame Z swept toward the door of the Magic and Curiosity Shop. Hurrying after her, Mary cast a glance at the old boot, but it was motionless.

Outside, in her new coat, Mary felt as warm as on a summer's day. Iris still seemed mostly asleep, although a sprinkling of tourists had appeared, taking morning strolls or darting into the few open shops. Mary felt the urge to join them, to explore. She took an eager step into the street.

Madame Z glanced at her and smiled. "Run along. I can see you wish to look around. I need to pick up some supplies anyway. Meet me back here when the bell tolls eleven."

"I'll be here," Mary promised.

"And, *devochka*—"

"Yes?"

Madame Z shook one bony finger sternly. "Be careful not to fall prey to any frauds or tricksters."

Mary had a home now, and a coat, and she wasn't about to lose either of them in Iris. She could see it was a tricky place. She fully intended to keep her eyes open.

FOUR

WITH MADAME Z'S WARNING IN MIND, Mary set forth to explore Iris. Most of the occult shops were closed, but she amused herself by reading the signs outside them. Next to Mr. Less's shop was **THE VOODOO QUEEN OF NEW ORLEANS**, and across from the Voodoo Queen's cottage was the Reverend Hezekiah, who offered **REMEDIES FOR ALL MANNER OF AILMENTS FROM GOUT TO GRIEF.** A few storefronts down was Dr. Edgar Shepherd, who was not in fact a doctor but a mind reader: THE MAN WHO KNOWS ALL; and Theodosia Spring, Spiritualist, who claimed to speak with ghosts. There were also some ordinary establishments in between—a grocer, a baker, a butcher, a bank. They were all open for business, but they interested Mary less than the others (although she noticed Madame Z stepping into the butcher shop, a hopeful sign of another tasty dinner).

Mary rounded the corner and found herself back on the main street. She steered clear of the fire-eater's black house, then cataloged the many other occult shops: THE FAKIR OF CONSTANTINOPLE, MYSTERIOUS CONJURER OF BYZANTIUM; Sybil von Hapsburg, who advertised **TAROT TRUSTED BY THE KINGS OF EUROPE**; Mr. Yu's Tea Shop (Tea-Leaf Reading Inside), its gables painted red and gold, with a pair of wooden dragons guarding its porch. But what caught Mary's eye was a group of sightseers clustered under the awning of the hotel next to Mr. Yu's Tea Shop. They were watching a man with a gray-streaked beard and wire spectacles who was holding a small rectangular birdcage in both hands. Beside him stood a slender boy who looked to be around Mary's age. The boy was dressed in a dark corduroy jacket and trousers. The plainness of this outfit contrasted with the outlandish top hat perched on his head.

Mary crept a few feet closer, curious, when the boy's eyes alighted on her. He tipped his top hat as if he'd been waiting for her. She knew she should continue on—these were probably the tricksters Madame Z had warned her about—but the boy was now shifting his eyes from her to the cage in the man's hands. "Behold the Illusionist Kagan," he said in a commanding voice. Then he flashed a mischievous grin. Mary had never been able to say no to Caleb when he'd smiled at her like that. She had even stolen a pie for him once, because he had asked and she was smaller and quicker on her feet. The memory of his dimpled grin as he had spurred her on blotted out the world around her until she heard a chirping sound. Her eyes found the cage and a single yellow finch perched inside.

"The cage is here in the material world," the man said. "The bird is here as well. You see them clearly before you."

The boy waved her closer. "Come, miss," he said warmly. "Touch the cage."

Mary found herself walking up to it. The bird inside had fallen silent, frozen on its perch. She reached out a hand and touched the cold wire.

"Does it feel real?" the man asked.

Mary ran her hands over the stiff steel cage. "Yes."

The man turned to the small crowd of spectators. "I have never seen this young lady before. Have you ever seen me?"

"No," Mary said.

The man looked back at his audience. "What she feels with her hands you must trust with your eyes. It is here. It is real. It is . . ."

"Not too close, miss!" the boy said.

Mary jerked around to see the boy raise his hands dramatically as if to shield her from the force of the magic.

"Gone!" cried the illusionist.

The cage vanished, bird and all.

Around her, Mary heard gasps, then ringing applause.

The magician bowed. "Thank you. Tell your friends to come see the Illusionist Kagan, here at ten, two, and six."

The show was over, but Mary did not leave. She was thinking about the birdcage. She had felt it with her own fingers. She imagined Madame Z laughing at her for believing that this little man with the wire spectacles could actually perform magic. She knew it had to be some kind of trick. But how did the illusionist make the entire cage and bird vanish into thin air?

She was so lost in thought that she did not notice the boy until he appeared right in front of her, almost like an illusion himself. He had straight dark hair and pale, lightly freckled skin. He held out his top hat, shaking it gently so she could hear the clink of the coins inside. Mary realized that in her fur-trimmed coat she looked as wealthy as the rest of the sightseers. That was probably why the boy had smiled at her—not out of any genuine interest, but because he was hoping she would give him a few extra coins. But Madame Z hadn't given her pocket money.

"I'm sorry," she said. "I don't have anything."

She expected him not to believe her, to beg and cajole. Instead, he grinned. "Figured as much."

Mary gave him a puzzled look.

"Your boots," he said. "Not a tourist in those."

Mary looked down at her scuffed orphanage boots.

"If you worked for another act, you would have brought a penny or two so as not to arouse suspicion," the boy continued. "So, seeing as you're not competition, miss, who are you? There aren't many children living in this town."

"I'm Mary. I just arrived yesterday with Madame Z. She adopted me."

The boy shook his head. "I don't know a Madame Z. But I've been here just a few weeks myself. I'm Jacob. That's my father." His eyes shifted to the Illusionist Kagan, who was packing various props into a case. Now that the performance was over, Mary noticed that he looked only at the props in front of him, as if the world around him held little interest.

"Why aren't there many kids here?"

"Magicians aren't usually family types," Jacob said. He cocked his head as if trying to figure out what to do with her. "Listen, Mary—I'll make you a deal. You tell me how the trick was done, and I'll give *you* a coin."

Mary tried to think of how the cage and the bird could have disappeared into thin air. Finally, she gave a shrug. "I don't know. Magic?"

Jacob laughed, then leaned in, speaking just above a whisper. "There's no magic in that trick. My father taught it to me long ago. The cage collapses; that's why he must hold it with both hands. I create a diversion." He gave a little bow. "Thank you for your help with that—a girl in danger always does the trick. Then the cage collapses and—whoosh!—he pulls a string that yanks it up his sleeve."

Mary was struck by the trick's cleverness. The illusionist literally had "a trick up his sleeve." But a disturbing thought occurred to her. "What about the bird? It must be killed when the cage collapses."

"It's a stuffed one."

"But I heard it sing!"

"Like this?"

Mary heard a series of chirps. Jacob's lips barely moved, but the sound was coming from his mouth.

"How—?"

"Basic ventriloquism." Jacob reached his hand behind her ear and pulled out a nickel. "But who is tricking whom? Turns out you had money after all."

Mary smiled. "I forgot to check my ears."

He nodded seriously. "Happens to me, too."

He held out his hand and tilted his head over it.

"Nothing's coming," she said.

Jacob sighed dramatically. "Stuck again. Hold out your hand."

He banged the side of his head a few times until several pennies appeared to fall out of his ear into Mary's cupped hand. The sound of her own laughter was almost as surprising to her as the pennies.

"You didn't figure out my father's trick, but now that you know the secret behind it, I need to keep you quiet," Jacob said with a conspiratorial wink. "Four cents should do it, I hope?"

Mary couldn't take four cents—it seemed too much, putting her in Jacob's debt. "You don't need to pay me off," she said. "I won't tell. And besides, now I finally have something to give you."

She reached out to drop the coins into the top hat, but Jacob yanked it away. "Keep them."

Mary wondered if the pennies were fake or whether this was the beginning of some more complicated swindle. But it was also possible that the boy was just being generous. If anything, he seemed a little lonely. She knew what that felt like. Before the fire, Caleb had always been nearby, as comfortable as a shadow.

"Thank you," she said. "I'm from Buffalo, by the way. And you?"

"Not from anywhere, exactly, but I've lived in"—Jacob began to tick off on his fingers—"Chicago, New Orleans, Atlanta, San Francisco, New York."

"So many places! I'd never left Buffalo until yesterday."

"I've been pretty much everywhere," Jacob conceded. But Mary noticed that there was no pride in his voice. If anything, he sounded a little wistful.

"Will you be in Iris long?"

"A few weeks, at least," Jacob said. He was himself again, grinning at Mary as he transferred the coins from his top hat into his pocket. Mary realized that there weren't many—he could scoop them up in one hand. She wished she had the sleight-of-hand skill to slip back the pennies he had given her.

"I should be going," Mary said, "but it was nice to meet you."

With a playful wink, Jacob made the top hat appear to float onto his head. It perched there at a jaunty angle, giving him a raffish look. "Until we meet again," he said with a bow.

Mary giggled. "Good-bye, Jacob."

The bell began to toll eleven. As Mary made her way back to Sivka, she decided she wouldn't tell Madame Z about this strange, charming boy. She did not want to be warned about how he might trick her. She had already made up her mind that his kindness was real.

FIVE

THAT EVENING, Madame Z prepared another scrumptious meal—a creamy cured pork belly, followed by thin pancakes with sweet cottage cheese and raisins fried in butter—blini, Madame Z had called them. After dinner, Madame Z played her balalaika, a three-stringed Russian guitar, and Yulik curled up in Mary's lap. Her stomach full, Mary's thoughts drifted back over the many wonderful moments of the day—her mended dress, her new coat, but most of all, meeting Jacob. It had been a long time since she'd had a friend. At the first orphanage, some of the girls had shied away from her, as if the misfortune of the fire might be catching. Others had teased her for sleeping with the *Household Tales*. Even in the days when she had a family and went to the crowded local school, she'd mostly played with Caleb and his friends, since her mother had made them promise to always stay together.

Mary wondered whether she would see Jacob again, perhaps at school. As she considered this, she realized she had very little sense of what her new guardian expected of her. Madame Z hadn't mentioned anything about school. Mary wondered if this was just a brief welcome before Madame Z assigned her the real work she had brought her home for—such as being a cook or maid.

"Is there work you need me to do?" Mary asked during a lull in the music.

"Work?" Madame Z said, sounding alarmed by the prospect. "Not at all!"

Mary wasn't sure she believed her. Preparing all those fancy dishes seemed like too much for one old woman. "You don't need help with the cooking?"

Madame Z leaped to her feet. "Let me show you something, *devochka*."

She scurried toward the kitchen, waving Mary after her. Mary had not yet been inside it and curiously followed. An enormous brick-and-mortar oven reached from floor to ceiling and took up half the room. It shared a wall—and no doubt a chimney—with the fireplace in the parlor. Madame Z licked her lips and pointed to it. "Let me introduce you to my *pech*. In Russia, almost every home has one."

She opened the arched door to reveal nearly a dozen dishes—from soups to pastries—bubbling and baking inside. Mary inhaled deeply as their delicious odors wafted out. "Tomorrow's supper, cooking slowly," Madame Z said. "You see, I hardly do anything. The *pech* does it all. There is no work here. Just play. You absolutely must join me for meals, but you have no other duties."

Mary delighted at the sound of these unfamiliar words. Mrs. Boot hadn't believed in leisure, only constant work. "How about school?"

"Alas, there are not enough children in Iris to support one."

"So just eat and play? That's it?"

"Eat and play," Madame Z repeated, a wistful look on her face. "Childhood is so short."

Mary couldn't believe the change in her fortune. She had warm clothes, plentiful food, all the time in the world to read and play. She didn't have to go to school. She wasn't going to be a cook or a maid. It almost seemed too good to be true.

The next morning, as Mary came down the stairs, she heard someone banging about in the kitchen. She figured Madame Z was getting a loaf of bread for breakfast out of the *pech* or monitoring the dishes slowly cooking inside.

"Good morning," Mary said, pushing open the door.

But the kitchen was silent. Only a half-chopped cabbage lay on a cutting board. She was tempted to peek into the *pech*, when she heard the clatter of dishes outside. That was it. Madame Z must have been chopping the cabbage when she heard Mary coming down the stairs and had rushed out to the porch with breakfast.

But when Mary stepped out onto the porch, there was no Madame Z, only Yulik balancing on the railing. A cup of hot tea, steam swirling off the top into the cool morning air, and a piping-hot loaf of bread with jam lay on the table. Beneath the jam jar was a note. Mary pulled it out and read it:

Devochka—
Chore to do. Back in an hour.
Mme. Z

Mary must have just missed her. But she didn't mind—it was peaceful eating her breakfast alone. Yulik didn't comment when Mary licked the jam spoon or slurped her tea, which tasted better than yesterday's. After she had polished off the last crumb, it occurred to her that Madame Z's absence was the perfect opportunity to explore the house and learn a little more about her new guardian.

She started her search upstairs, in Madame Z's bedroom, with Yulik prowling beside her. But the room offered little by way of its owner's history. There was a simple birch-frame bed, neatly made, and a dresser. On top of the dresser sat a worn leather halter, an old book with a peeling binding, and a triangular cone of thick black yarn. Mary opened the book, which was written in a different language. Some of the letters were familiar, but there were several she'd never seen before. Mary heard a muffled thump downstairs. She quickly closed the book and put it back on the dresser. She didn't want to be caught snooping, even if Madame Z didn't seem like the type to mind a child's curiosity. But the noise didn't turn into footsteps or Madame Z's voice.

With Yulik at her heels, Mary went back downstairs to explore the kitchen. Although she didn't remember them having been there earlier in the morning, the two samovars sat on the table. Mary took hold of the handles, but she could just barely lift it. Madame Z was stronger than she looked. Other than the samovars, Mary didn't find anything interesting in the kitchen—just a butcher block table, a set of knives, an icebox, and the *pech*.

She ran her hands across the loom in the parlor, strummed the balalaika. Looked at the spiders trapped in the gobs of amber. But she didn't find anything new in the parlor, either. Growing bored, she wandered out to the foyer as Yulik raced in front of her and scratched on the door. She was about to open it for him and join him on the porch when she decided to quickly glance around. That's when she noticed a small door by the staircase.

It was no wonder she had missed it before. It had a keyhole but no knob. She tried to pry open the edge, but it wouldn't budge. When she knocked on the door, the sound was hollow, confirming there was a space behind it. It was likely just a coat closet. But why, then, did Madame Z keep it locked?

Mary went out to the porch and scanned the yard. There was no sign of Madame Z. And anyway, she told herself, even if Madame Z caught her snooping, this was her house now, too. She slipped back inside, took out one of her hairpins, and wedged it into the keyhole. Caleb had taught her this trick (he had used it once to steal a cube of sugar from their landlady's storeroom; Mary still remembered how they had taken turns sucking it). But she could not engage the lock, and the pin came out bent. She pulled out another hairpin and gently prodded it into the lock. But this time it came out dented, no doubt from all her pushing.

With a growing sense of frustration, Mary poked the tip

of her pinkie finger into the hole, hoping to feel the mechanism inside it. Yulik, who had been watching her with interest, meowed plaintively, but she ignored him. She wiggled her finger, wedging in more of it—almost as if she were making the hole bigger. But she felt nothing except warm air. She shoved her finger up and down. It was then that something ridged and sharp pinched it. She acted instinctively, yanking out her finger. But before she could pull it out entirely, she felt a piercing pain, and her pinkie emerged with a tiny gash at the end of it.

Mary stanched her bleeding finger with the hem of her dress. As a small crimson stain began to blossom through the cloth, she couldn't shake the feeling that the keyhole had bitten her.

Footsteps sounded outside. Mary let go of her hem and swung around just as the door opened and Madame Z stepped inside.

"Good morning, *devochka*," she said. She gave a sniff. "Something smells good."

Mary sniffed, too. A rich, oniony scent was drifting through the house from the *pech*. "I couldn't help tasting one of the dishes," she said, hoping this might explain her red face and guilty expression.

"It's hard to wait," Madame Z said sympathetically. Then she scratched Yulik under the chin.

Mary was relieved that Madame Z hadn't seemed to notice the bloodstain on her dress. But she couldn't ask Madame Z about the closet now without tipping her off that she'd been trying to break in. She would have to wait until the timing was less suspicious.

Mary retreated to the parlor. But she noticed that Madame Z didn't follow her, remaining in the foyer. Mary tiptoed back to the door and peeked in. The old woman was standing by the closet door. As Mary watched, Madame Z reached out her hand toward the lock. But then she hunched over it, blocking Mary's view.

That afternoon, after a three-course lunch that ended with a warm cheese pastry topped with raspberries, Mary casually asked what was in the closet by the stairs.

"Nothing you'll ever need, *devochka*," Madame Z said cheerfully. "Just mops and brooms."

Mary smiled, but she wasn't sure she believed the explanation.

"But there is something you *do* need," Madame Z continued, peering under the table.

Mary followed the old woman's gaze down to her feet.

"New boots. Your soles are almost worn through. Those look far too small as well."

"They are," Mary admitted. She tried to wiggle her toes, but they were wedged in tight.

"Forgive me for not having noticed sooner, *devochka*," Madame Z said. "Today seems like an afternoon just to eat and rest. But tomorrow I'll send you back to Mr. Less. I'm sure he'll find something just right."

"Thank you," Mary said. Once again, she was touched by Madame Z's motherly devotion to her comfort. But she wondered if the old woman was also trying to distract her from the subject of the locked door. Mary decided she would have to figure out a way to open it herself.

SIX

THE NEXT DAY, after a lunch of thick pancakes served with sour cream, Madame Z sent Mary off to Iris.

"You're not coming with me?" Mary asked.

"I have a few things to do around the house," Madame Z replied. "And Less knows you now. He'll just put the boots on my tab."

Mary was surprised that Madame Z would send her out by herself, but she was happy to hear it. She could stop by the hotel and look for Jacob.

By the time she had reached town, though, her feet hurt so much that she decided to head to Mr. Less's shop first. She spotted him behind the counter, whittling a piece of wood in the shape of a bird. Two women in silk dresses leaned over the counter, watching with great interest. As one tugged on the other's sleeve, Mr. Less cupped his hands together over the bird carving and then opened them up. A live swallow flew out, swooping across the store and alighting on a pair of giant antlers in the back. Mary realized the competition Jacob and his father were up against—it was an excellent trick.

"Isn't that clever!" one of the women said.

"I told you," said the other. She slipped Mr. Less a large bill. "Have the tiger skin shipped to my house in Newport."

"You are comfortable with large cats?" Mr. Less said, his eyes crinkling.

"Oh, Mr. Less," the woman said with a braying laugh, "you are too much."

Crowing to each other about the charming little shop and its droll owner, the women swept past Mary and out the door.

Mr. Less turned to Mary with a playful smile. "Madame Z's girl. Still here, eh?"

"Why wouldn't I be?" she asked, more accustomed to his teasing tone. "And it's Mary."

"Of course," Mr. Less said with a deep bow. "How can I help you, Mary?"

"Madame Z sent me back for some boots. Mine are too small."

Mr. Less stepped out from behind the counter. There was something odd about his appearance that Mary couldn't put her finger on. He was dressed rather clownishly, with a red scarf around his neck, and loose, simple clothing.

"The picture is certainly not complete," Mr. Less agreed, looking down at her feet. "What are you looking for? No doubt something that will allow you to run." He chuckled. "That's what children are always doing, isn't it?"

"Not me," Mary said. "I like to sit and read. Do you want to measure my feet?"

But Mr. Less was already scurrying back to his storeroom. "Not necessary," he shouted back to her. "I can tell a size just by looking."

Recalling the perfect fit of her coat, Mary didn't doubt it. She wandered around the shop as she waited, picking up arrowheads and starfish and cracked-open quartz crystals. The swallow fluttered its wings atop the giant antlers, then sailed over the bric-a-brac and landed on her shoulder. Mary froze, not wanting to frighten it away.

"Look at that," Mr. Less said. He clapped his hands, and the swallow vanished.

"Where did it go?" Mary asked.

Mr. Less slipped a hand into his pocket. "Up in the rafters."

Mary craned her neck, but she couldn't see the bird.

"Here you go," Mr. Less said, opening a long white box and holding it out for her.

Inside was a pair of black leather boots. Mary lifted them out; they were shiny and soft. She yanked off her old ones and pulled these on with a contented sigh. She laced them, stood up, and walked around the store. The boots were so comfortable, it was almost like having new feet.

"Perfect, once again!"

Mr. Less bowed as if he'd expected no less praise. "Anything else?"

Mary shook her head—she didn't want to spend any more of Madame Z's money—but she couldn't help scanning the shop. Her eyes fell on the old boot. Mr. Less had moved it to another table, closer to the front. Mary stared at it, but it didn't move.

"Maybe you could put my old boots next to that one," she said, pointing to it. "So it could have friends."

Mr. Less smiled. "You're an interesting one." He looked down at her new boots. "You'll break them in faster than you think."

Mary nodded. The walk home would help. "Thank you."

She sprang out the door and dashed down the stairs, then stood and wiggled her toes. There was plenty of space.

"You definitely look like a tourist now!" a voice said behind her.

Mary turned around. Jacob was grinning at her new boots.

She smiled back at him. "It's just an illusion."

Jacob put his finger to his lips. "I won't tell. I was heading to Mr. Yu's for a cup of tea. Why don't you join me?"

Mary glanced over at Mr. Yu's Tea Shop, with its red-and-gold gables and wooden dragons. She had never been in a tea shop before and wondered if Mr. Yu's Chinese brew tasted anything like Madame Z's rotten-leaf tea. Even more intriguing was the sign Tea-Leaf Reading Inside. "Sure," she said.

Jacob led her up the stairs, past the wooden dragons and through a red door. Inside, the air was steamy and warm, with an unfamiliar nutty smell. Red paper lanterns hung from thin wires that crisscrossed the tearoom, and tourists sat on cushions around low wooden tables. A man with a black mustache down to his shoulders and a red silk robe greeted them with a deep bow.

"Two for tea?" he said.

Jacob handed him several coins. "Yes, Mr. Yu, if you will."

"You shouldn't pay for me," Mary said. "I still have your coins."

"Save them," Jacob said. "I invited you, so it's on me."

Mr. Yu led Mary and Jacob to one of the tables, then scurried over to a wall of wooden cubbyholes. In each one, Mary noticed, was a small clay teapot and a stack of teacups without handles. Mr. Yu brought a set back to their table and poured murky green tea into the cups. Mary noticed him watching her intently. "Drink tea," he instructed. "Read leaves after."

After Mr. Yu departed, Jacob turned to her. "He's very good," he said in a tone of respect.

"At reading tea leaves?" Mary asked.

"At reading people," Jacob said with a sly smile. "That's ninety percent of magic. Most people have tells—little clues that tell you something about them."

"Like my boots?" she said, thinking back to how Jacob was able to tell that she wasn't a tourist.

"Exactly. But there are even more subtle tells—the way someone stands, the look in her eyes. Is she skeptical? Preoccupied? Eager to believe?"

"What was I?" Mary asked, half afraid that Jacob already knew too much about her.

"When I first saw you?"

Mary nodded.

He sipped his tea, thought about her question. "Curious," he said finally.

"You mean about the tricks?"

"Yes, but also curious to me. You didn't quite fit here. I wanted to know more about you."

"So you were curious, too?" Mary asked.

"Of course," Jacob said.

Mary smiled politely and sipped her tea, but she didn't think he'd told the entire truth. Jacob hadn't just been curious; he'd been lonely. She realized she wasn't so bad at reading people herself.

"You can ask me anything, but I get to ask you a few questions first," she said.

"Fair enough."

"Is it just you and your father who travel around?"

Jacob nodded. "My mother died when I was six. After that my father started moving around more. I guess he figured if we never had a home, he couldn't miss her not being there."

"Do you miss her?" Mary asked. She realized it was a bold question; but knowing how much she missed her mother and Caleb, she had to ask.

Jacob sipped his tea. "For a long time I did. Now, most days I'm okay. What happened to your parents?"

"My father died before I was born, and my mother and brother died in a fire."

She waited for him to react with a look of horror, as some of the other orphans had when she'd told her story. But Jacob's dark eyes met hers directly and without fear.

"And then you were sent to an orphanage?"

Mary nodded and took another sip of tea. "Two of them, actually. At the last one, we were hardly fed and we had only the thinnest of blankets. I figured out how to run away, though. Last week, I crawled through the clean-out door of the kitchen stove, up the chimney to the roof—"

"No wonder you have a gift for magic."

Mary gave him a puzzled look.

"Magic is the art of escape."

Mary liked this idea, even though she couldn't honestly take credit for escaping. "Except I didn't escape. Mrs. Boot, the horrible matron, caught me once I made it down to the street."

She thought about mentioning the whirlwind but decided the story was too odd.

"But you're here now, not at the orphanage," Jacob said.

"That's true," Mary admitted. "I guess I did get away, because the next day Madame Z came and adopted me."

"Do you like her?"

"Yes," Mary said, thinking of Madame Z's kindness and generosity but also the locked closet. "She's just . . . a little hard to read."

"Perhaps you just need some practice. Watch Mr. Yu."

She drank the last of her tea. Then Jacob waved over Mr. Yu, who, Mary realized, had been studying his patrons from a stool in the corner as he smoked a long pipe. He glided over, tilted Mary's cup, and stared into it.

"Shape of a crescent: a journey, recent," he said, pointing to a shapeless clump of leaves near the rim, then to several others. "Steps: an improvement in life. Elephant: wisdom through a friend." Finally, he pointed to a clump at the very bottom. "Hen: symbol of domestic bliss."

Mary realized that Mr. Yu had read all these predictions not in the actual tea leaves, but in *her*. She was new to Iris—thus the recent journey. The mix-match of elegant coat and boots and thin frame might suggest a change in fortune. Jacob appeared to have befriended her. But Mr. Yu had also somehow seen her longing for a happy home. Perhaps that desire was so common that any child possessed it, but Mary thought his words proved what Jacob had said about Mr. Yu's great skill at reading people.

"Thank you," Mary said.

Mr. Yu gave a small bow and turned to Jacob, but he had placed his hand over his cup. "Not for me today, thank you," he said. "Just the tea."

Mary wondered whether he was hiding more than just loneliness. Mr. Yu gave a bow, and they rose and departed.

Outside, the air felt crisp after the steamy warmth of the tearoom. Jacob flipped his top hat so that it landed at a rakish angle on his head.

"I can show you around sometime if you like," he said. "Just meet me here after one of the shows."

Mary didn't even stop to think. "All right."

SEVEN

THAT EVENING, over a sumptuous meal of suckling pig and buckwheat porridge topped with nuts and fruit, Mary told Madame Z about her visit to Mr. Less's shop.

"He turned a carving of a bird into a living swallow," she said.

"One of his favorite tricks," Madame Z replied between bites. "The tourists love it."

"Later he said the bird was up in the rafters, but I think he turned it back again."

Madame Z laughed. "Turned it back?"

"He wanted me to think the bird was still up in the rafters, but the moment it vanished, he slipped something into his pocket."

Madame Z stopped chewing and studied Mary with her sharp gray eyes. "All part of the trick."

Mary felt her face flush. She realized how naive she sounded. "Is Mr. Less one of the tricksters you keep warning me about?"

"Not at all," Madame Z said, stabbing a piece of suckling pig with her fork. "They're far more clever."

Mary thought of Jacob—he seemed very clever. But she didn't think he was trying to trick her, unless it was into having a friend. He needn't worry about that. She was eager to see him again.

"May I go into Iris by myself again sometime?"

"Why not?" Madame Z said with a shrug. "Just beware the tricksters, *devochka*. They're always one step ahead."

The next day, when Mary mentioned Iris, true to her word, Madame Z waved her off. Mary reached the hotel just as Jacob and his father were capping off their two o'clock show with the collapsible-cage trick. The audience was slightly bigger than the one at the morning show she'd seen, but she still wouldn't have called it a crowd—six or seven tourists. One or two looked restless, as if they planned to wander off before the end. Mary could tell from the quick dart of Jacob's eyes and the smile that flashed across his face that he had spotted her; but he continued seamlessly with the trick.

Although Mary now knew how it was done, she was no less in awe—the ventriloquism was so subtle, the distraction perfectly timed yet seemingly unplanned, the sleight of hand as elegant as a series of dance steps that flowed each into the next. And the trick couldn't always be the same, Mary realized, because the audience wasn't the same—Jacob and his father had to adapt to the size and focus of their crowd. It took an observant eye and a quick hand.

After the show, Jacob dashed first to the tourists who had already begun to walk off, tipping his top hat. One reached into his pockets and dropped something into Jacob's hat, but another waved him away, which angered Mary. Yet Jacob seemed unperturbed—he circled back to the most enthusiastic members of the audience, shaking his hat and bowing with each coin they tossed into it. Still, Mary could see that he didn't take in much. When he finally caught her eye and darted toward her, she reached her hands into her coat for the pennies he'd given her, and held them out.

"No," he said upon reaching her. "Those are yours. And besides, you know how the trick is done."

"Doesn't mean I could ever do it myself," Mary said.

"Practice is all," Jacob said, reaching up to her head. "Like when I keep cleaning your ears, I find more inside them."

But Mary raised her hand to block him. "No," she said firmly. "I'll keep what you gave me, but no more. You're already showing me around."

Jacob broke into a grin. "Of course! Let me just tell my father."

He ran back to the Illusionist Kagan, who was packing props into a black suitcase beneath the hotel awning. From the cold stare the illusionist gave her, Mary could tell he didn't like the idea of Jacob showing her around any better than Madame Z likely would have.

A moment later, Jacob slid to a stop beside her. "The tour commences."

"He doesn't want you to go?" Mary asked.

Jacob exhaled sharply. "He doesn't trust anyone. And he thinks friends are a waste of time."

Mary had to hold back a smile. Jacob was calling her a friend. "He probably just misses your mother."

Jacob nodded. "I just wish . . ."

"What?" Mary asked.

He shook his head. "Never mind. Come on. Let's have some fun."

Mary wondered what he wished for, but she didn't want to press him. "Where first?" she asked.

Jacob pulled out a pocket watch with a cracked glass front. "Found it on the street in New York City," he explained. "Doing magic teaches you always to keep your eyes open. Good timing— we can catch the end of my landlord's act."

He led her up the steps of the cottage with the wand in the window, past the sign **THE GREAT DEBOSCO, BEHOLD TO BELIEVE!** Inside was a single large room set up as a small theater, with six rows of folding chairs facing a raised stage. A thin, rubbery-looking man with a pointy beard so black Mary thought he must have brushed it with shoe polish stood upon the stage, pushing a needle through his thumb. There were gasps from the nearly full audience, but the Great DeBosco just smiled as if spearing his finger with a needle felt no more uncomfortable than trimming his nails.

Jacob handed a couple of coins to a woman with dyed orange hair standing inside the doorway. She took Jacob's money but made a sour face as she pointed him and Mary to a seat in the very last row.

"She knows I'm competition," Jacob whispered as they sat down. "She thinks I'm here to steal his secrets."

"Are you?" Mary whispered back with a playful smile.

Jacob shrugged. "They're not worth stealing."

Onstage, the Great DeBosco gave the needle a final push, and it emerged on the other side of his thumb. There were shrieks from the audience, but Mary noticed that Jacob stifled a yawn. "It's a carrot. It's all in the angle."

"You're really good," she said.

"I've just had practice. I've been watching magicians my whole life. Give it a try yourself. Watch his hands."

Mary watched carefully as the Great DeBosco took a spoon and bent it until the bowl part broke off. After showing the audience the broken parts, he then made it whole again. But Mary thought she saw something silver flash in his hand.

"Is he hiding another spoon?" she asked Jacob.

"Good eyes," he said. "His palming is clumsy. He never actually broke the spoon. What he's hiding in his hand is the sawed-off bowl of another one, which he uses to create the illusion that he broke the first one."

For his next trick, the Great DeBosco lit a feather on fire; as he extinguished the flame, a dove appeared out of thin air.

"The fire is a diversion," Mary said. "But where did the dove come from?"

"You're learning," Jacob said with a wink. "He pulls it out of his coat. Next time, just keep your eyes on his sleeve."

After the show, the Great DeBosco stood by the door, bowing

and collecting extra coins. Jacob brushed past him as the magician closed his fist over the coins, then opened his hand to show that they had vanished.

"He's dropping them into his other hand first," Jacob said when they were outside.

Mary grinned. "Has there ever been a trick you *can't* figure out?"

Jacob considered this question. "Yes, actually. Do you want to see it?"

EIGHT

MARY HESITATED OUTSIDE THE BLACK COTTAGE. Of all the acts in Iris, Madame Petitsa's was the last one she would have chosen to see. Her stomach tightened at the very thought of fire, never mind someone eating flames. But she was also curious to see the one trick that a master magician like Jacob couldn't figure out.

Halfway up the stairs, Jacob seemed to sense she wasn't behind him. He turned around and, at the sight of her, raced back down. "I didn't think," he said gently. "Of course you don't like fire. We don't have to go."

But his kindness about her fear made her determined not to give in to it. "No," Mary said. "I want to see her."

Before she could change her mind, she marched up the stairs and opened the door.

Inside was a smoky-smelling, dark room, with heavy window shades that blocked out the light, and a small, unlit fireplace against one wall. A horseshoe-shaped arrangement of chairs, several occupied by tourists, surrounded a woman holding a flaming torch. She had a beaky nose and curly orange hair that cascaded down her back. Her lashless brown eyes passed over Mary to land on Jacob with a knowing flicker.

Mary felt a wave of dizziness as Jacob closed the door behind them. Caleb and her mother had been trapped in a small, smoky room just like this one. She fought off the urge to turn around and run out the door, counting as she breathed in and out to keep herself calm. She chose a seat as far away from the flaming torch and as close to the door as she could. As soon as she was seated, Madame Petitsa bowed, then leaned in over her torch and swallowed the flame, plunging the room into darkness. Mary instinctively swung her head in the direction of the door, tensed to make a run for it. Just then, there was a hissing sound, and the torch, which Madame Petitsa held out in front of her, burst into flame again. Mary lurched back in her seat.

As the audience applauded, Mary glanced over at Jacob, hoping he hadn't noticed her reaction. But he wasn't looking at her. His brow was wrinkled, his mouth set in a frown. "Watch closely," he whispered. "She'll do it again."

Mary wiped her clammy hands on her coat and watched carefully as Madame Petitsa leaned over her torch and gobbled up the flame. But this time, instead of relighting the torch, she breathed out a great cloud of flames, like a dragon. Mary ducked in her seat, heart thumping, but the cloud of fire vanished.

"That's incredible!" she said to Jacob, her voice shaking.

But he just sighed. "Basic fire-breathing," he whispered. "She could have lamp oil in her mouth, which she blows into the air and sets on fire. It's that first trick."

"I don't understand," Mary said.

As Madame Petitsa relit her torch and took a bite of the flame, Jacob watched her carefully. "There's one important rule in fire-eating," he whispered. "You always have to tilt your head back because flames rise upward. But Madame Petitsa—" He cocked his head at the fire-eater. Mary understood at once. "She leans over it!"

"Exactly. I can't figure out how she does that without burning herself or catching on fire."

Mary shuddered at his words, thinking about fire, her family burning in it, their cries, the smoke filling their lungs. The room felt closer than ever; the air around the flame wavered with heat.

"Are you okay?"

She realized she was grimacing and forced herself to smile. "I'm fine."

But Jacob didn't look convinced. "You've seen it." He stood up and left a coin on the chair behind him. "Let's go."

"Shouldn't we leave two?" Mary asked.

He shook his head. "I've come to watch her so many times she won't let me pay anymore."

Back outside, Mary took a deep breath of crisp air. But she felt guilty, too. Her mother and Caleb had never gotten that relief. If only there had been something she could have done—a spell she could have uttered to put out the fire, or a pair of magic wings she could have used to fly up and save them.

As they stepped into the street, Jacob flipped his top hat back onto his head and shrugged. "I can't figure it out. I guess I just have to keep watching. . . ."

Mary looked over at him, but he didn't continue. He looked preoccupied.

"It couldn't be . . . real magic?" she asked.

He looked surprised. "Real magic? But there's no such thing."

Mary immediately regretted the suggestion. Jacob clearly had been impressed with her sharp eye. Now he thought she was childish.

"Just kidding," she said quickly. "I'm sure you'll figure it out. Listen, I should go soon. Madame Z wants me home for supper. Thanks for showing me around, though."

"My pleasure," Jacob said, but he seemed lost in thought.

Mary hoped he wasn't too disappointed in her.

"Can we do something again?" she asked.

Jacob smiled in a way that instantly reassured her. "We have a room at the boardinghouse DeBosco owns. It's up the block, on the northern edge of town. I'm hoping we'll be here for a few more weeks at least. Stop by sometime between shows."

"I will," she promised.

He tipped his hat, and a carrot fell out from under the brim.

"The Great DeBosco's thumb," he said, handing it to her. "Keep it as a souvenir."

Mary laughed and put the carrot in her pocket for Sivka. But even Jacob's mischievous tricks couldn't completely banish the melancholy mood that was descending upon her. She could still smell smoke on her clothes.

As she headed back through town, Mary noticed that the sun had vanished and the sky had grown overcast, as if it were feeling the same way. A breeze had kicked up with the gathering storm. Even though she was still warm in her new coat, she shivered, thinking of her mother and Caleb. She didn't even bother to look at the occult shops but stared down at the ground.

"*Devochka!*"

Mary looked up. Madame Z was standing on the cottage porch of the Voodoo Queen of New Orleans. "Let me give you a ride."

Mary spotted the gig parked along the street. Sivka looked at her and shook his mane. "I didn't know you were coming to town."

Madame Z looked up at the sky and shrugged. "Weather is changing. Thought I'd get out while I could." She stepped carefully down the porch stairs, leaning on her birch cane and seeming more her age as tourists rushed past her. "So much foolishness here," she said as she reached Mary. "That one has dolls and bags of herbs to cast spells. Did you see anything interesting, *devochka*?"

"Not really," Mary said, wondering if Madame Z had spotted her and Jacob during their tour.

"Hungry?"

"Yes," she admitted.

With a nod, Madame Z scrambled up on the gig. "Me too. *Pora domoi!* Home."

NINE

THAT EVENING THE STORM BROKE, and for the next two days cold rain drummed at the windows, trapping Mary inside. Although she wished she could go visit Jacob at his boardinghouse, Mary didn't really mind being stuck inside. The house seemed even cozier in the storm, with a small fire crackling safely in the hearth and Yulik lounging on her lap like a soft, purring blanket. Mary read aloud to him from the *Household Tales*. His green eyes seemed so intelligent that she couldn't help imagining he appreciated "Cat and Mouse in Partnership" and some of the other stories. Mary asked Madame Z whether she had other books, and, minutes later, the old woman carried in a stack of them. Mary read those to Yulik, too.

With Madame Z home all the time, Mary had little

opportunity to tackle the lock on the door by the staircase. Once, she managed a surreptitious jab at it with a dinner knife, but the tip just came out bent. Another time, she spied Madame Z hunched over it. But the old woman instantly spun around and, with a cheerful firmness, led her into the parlor for supper.

Madame Z seemed to view the weather as the perfect excuse to cook one scrumptious meal after another. On the first evening of the storm, they ate a stew of salted beef and sour cabbage; on the next night, a fish, rice, and onion pie Madame Z called *kulebyaka*. (Mary enjoyed the soft, soothing sounds of Madame Z's native tongue and always repeated the words the old woman taught her.) There was also a continuous supply of warm, fresh bread; pickled vegetables; eggs; amber-colored berries that Madame Z called cloudberries and said were a favorite of the czars; and what Mary had come to think of as rotten-leaf tea, which she was growing to enjoy more and more. After supper, as they lounged in the parlor, Mary tried to read Madame Z the way Jacob had taught her, but the old woman's emotionless gray eyes were like mirrors in which Mary could see only herself.

At night, she watched the mysterious flickering light out her bedroom window.

She decided it was the magic light at the bottom of the witch's well from "The Blue Light"; then later, the dwarves' gold from "The Gifts of the Little People." She fell asleep—the *Household Tales* snuggled next to her, and Yulik at her feet—and dreamed of adventures in fairy-tale lands. On the first night, Caleb was with her; but on the second, she realized that the boy by her side was Jacob.

Sometime during that night, a bony hand shook her awake.

Startled, Mary nearly shrieked. She sat straight up, imagining she was back at the orphanage. Her heartbeat slowed only when she realized that instead of Mrs. Boot, Madame Z stood by her bed. She wore a kerchief on her head and sniffed ever so gently.

Did she have a cold? Had Mary not washed sufficiently? Outside, Mary noticed, it was still dark, but the incessant rain had finally ended.

"What is it?" Mary asked.

"Up, *devochka*," Madame Z said, sniffing again. "It's the perfect time."

"For what?"

Madame Z smiled. "Mushroom hunting. The hours before dawn after a heavy rain." She held out a straw basket lined with cloth. "Get dressed and meet me on the porch."

Mary scrambled out of bed, awake now and eager for a chance to explore the forest with Madame Z. She had never been mushroom hunting in her life, never mind been invited out while it was still dark. She dressed quickly as Yulik leaped off the bed and pranced down the stairs ahead of her, seemingly as excited for the adventure as she was.

After a quick cup of tea and bite of bread, Mary followed Madame Z into the forest. The old woman swung a lantern back and forth through the darkness, illuminating tree trunks and spindly branches. Mary noticed that Madame Z was sniffing again, but now she knew why. The air smelled wonderful—not like the horse dung and coal smell of the city, but like fallen leaves and ferns, fresh dirt and rain.

They passed a stable and paddock, which Madame Z said

were Sivka's. The forest grew thicker, and Mary saw a log hut with smoke drifting out of the chimney.

"Is that where your stableman lives?" Mary asked.

"Koshchey?" Madame Z said absently. *"Da."*

They passed the hut just as a light turned on in the window, and the door opened.

"You weren't just going to pass by?" Koshchey asked. Mary could see into the hut behind him. It was sparsely furnished— on the floor was a nest of blankets that seemed to serve as a bed, and there were cages, in various stages of repair, for game or birds. A high-backed chair sat by the dying embers of a fire.

Madame Z turned to him with a look of irritation. "We have mushrooms to hunt before sunrise."

Koshchey nodded, bending his long frame submissively. "Mushrooms, of course. But let me at least say hello to the child."

Madame Z opened her mouth as if about to say something, then closed it. "Go on, then."

Koshchey bent down, smiling eagerly at Mary. "Your first hunt, my dear?"

Mary nodded.

"Flowers grow by sunlight, mushrooms by moonlight. Did you know the moon rises and falls, east to west, just like the sun? A perfect night for a hunt—the clouds are clearing, the moon still high. Just take care not to pick a death cap and you will be fine."

"Of course, I will teach her to avoid them," Madame Z said.

"What's a death cap?" Mary asked.

"A very deadly mushroom—the most dangerous in the forest," Koshchey said.

"Why are you scaring her?" Madame Z said. "She will be fine with me."

Koshchey winked at Mary. "Just an old man's advice."

"Good night, Koshchey," Madame Z said curtly. "Come, *devochka*."

Madame Z turned away, raising her lantern as she threaded through the trees and back into the forest. Mary hurried after her, more afraid of losing sight of her guide than of poisonous mushrooms. Madame Z wandered, seemingly without direction, deeper and deeper into the forest. As she did, she lowered her lantern to show Mary how to identify different types of edible mushrooms—spongy brown morels; flower-shaped black trumpets; giant, pale puffballs that grew as large as supper plates. She demonstrated how to pluck them at their stems and place them gently in her basket.

As promised, she also pointed out more dangerous spores.

"This one with the red cap is a fly agaric," she said, pointing at what looked to Mary like a toadstool from a fairy tale. "It causes powerful hallucinations. Do not even touch it."

And deep in the forest, where the earth was covered with a carpet of ferns and moss, she hunched down to show Mary a greenish, white-gilled mushroom. "Death cap. Those who eat it get ill and then recover. But this is a cruel joke. Five days later, they die. Always."

Mary paid careful attention to these lessons. The word *hunting* had originally amused her, but now she saw that picking the wrong mushroom could be as fatal as a misfired shot. She paid less attention to their winding path, which seemed determined entirely by whatever trail of fungus and root Madame Z kept sniffing in the night air.

At last Madame Z stopped in the shadows near a fallen log and held up her lantern. The dew-covered caps of white mushrooms clustered along the lichen-covered log like a village perched on a grassy hillside.

"Oyster mushrooms!" Madame Z said, stepping over the log. "I shall gather on this side, *devochka*, and you gather on that one. I will place the lantern on top so that both of us can see."

Mary got to work. She couldn't see Madame Z on the other side of the log, but she could hear the old woman's soft humming and the squelch of leaves as she moved about. Mary carefully plucked a dozen oyster mushrooms, stopping a few times to give her basket a little sniff as Madame Z had done, appreciating the musty odor. Then she crouched down and plucked another few. She wondered if this was enough—her basket was three-quarters full. But before she could stand up and ask, a gust of wind shook the leaves above her and knocked the lantern off the log, shattering the glass and extinguishing the flame.

"Madame Z?" Mary called into the darkness.

No one answered.

"Madame Z?" Mary called again.

She listened for the humming but couldn't hear it anymore. Her stomach tightened.

She could make out the outline of the fallen log. Holding her basket in one hand, she felt along the bark with the other. The log was large, and by the time she reached the end of it, she was far away from where she had started. She called for Madame Z again, but no one answered. Had the old woman wandered off and couldn't hear her?

Mary became aware of the sound of her own breathing, fast and loud. Madame Z had said Mary would be fine with her, but now Madame Z was gone. Mary had no idea how to find her way home alone. This wasn't Buffalo, where there were people on the streets who could give directions. This was a forest that could stretch for miles and where wild animals, hungry animals, might be out hunting.

Something rustled in the overgrowth. A buck? A bear? She backed away just as a pair of yellow eyes flashed in the darkness and an enormous white wolf trotted out. Mary stood frozen. Her fingers tingled. She imagined other wolves surrounding her; in the stories she'd read, they hunted in packs. But no other sets of eyes appeared, and after a seemingly endless moment, the lone wolf wagged its tail like a dog. Then the animal trotted off, stopping and looking back over its shoulder at regular intervals. It seemed to be waiting for Mary to follow.

Mary wondered if she had fallen asleep and was dreaming. Or perhaps her fingers had brushed against a fly agaric and she had absently licked them? But she felt a mad instinct to follow, imagining that the wolf might show her the way. She grabbed the basket of mushrooms and dashed after the beast. She stumbled over roots and tore through brambles, sometimes losing sight of the wolf before catching a glimpse of its white tail. Its hulking, ghostlike shape slunk around trees, leading her in what felt like endless loops and circles, till Mary was breathless and almost dizzy.

She finally halted—the wolf wasn't leading her home, only deepening her confusion.

"Stop fooling me!" she said firmly.

The wolf stepped out from behind a tree. Its long snout made it look almost as if it were grinning. Then it grew in front of her, its fur turning brown, until Mary realized it had become a bear. She closed her eyes, then opened them. There was nothing in front of her. She was standing back near the fallen log. She pinched herself. The pain convinced her she was awake. She blinked her eyes again, but nothing unusual appeared.

"Enough!" she told herself. She couldn't let her imagination and fear get the best of her. She had to find her way home. The house couldn't be far. She looked up through the tangle of branches till she found the waning moon. What had Koshchey said? That it rose and fell, east to west, like the sun. At this time of night, so close to dawn, it would have begun to set toward the west. Madame Z's house was on the eastern edge of the forest. So she needed to walk with the moon at her back. His advice had turned out to be helpful after all. With a determined step, she set off.

She walked for some time, softly humming the same song Madame Z had hummed, both to distract her from any fears and to help Madame Z find her. It still didn't make sense that her guardian had just vanished with the light. Why hadn't she called out for Mary?

As the moon drifted behind her, Mary wound around trees, pushed through thorny undergrowth, squelched over moss. She heard a gurgling stream, though she didn't remember passing it with Madame Z. She stopped humming to listen to the water.

Just then, she heard a woman singing. She almost called out, thinking it was Madame Z, when she realized that the voice was higher and younger, a girl's voice. The girl sang a wordless tune that seemed familiar to Mary, but it kept changing just as she felt she could place it. Mary pushed her way past low-hanging branches and tangled underbrush to where a brook tripped over rocks in the moonlight. But the moment she emerged, the singing stopped. The only sound was the babble of water. Mary crouched down and dipped her fingers into the brook. A sucking current tugged at her fingers, gently at first, and then with a fierce yank that almost tipped her into the water. She broke away and leaped to her feet, imagining sinister forces at work. Picking up her basket of mushrooms, she followed the moon back into the forest.

The trees began to change—to grow spindly and white, like Madame Z's cane. Mary realized she was in a birch grove. Mist drifted over the ground. A glowing orange light appeared on the ground in the distance.

"Madame Z, is that you?" Mary called.

But no one answered. Mary wondered if the light was the first ray of morning sun hitting the forest floor. It seemed too bright to be anything else. But as she ran toward it, she realized that the light was shining up from the ground, not down from the sky, which was just beginning to lighten from black to plum.

She wondered if it was a bonfire. But there was no scent of smoke, and the light didn't flicker, but shone steady and bright. Could it be the dancing orb she had seen outside her window? As she drew closer, she stifled a gasp. A small orange feather lay on the ground. It glowed like a lantern. Mary knelt down and picked it up.

A twig cracked, and a voice drifted through the mist: "*Devochka*, are you there?"

Mary quickly tucked the feather into her coat. This was it! There was magic in this world—*real* magic. How else to explain a feather that glowed as bright as the sun? This was proof! She couldn't wait to show it to Jacob. She would tell him about the strange wolf-turned-bear, too. She thought of the Grimms' tale "The Golden Bird" and wondered if this bird was the dancing light she had seen outside her window. It would make sense that this was one of its feathers.

A gray shape darted out of the mist toward her.

"Yulik!" Mary cried.

The cat twined himself through her legs and purred.

Madame Z drifted out of the mist after him. "*Devochka*, are you all right? Lost in these woods, all by yourself!"

Mary knelt down and gave Yulik a kiss on top of his head.

"I'm fine. Where did you go?"

"Once I realized I had lost you, I went to find Koshchey. We were about to mount a search—" Madame Z stopped, blinked. "You're really fine?"

"Yes," Mary said. "I'm all right."

Madame Z narrowed her eyes as if she didn't quite believe her. "But you had no light. How frightened you must have been!"

"A little at first," Mary admitted. "But there was a bit of moonlight. It was even kind of . . ."

Madame Z cocked her head, waiting.

But Mary did not say the word *magical*. She just smiled.

"You are a peculiar child," Madame Z said. She studied Mary

with her gray eyes, then turned to Yulik. "What should we do with her?"

Yulik meowed.

"What did he say?" Mary asked, enjoying the now-familiar trick.

Madame Z shrugged. "Take you home. Cook up the mushrooms."

TEN

AFTER A HEARTY BREAKFAST, Mary asked Madame Z if she might take a walk into Iris. She was eager to find Jacob.

"Of course, *devochka*," Madame Z said absently as she sat on the porch, sipping a cup of rotten-leaf tea.

Mary waited for Madame Z to say something more, but the old woman looked lost in thought. Mary tried to read her face, hatched deeply with lines; it was like looking through a window-pane covered with frost.

"What are you making with the mushrooms?" she asked, trying to draw Madame Z out.

This friendly question received no response.

She tried again. "I'll be home in time for lunch. At noon?"

At this, Madame Z looked up, forced a smile. "Lunch, yes. Noon sharp. Forgive me, *devochka*—I am just *ochen oostala*, tired."

It was true that they had been up half the night, but Mary still thought that something more than exhaustion was bothering Madame Z. She set this problem aside, though. First, she needed to show the feather to Jacob.

The morning was beautiful, the light soft as Mary opened the white gate, which creaked as she pushed it. She walked along the rutted road, past stubbly yellow fields dotted with enormous bales of hay, and rolling pastures where sheep and cows serenely grazed. Lining the road were trees that competed to impress her with their red and orange leaves. Even the ordinary autumn day seemed capable of magic.

Mary hurried through town, which was still mostly asleep, until she reached a slender three-story building on the northern end that looked careworn enough to be a boardinghouse. Its shutters were all slightly askew, and a pair of dormers poked out of the roof. A man with a turban and a beard sat on the steps outside, a thick brown rope hanging around his neck and arms. As Mary drew closer, she noticed that the rope was moving. It twined around the man's shoulders and arms.

"Python," the man said, holding the snake out proudly. "Bit of indigestion, though."

He pointed to an enormous bulge in the python's middle.

Mary looked at it with alarm. "What is that?"

The man shook his head. "The neighbor's poodle, who'd been trained to count. It was a terrible misunderstanding. He's since

left Iris. But ever since she ate Socrates, Fanny has been too sluggish for me to charm. I've had to use less reliable snakes instead."

Mary tried not to imagine what a less reliable snake might
do. She was mostly just relieved that Jacob wasn't the neighbor
whose dog seemed to be giving the python indigestion.

"Do you know the Illusionist Kagan and his son?" she asked.

"Of course. They live in the top room. Right up the stairs.
They're out, though."

Mary tried to hide her disappointment. "Do you know when
they'll be back?"

"Kagan is scouting the neighboring towns. Thinks there are
too many magicians here. Fortunately, I'm the only snake act
in town—Dobbin, King of Serpents. But there's less demand for
snake charmers than for psychics and magicians." Dobbin shook
his head. "Most people don't know what they're missing with a
fine creature like Fanny. Can you believe how many people are
afraid of snakes? I'm sure Kagan and the boy will be back in time
for his noon show, though. . . ."

Mary nodded politely as Dobbin babbled on. This news
couldn't be worse. She had promised Madame Z she'd be back
by noon for lunch. She would have to come to Iris and find Jacob
another time.

"Would you tell Jacob that Mary stopped by?"

"The boy?" Dobbin said. "Oh, yes, quite like him. Quick with
his hands. Fanny likes him, too. I'll let him know."

Mary walked back through Iris. She hoped that Jacob's father
wouldn't decide to move right away. Jacob had told her they were
planning to stay for at least a few weeks. She had a feeling he

didn't want to leave, either. The residents of Iris clearly intrigued him—especially Madame Petitsa.

Mary looked around at the cottages. Now that she knew there was real magic—glowing birds and shape-shifting animals—they seemed more enticing and mysterious, the way they had when Mary had first awakened in Iris. Even the shabbiest cottage on the edge of town, the one that belonged to Rusalina, Spirit Guide, seemed powerful in a way it hadn't before.

Mary stopped in front of it. Its blue paint was chipped, and it occupied a low and muddy spot. Perhaps to make up for the undesirable location, a sign in Rusalina's window read TALK TO THE DEAD. ONLY FIVE CENTS.

Mary reached into her pocket for Jacob's pennies. There were only four. She could almost hear Madame Z's voice: *You're lucky,* devochka. *How silly it would be to spend five cents just to get fooled!*

But then Mary thought of her mother and Caleb. If there was even the smallest chance to speak to them again, to hear their voices, to tell them how much she missed and loved them. . . . She found herself drifting up the steps, peering through the window at a pale girl sitting alone in a cramped parlor. She looked just a few years older than Mary and was combing her long, stringy blond hair. Mary opened the door just enough to stick her head through.

"I'd like to talk to the dead, but I don't have five cents."

The girl stared at Mary with interest. "Never mind. I'll take what you have."

Mary stepped into the parlor. It looked as if it had seen better days. The floorboards were water-stained—the area was clearly prone to flooding—and the wallpaper was peeling. There were two worn velvet chairs with scalloped edges and a round pedestal table between them. Rusalina beckoned Mary to the chair across from her own.

"Whom do you wish to talk to?" the spirit guide asked.

Mary hesitated.

"My mother."

Rusalina took the small ivory comb in her hand and stuck it into one side of her hair. It was by far the most beautiful object in the dreary little parlor, its top encrusted with pearls. Mary noticed three other ones just like it already tucked into the sides of Rusalina's long, stringy hair.

"Speak to her," Rusalina said.

Mary had not expected it to be so simple. "Don't you need to summon her spirit?"

Rusalina looked at Mary and smiled impishly. "There is a spirit in the room. She'll pass on the message."

Mary didn't say anything. If she did, she might start crying. Claiming a spirit was in the room without even a knock or rattle was a pitiful trick for the most gullible of customers. But Mary knew she only had herself to blame. She had started imagining magic everywhere, magic that was far more powerful than a glowing feather—the type of magic that could raise the dead and bring back the family she had lost.

Mary stood up and began to fish through her pocket for the pennies. "I'm sorry, I've got to go. But I'll pay you."

"What's the rush?" Rusalina said with a tinge of annoyance. "Don't you want to talk to the spirit?"

Mary gritted her teeth, trying not to cry. "I just wanted to talk to my mother."

"Come here, poor girl," Rusalina said in a cooing voice as she reached out to her.

But before the medium could grab her hand, Mary dropped Jacob's pennies onto the round pedestal table and raced for the door. She did not look back, wiping away her tears as she ran to Madame Z's.

ELEVEN

MARY WAS QUIET DURING LUNCH, but if Madame Z noticed a change in Mary's mood, she didn't say anything. The old woman seemed back to her usual self, humming as she served Mary a bowl of thick and savory mushroom-and-potato soup, clucking unhappily only when she wouldn't accept a second helping.

Mary didn't want to rush back to Iris the same day, in case Madame Z began to wonder what she was up to. She hadn't told the old woman about Jacob—she was still afraid Madame Z would think he was one of the con artists or hucksters she seemed so worried about and would forbid Mary to see him. So, after lunch, while Madame Z banged around in the kitchen, Mary sat on the porch with Yulik and started reading him "The Goose-Girl" from *Household Tales*. But her voice quivered during the scene where the princess parts forever from her loving mother. She closed the book.

"Sorry, Yulik," she said softly, scratching him under the chin.

She knew it was silly to apologize to a cat, but Yulik rubbed his cheeks against her fingers as if he understood.

As she stroked him, her thoughts drifted away from the longing she felt for her mother to her current situation. Madame Z gave her plenty of food, warm clothes, a room of her own, time to play and explore. And yet there was something missing. Beyond attending to her basic physical comfort, Madame Z did not seem terribly interested in her. She never asked about her thoughts or feelings or discussed her dreams and hopes for the future.

Inside the house the oven door banged shut, and Mary wondered if she was being unfair. Perhaps Madame Z simply didn't know *how* to be a mother beyond feeding and clothing her. She had told Mary she had no family. But it was also possible that her family, like Mary's, had died. This would explain the too-long nightgown Mary had worn her first night—maybe Madame Z had once had a daughter and lost her and was afraid to love again. Mary remembered that her own mother had always told her, "Don't judge a person till you know him." She had been friendly with some of the most sullen and ill-tempered people in their neighborhood, and they had softened around her. In this spirit, Mary resolved to ask Madame Z a little more about her life.

She waited until that evening, after Madame Z had served another tasty meal—mushroom-and-potato *vareniki*, or dumplings, along with roasted duck and a salad of pickled onions and beets. Mary ate two helpings and praised the meal several times. Madame Z's gray eyes crinkled with pleasure.

After supper, Madame Z settled onto the couch and strummed her balalaika while Mary lounged before the fire with Yulik.

In the peaceful stillness after Madame Z had finished her last song, Mary turned to her. "Did you ever have children?" she asked.

Madame Z blinked. "Are you asking if I've ever been a mother?"

Mary nodded. "I just thought, since you adopted me—"

"*Devochka*," Madame Z said sharply, "I am no one's mother."

Mary stiffened. Madame Z had never spoken to her in this harsh tone, which seemed reserved only for Koshchey. Perhaps it was just the dying embers in the hearth, but the parlor suddenly felt cold.

In a flash, as if she'd realized her error, Madame Z's face reassembled itself—her eyes crinkled kindly, and a smile played on her lips. "I've never been a mother, if that's what you mean. But I'm happy you're here."

"That's all. I was just wondering," Mary said blithely, as if she hadn't noticed the old woman's first reaction. But she knew now that her instincts were right: Madame Z did not think of herself as a mother or of Mary as a daughter. So why had she adopted her?

But before Mary could ask another question, Madame Z stood up. "It's late."

Mary nodded. The turn in the conversation had clearly made the old woman uncomfortable. Mary bid her good night. She headed into the foyer, and her eyes fell on the locked door by the staircase. She was certain that something besides mops and brooms lay behind it. She had to figure out a way in.

TWELVE

THE NEXT MORNING, as Mary ran to Iris, she half-feared she would arrive to find that Jacob and his father had moved away forever. It had been four days since she'd last seen him. She was panting by the time she saw Dobbin, sitting on the front stoop, with Fanny draped lazily around his shoulders.

"Mary!" he greeted her. "In a big rush. Never good for the digestion. Though, hopefully, your meals are not as big as Fanny's."

"Is Jacob home?" Mary managed to gasp.

"I believe so," Dobbin said. "I passed along your message this morning. Though he seemed a little cross I hadn't told him last night. Wonderful boy, though. Very understanding about the doves."

Mary wasn't sure which doves Dobbin was referring to,

but the important information was that Jacob was still in Iris. "Thank you!" she said.

Keeping a wide berth between herself and Fanny just in case, she raced up the stairs, through the door, and into the main stairwell. The staircase was drafty, and the floor was scuffed and covered with dirt and leaves. An animal smell pervaded the air. As she was passing the second-floor landing, a door swung open and a short man with a monocle came running out.

"Your unique and lovely head caught my eye," he exclaimed in a British accent. "Professor Horatio St. John. Normally, I charge a fee, but for you, dear girl, I will give a phrenology reading gratis."

Mary must have looked puzzled, because he continued, "That's free, my dear. Phrenology, the art of reading the bumps on one's head to determine such qualities as parental love, combativeness, mirthfulness, alimentiveness, et cetera and et cetera, of which I am a renowned expert. Now, please, lower your head!"

Mary barely had time to consider this request before Professor St. John had placed his hands on her head. She could feel his fingers run across her skull as he exclaimed, "A veritable dynamo of bravery, persistence, occult potential, strong stomach!"

"Harry," said a familiar voice from behind them, "she's my guest."

Mary was relieved to see Jacob coming down the stairs.

Professor St. John quickly withdrew and held out his hands, palms up. "My apologies, dear lad. Thought she was a customer. No harm done."

Jacob nodded as the professor scurried back into his apartment.

"Sorry about that," Jacob said. "I didn't see him take anything, though."

Mary's face reddened as she remembered the pennies. She didn't tell him about Rusalina. She didn't want him to know how foolish she had been.

"So 'Professor St. John' is not a renowned head-bump reader?"

"No, but Harry's quite a gifted pickpocket. His English accent is pretty good, too, considering he's from Georgia." Jacob grinned. "Sorry I missed you yesterday. Come on up. My father went to pay the rent, but he'll be back soon."

Mary took this as a welcome sign. If Jacob's father was paying the rent, they weren't leaving yet.

"Does everyone who lives here have an act?" she asked as he led her up the final flight of stairs.

"Pretty much. It's the cheapest place to stay if you're new to Iris. Everyone here takes turns performing in front of the hotel, which is the best spot in town if you don't have a storefront of your own."

"I met Dobbin yesterday," Mary said.

"You probably met Fanny, too. She occasionally escapes, which can be a problem. We lost two doves, and you probably heard about the counting poodle—"

"Socrates?"

Jacob shook his head sadly. "It took less than five seconds for Fanny to swallow him whole."

"Someone was counting?"

"Socrates himself, naturally."

At the top of the landing, Jacob opened a door into a small room with a sloped ceiling. Mary guessed it had been part of the attic till the Great DeBosco decided to add dormers and rent it as a room. One thin feather mattress lay against the wall, and another lay beside the dormer windows, which provided a little light. The beds looked about as comfortable as those at the Buffalo Asylum for Young Ladies. There was a small stove with a worn-out pan and pot on top; a few bags of sugar, flour, and millet sat in the corner. A couple of boxes with a steamer trunk in between them served as a table and chairs. The only other furnishings were the chest of magic props Mary had seen at the Illusionist Kagan's show and the birdcage with the stuffed bird perched stiffly inside it.

"Not exactly homey," Jacob said.

"But it's still more of a home than an orphanage," Mary said.

"The one you told me about sounded awful. It's kind of you, though, to try and cheer this place up a little."

"What?" Mary asked, not following.

Jacob reached into her pocket and pulled out a red chrysanthemum. "Thanks for this. You're lucky Harry didn't filch it."

She laughed. It felt good to be with Jacob again.

He filled a glass with water and put the mum in it, propping the bloom over the edge.

Mary knew she didn't have much time—the Illusionist Kagan might be back at any moment. "Have you figured out how Madame Petitsa does her fire-eating yet?" she asked.

Jacob shook his head. His brow wrinkled. "Why do you ask?"

She took a deep breath. "I wasn't totally kidding about real magic. There's something I want to show you."

She drew the feather out of her coat sleeve, then held it against the inside of her coat so he could see it glow.

Jacob's eyes widened. He silently held out his hand, and she passed him the feather. He took it into the corner of the apartment, away from the window, and ran his fingers over it.

Finally, he looked up at her. "Where did you get this?"

Mary told him about the mushroom hunt. "I know it sounds crazy, but—"

"Are you sure you weren't dreaming?" Jacob asked.

"Even if I dreamed up the bear and the wolf and getting lost in the woods, there's still the feather. Can you explain it?"

Jacob shook his head and turned the feather over in his hands. "I've never seen anything like it."

"What if there's magic here in Iris—real magic?"

"There can't be. My father says there is no—"

But Mary could tell from the way his brow wrinkled that he had already begun to doubt this.

"Your father doesn't see it! But you do. I know you do."

Jacob looked straight at her. "I've watched Madame Petitsa do that trick over and over." He held up the feather. "And now this."

Mary's heart thumped. "What other explanation is there except—"

"Real magic," he said softly, a smile playing on his lips.

He had reached the same conclusion. They couldn't both be wrong.

"Madame Z also claims there's no such thing," Mary said breathlessly. "But I'm starting to wonder if she knows more than she admits."

She quickly told Jacob as much as she could about Madame Z—that she had come from a land near Russia, that she didn't have a family, that she provided Mary with every comfort but didn't seem to want a daughter. Finally, Mary told him about the locked door by the stairs.

"You need to get in there," Jacob agreed.

She shook her head. "I can't pick the lock."

Jacob's brow wrinkled as he considered this. "I often figure out a trick simply by observing where something is. Is it on a table that might have a trapdoor? Is it positioned in such a way as to hide another object behind it? Consider where the closet is in space."

"You mean what's around it?" Mary asked.

"Exactly," Jacob said. "You're focusing on the obvious way in. But perhaps there's another."

Before Mary could fully consider this idea, footsteps padded up the stairs and the door opened. The Illusionist Kagan stepped heavily into the room.

"Father," Jacob said, "this is Mary."

Mary stuck out her hand, eager to make a good impression, but the illusionist did not take it. Instead, he bowed stiffly, as if the only greeting he knew was the one he gave at the end of his show.

"Lev Kagan," he said. "Did I hear you discussing magic?" He glanced sternly at Jacob. "Not giving anything away, I hope."

"Not stage magic," Mary said quickly. "Real magic."

The illusionist laughed dismissively. "There's no such thing, as Jacob knows. He's very talented. I trained him from an early age. He's better than I am. Nothing gets past him."

Mary avoided looking at Jacob.

"There are magicians everywhere here, though," Mr. Kagan continued, "like DeBosco, who charges me one rate one week, then changes it the next. We need to earn more tomorrow, Jacob, or I may change my mind again about staying any longer."

"We will!" Jacob said in a confident tone. "I'll drag an audience over if I have to."

Mary felt a pang of guilt about the pennies. She knew how much Jacob and his father needed them.

"I should get going before Madame Z wonders what I am up to."

"Come back soon," Jacob said, with a meaningful glance. "Tell me how it goes."

But his father did not extend an invitation. "Madame Z?" he asked as if this was the first time he had heard the name. "What's her game?"

"I don't know," Mary said.

The Illusionist Kagan gave a snort. "Everyone in Iris has one. You just haven't figured it out yet."

THIRTEEN

WHEN SHE OPENED THE GATE and stepped into Madame Z's yard, Mary paused to take a closer look at the house. She kept in mind what Jacob had said about considering exactly where the closet was. And that's when she saw that the house's other chimney appeared to be directly above it. She wondered if the closet concealed an old fireplace. Why did the house have a second fireplace, and why was the chimney above it even larger than the one over the *pech* and the parlor fireplace? In any case, it was a way in. But climbing onto the slanted roof seemed dangerous, and she did not relish the thought of reliving, in reverse, her failed escape from the Buffalo Asylum for Young Ladies.

She heard a meow and noticed Yulik balancing on the porch railing. She started walking toward him when something else occurred to her. The porch and first floor were set up above the ground, which meant there had to be something beneath them—either a basement or a crawl space. Rather than breaking into the closet from above, she wondered if she could figure out a way in from below. The first step, she decided, was to crawl through the rosebushes and see what was beneath the porch. But she would have to wait till Madame Z went out.

For lunch, Madame Z served a sweet, blood-colored beet soup called borscht, and black bread. Mary gobbled it down but noticed that Madame Z didn't eat much. Instead, she sat back in her chair and smiled at Mary. "You are looking so much better, *devochka*. Not all skin and bones."

After lunch, Madame Z took a nap on the porch and Mary read the story of Rapunzel from the *Household Tales* to Yulik. The old woman appeared to have no plans to go out. This was just as well, since reading about how the prince poked out his eyes on thorns did not make Mary eager to push her way through the rosebushes.

But just after four, Madame Z stretched and yawned, then stood up. "There are a few more ingredients I need for tomorrow night's supper. I'm going into Iris. Would you like to come?"

Mary leaped at this opportunity. "I was just there this morning. Is it all right if I stay home and rest instead?"

Madame Z's sharp gray eyes crinkled. "Of course, *devochka*. I will be back by sundown."

Koshchey stepped out of the woods, holding Sivka's reins. He waved at Mary, who stood on the porch. Remembering the helpful advice he had given her on the night of the mushroom hunt, she smiled and waved back.

Madame Z headed down the stairs to the gig. Yulik wove around her and meowed plaintively.

"Stop it," Madame Z said, giving him a nudge with her foot. "You're too attached."

The moment the gig was out of sight, Mary took off her coat so it wouldn't get dirty or torn and hung it on the porch railing. Then she raced down the stairs and surveyed the rosebushes with their bluish-white blossoms. It had grown chilly despite the slanting rays of late-afternoon sun that bathed the yard. She ignored the cold and pushed her way through the smallest of the bushes as Yulik brushed up behind her. The thorns scratched her hands and caught on her dress, but she soon discovered a white wooden lattice, half-entangled in rose vines. She pried open a section of it just large enough for her to crawl through, then replaced it behind her so that Yulik couldn't follow. She didn't want him to get stuck under the house. Yulik poked a paw through the slats and meowed loudly.

"I'll be back in a minute," she told him. At this, he just cried louder.

Some light filtered in through the lattice, but the space under the porch was dim and the dirt beneath her hands was cold. A few serpentine white roots popped up from it; potato bugs skittered around them. Mary could hear Yulik batting the slats and meowing frantically behind her.

She crawled away from the light, back through the cobwebs toward the center of the house. She expected to hit a wall—where the foundation or basement was—or a support beam, but there was none. The farther she went, the less she could see, so she felt around every few feet in front of her. She wished she had thought to bring a lantern or even the feather, which she had foolishly left inside her coat. Her fingers grazed the hard shells of bugs and shrank away from large, wet indentations she began to discover in the earth. She hoped they weren't the trails of snakes or, even worse, rats. Caleb had once been bitten by a rat in the boardinghouse kitchen—it was one of the few times she had seen her mother become upset.

The air smelled dank and there was a fetid odor, as if a bigger animal lived—or had died—beneath the house. Even if it was dead, Mary preferred not to run into it. She focused instead on keeping track of how far she had crawled. After several minutes, she calculated that she should be almost at the center of the house, roughly beneath the closet.

She still had not run into a supporting pillar or beam. The house could not simply be floating above the ground. It had to be held up by something.

At the very moment she thought this, her fingers jammed into something hard. She was certain it was part of the house's foundation. But when she reached out with both hands to inspect it, she realized it was slender, like a pole, and covered with some sort of hard bark that felt almost like scales. She ran her hands down to the bottom of the pole-like thing and discovered that it branched off into three roots, the ends of which were sharp and pointed like . . . claws.

Mary gasped. But before she could even yank her fingers away, something even more disturbing happened: the scaly, claw-tipped pole suddenly lifted itself off the ground and pulled away from *her*. Above her, the house shook and rumbled. Dirt sifted down upon her head. She scrambled away from the pole. But she made it no more than a few yards before she crashed into another scaly, claw-tipped pole. It too jerked away from her, sending a second series of shock waves through the house above.

Mary was certain that at any moment the house would come down on her. She and the creature—for it became terribly clear to her that the scaly, claw-tipped poles were a pair of legs—would be entombed together.

She crawled frantically toward the porch, not stopping to see whether the creature was behind her, ignoring the rain of dirt and dust. She could hear Yulik's frantic cries and used them as her guide. Light began to filter in until she could make out the brighter space under the porch. Just as she reached it, the house stopped shaking. She popped open the lattice, wiggled through the hole, and fought her way through the rosebushes, oblivious to the thorns tearing at her dress and skin. She scrambled to her feet, and Yulik raised his tail and butted his head against her shins.

Mary looked at the house. It appeared as stable and still as ever. But she knew she hadn't imagined it moving.

There was a creature—an enormous monster, by the feel of it—under the house. But if its scaly legs and feet were so large, how could the rest of it fit? A terrible thought dawned on Mary: the house itself was the monster, with enormous chicken legs.

This was real magic, but it seemed nightmarish, not wondrous and good. Madame Z had to know that her house was a monster—how could she not? Mary felt the hairs on the nape of her neck rise. She had a bad feeling that whatever the old woman had planned for her wasn't very nice after all.

She had to find Jacob. Now.

Mary yanked her coat down from the railing and threw it on.

But she'd barely started running when she skidded to a stop. Koshchey was standing between her and the gate, blocking the way.

FOURTEEN

THE SUN WAS BEGINNING TO DROP behind the house, and shadows fell across the yard. Koshchey loomed in front of her, taller than she remembered.

"What are you doing?" Mary asked. She tried to keep her voice calm.

Koshchey looked around as if to make sure no one was listening, then leaned in closer. "Giving you some advice."

Mary wondered if she could make a run for the gate. But Koshchey's legs were long, and he seemed tensed, ready to spring after her if she bolted.

"Advice about what?"

"About Madame Z. My advice helped you find your way in the woods, did it not?"

Mary considered this. She still wasn't sure she trusted him. "How did you know I would need it?"

Koshchey laughed. "Madame Z loses all the girls in the forest for a night. Most of them are scared out of their wits. But you surprised her!"

All the girls? Mary's legs felt weak. She was the latest of many. The too-long nightgown made sense now. She could barely bring herself to ask what Madame Z had done to the others.

"What happened to them?" she asked.

"The other girls? I told them who Madame Z was, and they ran for it."

"Did they make it?" Mary's voice was barely a trembling whisper.

"Let us hope so," Koshchey said.

Mary's breath sounded loud, and her skin prickled with cold sweat. "Who is she?"

"Normally, I might ask who *you* think she is," Koshchey said. "But I won't play with you. Have you ever heard of Baba Yaga?"

Bah-bah Ye-GA, he pronounced it. Mary shook her head.

"Of course," Koshchey said with a shrug. "The name means nothing to Americans. But any Russian child could tell you that Baba Yaga is a witch."

This made the worst kind of sense. It explained everything.

Madame Z lived alone on the edge of the woods. She seemed ancient and yet full of vigor. Her only companion was a cat—a cat who followed Mary around the house like a guard and was currently twining around her legs as if he owned her. Mary had read about witches in the *Household Tales*. They were always bad news, especially for children. She thought of the disobedient little girl in

"Frau Trude," thrown onto the fire by a witch, and of Hansel and Gretel, whom the witch in the cake house tried to eat. Mary could barely breathe. The succulent meals meant to fatten her up. All that sniffing! The enormous oven—large enough to fit a child inside.

"I see you've finally figured it out," Koshchey said, his blue eyes gazing at her with an eerie calm.

The yard fell fully into shadow, and the chill of the coming night filled the air. The trees seemed to lean in around her, the house to crouch over her, waiting to pounce. Mary imagined the fiery inside of the oven, the heat roasting her alive.

"Thank you," she said. "I'm going now."

But Koshchey did not move out of her way. "Wait!" he said, holding up his hand. "That's what I wanted to tell you. Don't run."

She eyed him distrustfully, suspecting a trick.

"Baba Yaga instructs me to tell the girls who she is. She likes them to know. She wants them to run."

So Koshchey hadn't helped the other girls. He had just followed Madame Z's orders. But it made no sense.

"Why would she want that? Wouldn't she want you to stop them?"

Koshchey gave a hearty laugh that seemed familiar, although Mary could not remember when she had heard it before. "It would ruin all her fun!" he exclaimed.

A cold wind shook the trees, swirling leaves around Mary. Her coat no longer seemed to keep her warm. "Fun?" she forced herself to ask.

Koshchey shook his head as if her ignorance amazed him. "Baba Yaga enjoys the hunt."

If Madame Z let her prey go, she had to be pretty confident

she could catch it again. With a sickening feeling, Mary realized that the previous girls had not escaped after all. She became aware of Yulik twining around her legs faster and faster. He probably enjoyed the hunt as much as his mistress did. Mary glanced behind her. The sun was sinking into the trees. In less than an hour it would be completely dark.

"But if I don't run, she'll eat me," Mary said.

Koshchey looked at her for a moment without speaking. Then he sidled closer to her. His voice was quieter, hushed.

"I liked you, Mary, the first time we met. You seemed different. So I will tell you this."

Yulik stopped circling her and yowled at Koshchey.

"What?" Koshchey said to him with a shrug. "Why not tell her? *You* like her, too."

Yulik purred, head butting Mary's legs in answer. Was this an act they were putting on together? With every minute, night was growing closer. Perhaps a few of the girls had escaped and Koshchey was delaying her. She took a step, then hesitated. Madame Z *had* said that Yulik never slept with anyone before. Mary had been kind to him, giving him scraps and petting him. And Koshchey had helped her in the forest.

"What?" Mary asked.

"I really shouldn't," Koshchey said. "Baba Yaga would be angry with me."

Yulik looked up at her and meowed, as if trying to tell her himself.

"Tell me," Mary pleaded. "Please."

"Most of the time, Madame Z eats children. Sometimes, however, she helps them."

A child-eating witch who was sometimes helpful? That made no sense. The Grimm brothers' witches were evil, no two ways about it.

As if he'd guessed what Mary was thinking, Koshchey said, "I am telling you the truth—I swear to you. Perhaps you will find my words useful."

She wanted desperately to believe him. But Koshchey was Madame Z's servant. Plus, she couldn't imagine how she had managed to impress him when Madame Z had first brought her home. They had been together only a few minutes. As he bowed deeply, she wondered again if this was just a trick to get her to stay. Perhaps Madame Z was just feeling lazy about the hunt. Mary decided she wasn't going to stick around to find out.

She gently pushed Yulik away. She took a step forward, then another, past Koshchey. Was he going to chase her? She glanced back, but Koshchey made no move to follow.

"One more thing you should know," he called after her. "She can smell your fear. So whatever you do, try not to be afraid!"

In the dark, with a witch chasing her? Was that even possible? Maybe he was just trying to frighten her so she'd stay. Mary picked up her pace, walking faster, then broke into a run. She listened for Koshchey's footsteps but heard nothing, and when she glanced back, all she saw was Yulik padding silently after her. Her hands were shaking so hard that the gate rattled as she slammed it shut behind her. She expected Yulik to jump through the slats and chase her down the road, but he stopped at the gate and meowed piteously.

"I'm sorry!" Mary called to him before she could stop herself. She knew he might be crying because his supper was escaping, but the affection between them had seemed real. She fought a foolish pull to turn back and embrace him, but then she reminded herself exactly whose cat he was.

Mary's legs pumped faster as she ran along the edge of the road, ready at any moment to leap into a gully or behind a tree if she caught sight of Madame Z's gig. The night was falling fast; color was beginning to leach out of the sky and fields, and the branches of the trees were turning into tangled silhouettes. Mary thought of the too-long nightgown she had worn the first night— would she meet the same fate as the last girl who had worn it? She pushed away the thought.

At last, as darkness fell, she staggered into Iris. She crept from house to house, joining the parties of tourists where she could. There was no sign of the gig or the giant golden-brown horse. She reached the boardinghouse and ran up the stairs, gasping for breath as she pounded on Jacob's door.

Jacob opened it, a gas lamp in hand. His eyes widened with concern. "What happened?"

"Tell him I've paid!" Mr. Kagan shouted from inside.

"It's not DeBosco," Jacob called back, stepping out into the stairwell. "Just Mary. I'm going to talk to her outside."

"Fine," Mr. Kagan said, sounding less interested.

Jacob closed the door and led Mary down a few steps, then pulled her to sit. As soon as she caught her breath, she told him everything that had happened. Jacob didn't interrupt but listened silently. When she was finished, he still didn't speak. Mary wondered if he thought she had lost her mind.

"You believe me, don't you?" she said.

"Of course I do," Jacob said, looking her firmly in the eye.

Mary was grateful, at least, for this. She wasn't alone. Jacob believed her. She wasn't like all the other orphans who had no one to confide in, no one to help.

"What am I going to do?"

Jacob glanced back at the door to his room. "I'll ask my father if you can stay with us."

But Mary knew that there was barely enough space for the two mattresses already on the floor. She also doubted Mr. Kagan would believe her story about a witch and give her refuge.

"No. I can't stay in Iris. Madame Z would look for me here. How far is the next town? You've been there. Perhaps if I can reach it . . ."

Jacob stood up, began pacing the cramped stairwell. "But what if you can't outrun her, like Koshchey said?"

"Even if he's telling the truth, how could I ever trust her? She's a witch! She could agree to help me and then just eat me later."

"You'd have to be clever," Jacob agreed. "You'd have to stay one step ahead of her."

His tone was thoughtful. Was he really suggesting she stay?

"You're crazy."

Jacob nodded as if he realized how insane such a plan seemed. But Mary could tell from his worried eyes that he didn't have much faith in the alternative.

"Did any of the others escape?" he asked.

"I don't know," Mary said, although she was skeptical.

"Well, I guess running is your best option," he said with a loud exhale.

And that's when it hit her: he didn't want her to go. Mary felt her face flush. No one had cared about her in years. How cruel to find out that someone was on her side just as she had to leave his. Whatever happened, it was unlikely she would ever see Jacob again. It made her angry—Madame Z had not only tricked her into thinking she had a home but was forcing her to abandon her first real friend since Caleb's death. Mary was afraid to look at Jacob, afraid he would see the tears filling her eyes.

"It's all right," Jacob said, touching her arm.

But Mary couldn't bear being comforted. "How far is the next town?" she asked, standing up.

"About five miles east along the main road," he said, getting to his feet along with her.

If only he could always be beside her. She couldn't look him in the eye. "It's best I go. You don't want her tracking me to you."

"Are you sure?"

Mary nodded.

Jacob looked at her solemnly. "If you're going to go, you'll need more money." And with a tap of his ear, coins rained into his palm. Mary allowed herself a small smile. She would always remember this trick. But when he tried to pass the money to her, she pulled her hand away.

"I can't take that."

"Why not?"

"It's probably everything you and your father made today! You'll have to move."

Jacob shrugged but didn't deny it.

"I have enough," Mary lied. She had to get away before she broke down. She forced herself to smile and reached out a hand. "Good-bye, Jacob. I hope you find a home someday."

But he didn't take her hand. Instead, he put his arms around her, drawing her into a hug. Mary closed her eyes, allowed herself to sink into his embrace.

"You should be the one she helps," Jacob said.

"Thank you," she managed to choke out. Then she reluctantly let go of him and ran.

FIFTEEN

MARY'S BREATH HEAVED as her new boots pounded the dirt. The road out of town felt like a bridge stretching across a dangerous sea of woods and fields. But as fast as she ran, when she looked up at the stars, she felt she had gone no distance at all; it was as if she were in a nightmare where she was being chased but her legs would not work or she was running knee-deep in sand. She couldn't even use her glowing feather for fear that the light would draw Madame Z's attention.

Mary tried not to think about Madame Z; it was the only way to suppress her fear and hide its dangerous scent. But thoughts kept popping into her head—the old woman sniffing at her outside the orphanage; the giant scaly legs beneath the house; the huge oven, big enough to roast a child whole. Mary imagined herself trussed and oiled for roasting and was seized by terror, which only became worse when she pictured Madame Z catching the scent of it with her large nostrils and licking her lips with glee.

At last Mary came to the town line, which was marked by a small white sign. She knew it didn't guarantee safety, but she had to catch her breath. As she crouched, pain stabbing her sides, she began to think for the first time about the life that awaited her if she actually survived. Even if she made it all the way back to Buffalo, where would she go? Not to Mrs. Boot and the Asylum for Young Ladies. She could hop a train to New York City or even out West, but a girl traveling alone was likely to attract dangerous company. At best, she might end up at another orphanage or a workhouse. Certainly, those places were better than the inside of Madame Z's oven, but they were a far cry from the only real home she had known in years.

The snap of a twig in a dark grove of trees off the side of the road made Mary start. A raccoon appeared and waddled across the road. Mary knew it was a sign to get going, but she could not will her feet to move. Everything she longed for—a cozy home, a kind friend—was behind her. She suddenly wondered if Jacob was right and the challenge before her was not how to escape but how to safely remain.

She knew from the *Household Tales* that witches were powerful creatures. Koshchey may well have been telling the truth when he suggested that it was pointless to try to outrun Madame Z. However, children sometimes outwitted witches. She thought of Hansel sticking out a bone instead of his finger to trick the witch into thinking he wasn't getting fat, and Gretel tricking the witch into climbing into her own oven. Jacob was right; she would have to stay one step ahead, but she wouldn't have to do it alone. He had a talent for tricks and illusions, and he would help her.

But this would work only if Madame Z kept her alive in the first place. Mary thought about what Koshchey had said: that Madame Z liked children to be afraid. Mary imagined the other girls steeped in the brine of their own tears and terror. This was why Madame Z *had* seemed surprised—confused, even—by Mary's calm after her night alone in the forest. And shortly after, when Mary had asked her about being a mother, the witch's mask of good cheer had slipped. Had she imagined herself in such a role with Mary? Koshchey had said Mary was different. Then there was Yulik. Madame Z had said he'd never slept in anyone's bed before.

What if she didn't run, as Koshchey said; what if she went back willingly and asked Madame Z for her help? This would ruin Madame Z's hunt, and it would also demonstrate Mary's bravery, possibly spoiling Madame Z's appetite as well.

As Mary peered up at the night sky, she realized that she wanted a home so badly that she was willing to face down a witch for it. She took a step back toward Iris, then another. It was easier than she thought. She felt her courage grow, the stench of her fear fade.

She had not gone more than thirty yards when she heard the distant rumble of wheels. As if she had summoned Madame Z with her very thoughts, the gig appeared around a curve, Sivka galloping toward her. An orange flame shot from his mouth, illuminating the darkness. Mary shuddered, knowing now why the horse's breath had been so steamy outside the Buffalo Asylum for Young Ladies.

Yanking on the reins, Madame Z brought the gig to a halt directly in front of Mary. Sivka pranced in place, his eyes white and strained as smoke drifted up from his mouth. She imagined that if Madame Z ordered it, he could roast her to a tasty crisp. But the witch gave no such command. Instead, she shook her wizened head and frowned.

"Where are you going?"

Mary studied the old woman as if for the first time. Her large nostrils reinforced that she had acute powers of smell. The silver braid wrapped into a bun and the gray eyes reminded Mary of autumn skies and swamps, mists and gravestones. But she refused to allow herself to be afraid. Madame Z wasn't sniffing. Mary was heartened, too, by the sight of Yulik, who meowed in greeting and raised his tail.

"Back to you."

Madame Z's eyes narrowed. "And why would you want to do that? You know who I am."

Mary wanted to shrink back, but she forced herself to square her shoulders and look the witch straight in the eye.

"I need your help."

Madame Z laughed. Mary noticed for the first time that her teeth were sharp and plentiful. "What makes you think I help anyone, *devochka*?"

Had Koshchey lied? Perhaps Yulik was just happy to see her because Madame Z had promised him a few scraps after she was done. But Mary knew the witch could also be testing her. "I've heard you sometimes help children."

"Who told you that?" Madame Z asked, her voice slightly cross.

"It doesn't matter," Mary said, not wanting to tell on Koshchey. "All that matters is that I think you should help me."

Madame Z gave her an imperious look. "Why is that?"

"Because I am not afraid of you." This was a lie, but there was still a certain power to saying the words out loud.

Madame Z smiled in a way that managed to be both appreciative and exasperated. "You are challenging, *devochka*."

"Will you help me?" Mary asked again.

Madame Z leaned down and offered Mary her hand. "Come sit beside me and we will discuss."

"Wait," Mary said, thinking quickly. "First you must promise not to eat me."

Madame Z gave a snort. "Trust me, there is nothing at all appetizing about you at the moment."

"And you must promise that nothing else can, either, including your house or that lock on the closet door," Mary added.

"Then don't tickle its feet, and keep your fingers where they belong," Madame Z said with an arch of one bristly gray eyebrow.

Reaching up, Mary grasped the ancient fingers, their nails twisted and yellowed. With a strength that no longer surprised Mary, Madame Z heaved her up onto the bench. Yulik rubbed himself against Mary and purred. She scratched him under the chin. Then she turned to Madame Z.

"Here's how you can help me, then. I want to go home."

Madame Z shook her head. "You have no home, *devochka*."

"Yes, I do. Yours."

Mary expected Madame Z to laugh at this outrageous claim, but a flicker of some emotion Mary had never seen before passed over her face. "You want to live with *me*?"

"Yes," Mary said. "I liked it there. At least I did before I knew you planned to eat me."

Madame Z's old brow wrinkled more than Mary thought was possible.

"Very well," she said, after a long pause. "I shall take us home."

Mary accepted this answer with a regal nod, as if she had expected no other. But inside, she was trembling. Her own words had convinced a witch!

Madame Z turned the gig around, and Sivka, with a fiery whinny, set off at a brisk trot. As they veered onto another road that skirted Iris, Madame Z began to sing one of her nonsensical lullabies. A wind kicked up and blew in harmony as dried leaves rose up from the road and took the shapes of giants and dragons, then collapsed, then rose again, in a riveting ballet. Only then did Mary understand that the lullabies were not songs at all, but enchantments.

As if Madame Z knew Mary had just figured this out, she began to sing more vigorously, increasing the magic around them. A flock of crows burst out of the trees and flew after the gig, croaking Mary's name with human voices. Forks of lightning flashed in the fields, and when Mary looked up to search for clouds, the stars began to leap toward her. She realized that the witch was showing off, demonstrating how powerful she truly was. She felt a vague unease over the spectacle. Could she really trust Madame Z's promise not to eat her? But her anxiety mixed with exhilaration. If Mary had power like this, she would never lose the people she loved the way she had lost her mother and Caleb. She could protect them from anything.

"There's one more thing I want," Mary said.

With a grin, Madame Z ceased her singing. The stars retreated into the sky, the lightning disappeared, the crows settled into the trees, and the leaves fell to the ground, crunching under the wheels of the gig as the wind sighed softly and was still.

"What is it, *devochka*?"

"Some magic of my own," she said.

Madame Z did not answer. She seemed to be thinking. At last, she spoke. "You want me to teach you magic?"

"Yes."

"I can. But magic must be earned, so you need to be patient."

"I am patient."

Madame Z nodded. "Very well."

As the gig sailed down the last quarter mile of road, Mary felt she had played her hand well. But she knew she would have to remain watchful and always one step ahead.

Madame Z tousled Mary's hair. Mary was almost able to enjoy this caress—especially as there was no sniffing to accompany it—when she noticed blazing lights up ahead. The gig rolled to a stop in front of Madame Z's gate, and a shiver passed through Mary as she realized its source. Perched on top of the wooden slats of the gate were human skulls, light flooding out of their eye sockets.

SIXTEEN

"THIS FENCE IS THE BORDER between my world and yours," Madame Z explained as the gate creaked open on its own and the skulls rattled their welcome.

Mary tried not to think of who they had been—the witch's past victims, no doubt.

"Why did I never see it like this before?" she asked.

A peevish, high-pitched voice responded, "There are many things we conceal from guests. We don't want them to feel uncomfortable."

Mary nearly fell off the gig.

"You talk?!" she asked the cat.

"You prove the point exactly," Yulik said, squinting his gooseberry-green eyes at her.

Mary collected herself. She was in a magical land with a witch. Was it really so extraordinary that a cat should talk? She decided to try to do a better job of hiding her amazement.

"I am not uncomfortable with your talking," Mary said. "Merely surprised."

But she was alarmed when the gig pulled into the yard. The home, the one she had wished for, was nowhere in sight. The forest stood in its place.

"What happened to the house?" she asked, trying to keep the panic out of her voice.

Madame Z gave her a sidelong glance. "Perhaps it did not like you poking its feet."

Mary ignored the old woman's teasing tone. "It can run away? Isn't that a bad quality in a home?"

"It hasn't gone anywhere," Yulik said, sounding offended on the house's behalf.

Before Mary could ask him where it was, Koshchey ran out to the gig. Flashing a triumphant smile at Mary, he began to unhitch Sivka.

Madame Z's gray eyes settled on him. "Koshchey," she said, "the child asked me for help. Curious, isn't it?"

Koshchey's smile faded. Mary realized the trouble he was in. Madame Z spoke quietly, but there was no mistaking the displeasure in her voice.

"A Russian child, perhaps, might know such a possibility exists. But an American one?" she continued.

Koshchey held Sivka's reins slack in his hand. His eyes darted from side to side. Mary looked at Yulik. Even without words, he had encouraged her to listen to Koshchey. But now the cat stared mercilessly at the old man, flicking his tail and saying nothing in Koshchey's defense.

"I am sorry, Baba Yaga," Koshchey said, clearing his throat. "The girl just seemed different, harder to frighten. She asked if there was a way—"

"You were careless with this one!" Madame Z interrupted. "From beginning to end."

Koshchey opened his mouth, but before he could defend himself, Madame Z made a scooping gesture with her hand and he was yanked, feet first, up into the night sky. As he dangled high above the ground, his arms and legs began to fade.

"What are you doing to him?" Mary cried out.

"He is doing that to himself," Yulik said.

Mary watched Koshchey's long gray beard dissolve into tendrils of wind, and his arms and legs twist together, forming a funnel. No wonder his laugh had seemed familiar. They had met before. She had told him to move along.

"That was him—the whirlwind in Buffalo!"

"No doubt," Yulik said, sounding slightly bored by the conversation. "He often takes that form when he is searching for orphans."

Mary could understand now why she'd made an impression on him. Most children probably hid their faces or sobbed at the sight of him.

Now fully transformed, Koshchey tried to right himself. But Madame Z merely laughed and closed her fist, then circled it around. The funnel of wind was spun sideways and upside down like a lasso. If this was what Madame Z could do to another magical being, Mary could only imagine what the witch could do to a human child like herself. But it didn't seem right to turn her back on someone who had lent her a hand.

"Let him go!" she said.

Madame Z raised her eyebrow but lowered her hand, and the whirlwind righted itself and wobbled back down to the ground. As soon as the funnel touched the earth, the translucent air swirled into the shape of a man. The tendrils of wind became Koshchey's long gray beard, and the funnel of air solidified into arms and legs.

Koshchey stared at the ground, looking a little green and wobbly. Madame Z hopped down off the gig and led Sivka over to him.

"If you want him someday," she said, handing Koshchey the horse's reins, "you must remember your place."

"He's working for Sivka?" Mary whispered to Yulik.

Yulik swished his tail. "Once he has served Baba Yaga for three hundred years, the horse will be his."

"How many years has he worked so far?" Mary asked.

"About a hundred and fifty or so," Yulik said.

Mary knew from the *Household Tales* that such bargains were struck in the fairy-tale world. But three hundred years of servitude seemed like a high a price for a horse, even one that breathed fire. She wondered what else Sivka could do.

Koshchey took Sivka's reins and bowed deeply. "It will never happen again."

Madame Z sighed. "I suppose you're not the only one who went soft on the child," she said with a glance over her shoulder at Yulik.

"Whatever could you mean?" asked the cat innocently. He jumped down from the gig, and Mary hopped down after him.

As Koshchey retreated into the forest with Sivka, Mary tried to catch his eye, but he didn't look back at her. She resolved to find him later, when Madame Z wasn't around, and thank him. He had put himself in jeopardy to give her a chance. She wondered why.

"*Izba!*" Madame Z shouted. "Turn your back to the forest and your face to me!"

Mary forgot about Koshchey as loud cracks and crunches filled the air. All around them the trees, like creaky old women, slowly straightened, revealing the back of the house concealed beneath their branches. But the rosebushes were gone, and Mary could now see straight under the house to the two giant chicken legs with their three-clawed orange feet. They stomped in circles, spinning the house around and around. At last, they stopped this dizzying dance just as the front part of the porch and door faced Madame Z. The house shuddered once or twice, then settled. The porch stairs unfolded with a series of clacks.

"Baba Yaga can move her house and the kingdom surrounding it to whatever country in the world she likes," Yulik explained with a hint of pride. "We've been practically everywhere!"

"But why do you move around?" Mary asked.

"Variety," Madame Z said, charging up the steps. "After a century or two in the same place, the children begin to taste the same, and the townspeople grow suspicious."

Yulik dutifully scampered after Madame Z, but Mary hesitated. Was she crazy to step back into the house when the witch had just admitted that she traveled the world with the sole purpose of sampling the local children?

As if she'd guessed Mary's thoughts, Madame Z turned

around and waved her up. "Come, *devochka*. I've already promised not to eat you. And it's getting cold."

As Mary followed her onto the porch, she wondered if a witch's promise was really worth all that much. Her gaze fell on the ivory wind chime. With a shudder, she realized that it had transformed into the delicate bones of a child's hand. It waved to her in the breeze as if in greeting.

"Give me your hand," Madame Z said.

Mary hesitated, then steeled herself and took a breath. She couldn't be afraid. She held out her hand.

The witch led her to the door and placed Mary's hand over a carved bird in the center of it. Then she placed her own bony one over it and began to whisper softly. For a moment, Mary felt a small heartbeat beneath her palm, then a warm, feathered body. But when she wiggled her fingers against it, the bird turned back into wood.

Madame Z released her hand.

"There, *devochka*," she said. "Now the door will always open for you, not just when I command it."

At the words *always* and *open*, Mary had an urge to throw her arms around Madame Z. But she realized that affection was a ridiculous emotion to feel for someone who up until a few hours earlier had been planning to eat her. She blinked back her tears.

"It's nothing, *devochka*," Madame Z said, looking slightly alarmed.

"It's not nothing," Mary said quietly.

The witch's gray eyes bored into hers. "There is only one way you could ever lose the power to open the door. Do not let anyone else in, not even Koshchey."

"I won't," Mary promised.

"*Otkroy*, then," Madame Z said. "Open."

Mary placed her hand across the bird till she felt its tiny heartbeat. The door popped open, to the sound of a hearty round of applause. As she stepped into the foyer, she looked to see who was applauding. Three sets of disembodied hands floated in the air, banging their palms together.

"Enough," Madame Z said in a voice of cranky affection. "Busy hands must have other things to do."

"These are the busy hands?" Mary asked.

In answer, the hands, one by one, offered themselves for an introductory shake.

"Who do you think does all the work around here?" Yulik said. "They are Baba Yaga's servants."

Reminded of their station, the hands began to help Madame Z and Mary take off their coats.

"I thought you were her servant," Mary said to the cat.

Yulik flicked his tail and gave her a haughty look. "*I* am her liege. It is a different thing altogether."

"You do as I tell you, like the others," Madame Z said with an amused smile. "*Devochka*, where would you like to take your supper? In the parlor or in bed?"

Madame Z had never offered her this option before. But the idea of lying in her warm bed with a bowl of mushroom stew or warm beet soup seemed too perfect to turn down.

"In bed, if I may," Mary said.

Madame Z nodded her approval at this choice. "Very well. You must be tired. Take her up to bed."

A pair of hands took Mary's. They were as large as a grown woman's and surprisingly warm and solid. They gently led her up the stairs while the others flew off in the direction of the kitchen. Perhaps to demonstrate his independence, Yulik did not come up at once, appearing only when the hands had finished undressing Mary, turning down her bed, and pulling the nightgown over her head. The hem, Mary noticed, had been shortened so that it fit her perfectly.

"Thank you," Mary said.

One of the hands patted her gently on the head.

When the hands had tucked her into bed, another set appeared with a tray covered by a silver lid, which they set on her lap, while the third set of hands tucked a napkin beneath her chin. Then, with great ceremony, they removed the lid to reveal warm, fresh-baked bread and mushroom stew, just as Mary had hoped.

When Mary had finished every last spoonful, the hands took the tray and departed, but Yulik, who had been supervising from the floor, stayed on. As Mary sighed deeply, enjoying a full stomach and the comfort of her own bed, he leaped up and began to circle her feet.

"I admit I rather enjoyed sleeping with you," he said stiffly.

"Me too," Mary said.

She fell asleep almost immediately to the hum of his purring.

SEVENTEEN

WHEN MARY AWAKENED THE NEXT MORNING, Yulik was gone. She dressed and ventured out to the porch, expecting to find Madame Z there with bread and jam, but the witch was nowhere in sight. Neither was Yulik, nor the hands. Only the child's skeletal hand greeted her, tinkling ever so softly in the gray mist that shrouded the forest and the house.

Mary wondered if she should take the opportunity to slip into Iris and tell Jacob she was safe and had decided to stay. But she didn't want Madame Z to think she had changed her mind and run away. Plus her stomach had begun to rumble. Best to eat something first, then figure out when to sneak into Iris.

Mary slipped back into the house, through the parlor, and

toward the kitchen door. Behind it, she could hear chopping interspersed with the thump of an oven door closing. With a sickening lurch of her stomach, she pictured Madame Z preparing a child for supper, before she realized that the odor wafting through the air seemed harmless. It was the smell of something yeasty, like bread or perhaps cake. Feeling a little like Madame Z, Mary sniffed appreciatively, then flung open the door.

Once again, her guardian was not there. But the disembodied hands were hard at work. One hand steadied a green cabbage as large as a human head while the other hacked at it with a silver-bladed cleaver. Another set of hands rolled out yellow dough, like a huge sheet of skin, with a rolling pin. A third set of hands, its fingers stained bloodred, peeled the skin off roasted beets. A teapot sat on the sill of an open window, and dried leaves, tangled in cobwebs and speckled with mold, blew through the window and into the pot. Mary realized that the autumn leaves must be what accounted for the musky flavor of Madame Z's tea. She ground her teeth, imagining the mold and rot in this witch's brew. Yet she felt just as thirsty for it.

"You didn't think I did all the cooking around here?" said a voice behind her.

Mary spun around to find Madame Z watching the hands at work. The witch could move so silently!

"Could you not creep up on me?"

Madame Z laughed. "'Don't eat me,' 'Don't creep up on me.' So many demands. I suppose you want breakfast, too."

Mary could tell that Madame Z was teasing, but her heart still pounded from the surprise of finding the witch behind her. Mary couldn't fully trust her—not yet. But she also knew there was power in treating Madame Z like an ordinary guardian. The witch was used to children being afraid of her, not standing up to her.

"Actually, I do," Mary said.

Madame Z nodded and said something in her language. Dutifully, the hands rolling out dough put down their rolling pin and flew over to the *pech*. They opened the door and waved over Madame Z, who began to sniff busily at something inside. Although the smell was encouragingly sweet, Mary still worried.

"What are you cooking?"

With bare fingers that seemed immune to the heat, one of the hands pulled out a piping-hot plate. Atop it sat a tall, round bread.

"*Kulich*," Madame Z said.

On her order, the hands with the cleaver took a break from hacking at the cabbage to slice the *kulich*. Back out on the porch, Mary and Madame Z ate the warm, sweet bread, together with a savory spread of farmer's cheese and raisins, and they drank the rotten-leaf tea.

They ate in a companionable silence until about halfway through breakfast, when Yulik trotted in from the mist carrying a mouse and dropped it at Mary's feet. The poor creature trembled but did not move, playing dead.

"No, thank you," Mary said, trying to hide her disgust.

"Mouse is not to everyone's taste," Yulik said diplomatically. Then he carried his breakfast to a spot behind Mary's chair, where a pouncing sound followed by a squeak made Mary's stomach turn.

"Eat it already!" she implored.

Madame Z sighed deeply. "I am afraid we are a family that plays with its food."

Was Madame Z playing with *her*? Mary put down the delicious bread, her appetite gone as she heard tiny claws scrabbling against wood, trying to escape. Madame Z had promised not to eat her. But what if the witch didn't mean to honor that promise? It was time to test her.

"So," Mary said matter-of-factly, pushing away her plate, "I'm ready to learn magic. When can we start?"

She waited for Madame Z to make up some excuse, but to her surprise, the old woman stood up eagerly. "Right now, if you like! Come to the parlor, *devochka*."

"Must everyone rush me?" Yulik groused. But, to Mary's relief, a crunch ended the pitiful noises behind her chair.

As she followed Madame Z back into the house, Mary wished she'd had a chance to go to Iris first and at least tell Jacob where she was. But she couldn't run off now, not when Madame Z was offering to start her magic lessons. She felt excited as she imagined learning how to enchant someone with a song or to control the wind.

Madame Z led her to the writing desk with the slender, coltish legs. On top of it sat a black feather quill, an inkpot, and a stack of heavy white paper. She pulled out the simple wooden chair.

"Sit, *devochka*."

Mary sat down as Madame Z pushed her chair in. She could feel the old woman's nose graze her head, but at least she didn't hear her sniff. Madame Z placed the old book with the peeling binding in front of her.

"What's that?" Mary asked, pretending she'd never seen it before.

Madame Z smiled. "Open it, take a look."

Mary flipped open the book to the middle, ready to say that she couldn't read the language inside. But the writing on the page in front of her was unmistakably in English.

"'Place whole cabbage in a large kettle filled with boiling water,'" Mary read. "'Cover and cook for three minutes. Remove leaves.'"

She looked up at Madame Z. "This just looks like a—"

"Recipe, *devochka!*" Madame Z said.

"A very good one," Yulik added from where he lay by the hearth, licking his paws. "For stuffed cabbage rolls."

Mary paged through the book, saw lists of ingredients and instructions. "So it's a cookbook?"

"Exactly!" said Madame Z. "And I need you to copy it. The print is fading."

Mary stared at her in disbelief. "But what about teaching me magic?"

"Magic can't be rushed," Madame Z said. "In the meantime, you might as well learn something about cooking."

"It's a useful skill," Yulik agreed. "Especially if you happen to have opposable thumbs." He looked down regretfully at his paws.

Mary ignored his self-pity and flipped through the cookbook till she reached the last page—363. "You want me to copy *all* of this?"

"Of course," Madame Z said. "But you don't have to stay in

the parlor. The desk and chair move. You can work on the porch, in the kitchen—"

She whistled sharply, and the desk sidled off on its delicate legs like a crab, repositioning itself around the parlor as the chair tottered after it. But having a magical desk and chair didn't seem like much of a consolation to Mary. Copying the entire cookbook would take her weeks—or months, even—and she needed to find Jacob as soon as possible. He was probably sick with worry wondering if she was still alive. Plus she needed his help to stay one step ahead of Madame Z, especially since the witch didn't seem to be honoring her end of the bargain—at least not yet.

With a shrill whistle, Madame Z sent the desk scurrying back to Mary.

"Go on. Let's see how you do."

What choice did Mary have? She couldn't tell Madame Z about Jacob—it seemed dangerous to admit to having a friend, especially since the witch hadn't promised not to eat other children. Mary would just have to wait for an opportunity to sneak out to Iris and see him. Turning back to the first page, Mary took the quill, dipped it in the black ink, and began copying onto the paper. The recipe was for bread. Sugar, water, yeast, milk, eggs, flour, salt. Cover, let rise. Punch down. Repeat. Bake for one hour. There certainly wasn't anything magical about it. Mary copied down a recipe for black bread and one for the cake-like bread she'd just eaten. Madame Z nodded her approval.

"Now I'm afraid I have other business to attend to, *devochka*, but I'll be back by lunch. Come, Yulik."

Madame Z vanished into the foyer. Mary raced after her. She

wanted to be absolutely certain that the witch would be away. "You're leaving me here all morning to copy?"

Madame Z spun around. Her gray eyes flashed at Mary. "Idle fingers can find themselves in dangerous places."

Mary felt the tiny scab on her fingertip, then glanced at the biting lock. "What's really behind that door?"

"Is every child so curious?" Madame Z asked Yulik.

"It is a common trait of their kind," he replied, squinting his eyes playfully at Mary. "As well, I suppose, of my own."

Madame Z bustled out the front door. Seconds later, she and Yulik disappeared into a mist that Mary was certain had not been there before.

There was a clicking noise behind her, and Mary swung around. But it was only the writing desk, which had followed her into the foyer.

"Not now," she said, waving it back into the parlor.

She waited a few minutes to make sure Madame Z and Yulik had gone. Then she grabbed her coat and headed out the door.

EIGHTEEN

As soon as Mary stepped off the porch, the house spun around, turned its back on her, and stalked off into the forest. Although Mary sensed it was temperamental by nature, she couldn't help feeling she had irritated it by leaving. But she put this out of her mind as she ran. To her relief, neither Madame Z nor Koshchey appeared to stop her. Scarlet leaves tumbled down, catching glints of afternoon sun, as she closed the gate of skulls behind her.

Mary reached Jacob's boardinghouse just as a woman with a nest of frizzy black hair leaned out an open window, her neck craned up at the sky.

"Do you see it?" she called out excitedly to Mary, pointing overhead.

Mary looked up, trying to figure out what the woman was looking at.

"There!" the woman said.

Mary followed the woman's finger, and this time she noticed a large bird circling high over town.

"A peregrine falcon," the woman said.

"How nice," Mary said, smiling politely.

But the woman shook her head and cried out dramatically, "Not at all! It's hovering right above you on the left—a sign of underhanded treachery. Woe to you!"

Mary felt a little jolt of fear before she reminded herself that, like Professor Horatio St. John/Harry the pickpocket, the woman was probably just another fraud.

"I don't have any money," she said. "I'm just here to visit Jacob."

The woman's head vanished, and her window slammed shut. She had probably been trying to con Mary, but an unsettled feeling remained.

At the bottom of the stairwell, Mary ran into Dobbin, who was pacing around and eyeing the door, with Fanny entwined around his shoulders and arms.

"Is it gone?"

"What?" Mary asked.

"The falcon. Fortunately, Cassandra alerts me to all birds of prey. She's an augur."

Mary had never heard this word before. "What's that?"

"She predicts the future through birds."

"You believe in that?"

"I believe in falcons. They'll snatch up a snake—usually not one as big as Fanny, but you can never be too careful."

Mary nodded. At least Dobbin's fear was based on reason.

As Mary took the stairs two at a time, she thought about Jacob. He probably had given up hope that she had survived. She couldn't wait to see his face when he opened the door and found her standing there, safe and alive. But then a shadow of doubt crossed her mind. What if he had left Iris already? Perhaps he didn't even miss her that much. He was certainly used to a life of moving on and forgetting people.

A rush of footsteps from above interrupted her thoughts.

"Mary!" a voice cried. "Is that you?"

All her doubts vanished as Jacob hurtled down the stairs and threw his arms around her.

"You did it, didn't you?" he said. "You persuaded her to help you, to give you a home?"

Mary rested her head on his shoulder with a dizzying sense of relief. The way he kept still, letting her remain there, reminded her of the night Caleb had read her "The Juniper Tree." It was one of the most terrifying stories in the *Household Tales* (about a boy murdered by his stepmother and served up as a stew before his sister brought him back to life), and he hadn't said a word when she'd curled up against him, even staying beside her till she fell asleep.

Just like that night, for a moment, Mary felt safe. Then she remembered Madame Z. Pulling away, she told Jacob everything that had happened since she'd last seen him—ending with how Madame Z had said she would teach Mary magic but was first making her copy an old cookbook.

"Perhaps it's some sort of test," Jacob said.

"It could be," Mary said. "But what if she's just playing with me the way Yulik played with that poor mouse? She promised not to eat me, but she is a witch. Can I trust her?"

Jacob thought about this, then nodded. "We need to have a plan in case she breaks her promise."

We. It was a powerful word, one Mary hadn't used in a long time. But she feared it wasn't as powerful as Madame Z. She pictured the witch tossing her in the air with a single wave of her hand.

"But what kind of plan could keep me safe if she turns on me? Especially if she never teaches me anything—she'll have all the magic and I'll have none."

"We need some help," Jacob agreed. "But there's someone else in Iris who does real magic. We both saw her—"

Mary realized at once where he was going. "Madame Petitsa!"

"Exactly. What if she could give us some real magic of our own?"

"You think she'd help us?" Mary asked.

"I don't know," Jacob said honestly. "But it's worth a try. I'd like to at least find out who she really is."

Mary nodded, though she didn't relish the idea of going back to the black cottage with its stench of smoke.

Jacob seemed to sense this. "Don't worry," he said. "We'll be together. And I have a good feeling."

His optimism was as contagious as his showman's grin. With a flourish, he clapped his hands and his top hat popped up between them.

"How did you—?" Mary asked.

"Like the cage," Jacob said as he set it at a raffish angle on his head.

"It collapses?"

Jacob linked his arm through hers. "You're learning fast."

Ten minutes later, they were in Madame Petitsa's parlor, watching her swallow flame after flame. But this time, Mary noticed that Jacob wasn't focused as much on Madame Petitsa. Instead, his eyes kept flickering over to Mary. She smiled reassuringly at him. It wasn't even an act. Perhaps it was just the draft from the fireplace, but the dark room seemed airier, the smoke less suffocating.

They waited behind as the crowd drifted out. At last, the final tourist closed the door behind her, plunging the room back into darkness.

"Madame Petitsa," Jacob began, "we—"

"The show is over."

Mary realized she had never heard Madame Petitsa's voice before. She'd performed her show in silence. It was surprisingly sweet and musical, considering how much fire she ate.

"We know," Mary said. "But we need to talk to you."

"We need your help," Jacob added.

Mary worried that he'd broached the subject too directly and that the fire-eater might be frightened off. She could easily slip out in the darkness. But, after a moment's silence, there was a hiss. Madame Petitsa blew a flame out of her mouth and lit the torch in her hand. The flames illuminated her crooked nose and lashless brown eyes. Her gauzy orange robes shimmered in the light. "What kind of help?"

"There is a witch named Baba Yaga—" Mary said.

Madame Petitsa interrupted her with an incredulous laugh. "A witch?"

"You don't believe in magic?" Jacob asked.

Madame Petitsa stared at him. "Tricks, yes," she said. "Not real magic—"

"But you don't do tricks," Jacob said quietly. "I've been watching you long enough to know."

Madame Petitsa gave a tight smile. "You just haven't figured them out."

"You lean over the flame . . ." Jacob pressed. "You don't get burned. . . ."

The fire-eater's eyes darted to the side. "There's no witch in Iris."

"Look," Mary said impatiently, "I know there's a witch here, because I live with her! She eats children, but she's made an exception for me. She's promised to teach me magic, but she hasn't yet."

With a powerful gust, Madame Petitsa's torch blew out. Mary tensed and grabbed Jacob's arm.

"I think we scared her away," she whispered.

"No," Jacob whispered back. "She's here."

Mary listened, heard the swish of robes.

"Please," she said into the darkness. "If there's any way you can give us some magic. Just in case Baba Yaga changes her mind about me."

The swishing sound stopped, but there was no response. Just as Mary was about to turn toward the door, the room flooded with light. She squinted and blinked her eyes. A glowing orange bird the size of a swan was flapping in the air in front of them.

"I've seen you before!" Mary shouted, remembering the dancing light outside her window. It all made sense now. Pulling the feather out of her pocket, she waved it in the air. "You live in the forest behind the house."

"It's *her* feather!" Jacob said. "Of course!"

Mary slipped the feather back into her pocket and turned to the glowing bird. "You must know how powerful Baba Yaga is. Can you help us?"

In Madame Petitsa's musical voice, the bird began to sing:

> *A wish the Firebird may grant*
> *But only to humans, who cannot enchant.*
> *First they must catch me, then I will trade*
> *A wish to each captor for freedom repaid.*

Mary's pulse quickened. "She's offering us a wish!" she said.

A wish was far more powerful than a magical object that had only a limited use. It could solve everything. She could wish to become more powerful than Madame Z if the witch ever turned against her. That way, Mary would be able to defend herself. She would no longer have to worry about Madame Z's real intentions.

The Firebird hovered right in front of them, no more than a few yards away.

"We just have to catch her," Jacob said under his breath.

Mary's eyes locked onto Jacob's. He gave an imperceptible nod, and together they rushed forward to grab the Firebird. But just as they were about to seize her, there was a loud *pop* and the bird burst into flame.

Mary lurched backward, pulling Jacob down to the ground. Seemingly unbothered by the fire engulfing her, the bird flew over their heads.

"Don't touch her!" Mary warned, keeping her arm over Jacob's.

The bird flew into the fireplace, plunging the room back into darkness as she vanished up the chimney.

With shaking hands, Mary sat up and reached into her pocket. Then she took out the feather, flooding the room with light.

"Are you all right?" Jacob asked.

"I think so," she said. "You?"

He nodded. "You pulled me away pretty quickly." He was sitting up now, too, looking at the fireplace, which bore a small scorch mark. "But there's nothing like having a wish blow up in your face."

Mary was surprised to find she could laugh.

"We're going to have to catch her, though," Jacob said matter-of-factly, standing up and pulling Mary to her feet. "You need that wish."

"I know," she agreed. "But how? We can't even touch her."

"We'll think of something," he said, leading Mary out of Madame Petitsa's cottage. "We just need a little time."

Mary started at the word. "Your father's not planning to leave Iris anytime soon, is he?"

Jacob laughed bitterly. "He's always planning to leave. But he's paid up through the week."

"I thought you were here a few weeks at least!" she said, trying to keep the panic out of her voice.

He looked away. "I don't know."

"What if we don't have enough time?"

He sighed quietly. "Let's not think about that now. Just meet me back here tomorrow if you can. And in the meantime, you know where to find me—day or night."

"Wait," she said as he turned down his street to the boarding-house. "What's your wish? If we catch the Firebird together, you'll get one, too. You once said you wished for something."

He looked back at her and smiled. But his eyes seemed sad, as if he didn't believe his wish could ever come true.

"A home I'd never have to leave again."

NINETEEN

THE SUN WAS STILL OVERHEAD when Mary opened the gate topped with skulls and crossed back into Madame Z's realm. She hoped Madame Z had not returned home already. As Mary stopped in the yard and opened her mouth to call the house out from the forest, she heard footsteps behind her. She swung around, fearing the witch's fury, but it was only Koshchey.

"Didn't mean to startle you!" he said with a chuckle. "Where have you been?"

Mary thought about lying, but she had the feeling that Koshchey must have seen her come through the gate.

"Iris," she admitted. "I just had to get out, take a walk."

Koshchey leaned in and smiled. "Don't worry," he said quietly. "I won't tell Baba Yaga."

"Thanks," Mary said, feeling grateful but at the same time a little strange about sharing a secret. "And thank you for telling me Baba Yaga might help me. I'm sorry she punished you for it."

"It's nothing," Koshchey said with a wave of his long, skinny hand. "Baba Yaga is often displeased with me, but she knows she can't hurt me. I keep my soul outside of my body, in an egg. It's hidden away where no one—not even Baba Yaga—can find it."

Even though Mary could see the wisdom in Koshchey's protecting himself from Madame Z, it disturbed her to think that his soul wasn't in his body. "What are you, exactly?"

"I think you'd call me a wizard, though I'm not nearly as powerful as Baba Yaga. Her magic is far greater than mine. But I had a feeling she might give you a chance."

"Why have you helped me?" Mary asked.

"You just seemed different from the other girls," Koshchey said. "More like someone she might respect."

Mary didn't feel as if he had fully answered the question—she had meant to find out what was in it for him—but it seemed rude to press the subject further. "So you don't think she'll change her mind about me?" she asked instead.

Koshchey shook his head. "I've been serving her for many years now. I think she's grown lonely in America, although she would never admit such a thing. It seems possible here for anyone to have a family, to belong. How is she treating you?"

"She said she'd teach me some magic—"

"Wonderful!" Koshchey said, clasping his hands together.

"—but she's just having me copy an old cookbook."

Koshchey considered this. "It's probably a test. Of your patience."

"Perhaps," Mary said. But she didn't feel certain enough to abandon her and Jacob's plan. She suddenly remembered seeing birdcages in Koshchey's hut. "Do you know anything about the Firebird?"

"The Firebird!" Koshchey said happily, as if Mary had mentioned an old friend. "Of course. Lives in the forest. Gives a wish to a mortal who can catch her." Koshchey shook his head as if he was just realizing something. "A wise idea! I knew you were clever. But catching the Firebird . . ."

He paused, locked his pale blue eyes on hers.

"What?" Mary asked.

"It's close to impossible. Mortals have wasted decades of their lives chasing the bird. I would focus instead on endearing yourself to Madame Z. Do this task she asks, even if it's pointless. Prove that you deserve her trust and affection."

Mary studied his face, trying to decide whether to believe him. On the one hand, if Madame Z planned to eat her, and Koshchey was in on the game, it would make perfect sense for him to discourage her from trying to catch the Firebird. But on the other hand, he had given her advice that had helped her find her way out of the forest, and that had seemed to truly anger Madame Z.

Mary glanced back over her shoulder. She wanted to call the house and retreat inside, where she could mull this over in private. But she didn't want to explain to Koshchey that Madame Z had said she couldn't invite him in. He seemed to sense her conundrum, because he put one hand on her shoulder and gave it a friendly squeeze.

"I should go."

As soon as he'd disappeared into the woods, Mary called

to the house, using the same words Madame Z had used. "*Izba!*
Turn your back to the forest and your face to me!*"

At first, she wasn't sure the words would work. But a few seconds later, there were thunderous cracks as the trees straightened their limbs, revealing the house beneath them. It spun around, like a dog excited by its master's return, before coming to a stop with its front door facing Mary.

The moment the wooden stairs clacked down, Mary was up them. She thrust her hand against the little bird at the center of the door. Her fingers began to tingle, and the wood grew supple and warm beneath them. Seconds later, she could feel silky feathers and a racing heartbeat. The door popped open. It was time to get back to work.

All afternoon and late into the evening, Mary copied the cookbook. Whenever her hand tired of writing, or the desk and chair started to wiggle and grow restless, she let them move around from the parlor to the porch to her room (she found they could climb the stairs quite ably) for a change of scene and a break. Madame Z, who had returned home with Yulik right before lunch, watched her without comment, but Mary could tell from the smile that played on her wrinkled lips that she was pleased with her effort.

As she copied, Mary paid closer attention to the recipes than she had earlier that morning. In the boardinghouse where she had lived with her mother and Caleb, the owner, Mrs. Walsh, had always made the meals—usually a bland combination of porridge and vegetables, or a watery soup. Mary's mother had never had the opportunity to teach Mary to cook, and working in the kitchen of the orphanage was a prized duty assigned to Mrs. Boot's favorites. For the first time, Mary considered the elements of a recipe. There was always a list of ingredients to be combined in a particular order, blending flavors to create something new. But each ingredient had a role. Miss one and the dish was incomplete.

The next morning, Mary was up at sunrise, leading the sleepy desk and chair out to the porch to copy. By the time the hands set out bowls of thick, creamy buckwheat porridge that she recognized from the cookbook as kasha (1 cup buckwheat groats, 1 teaspoon salt, 2 tablespoons sugar, 2 ounces butter, 3.5 cups milk), she had made it a quarter of the way through the book.

"*Oomnichka!*" Madame Z said, joining her on the porch and observing Mary's work.

"Well done!" Yulik translated, digging his front paws into the desk as he peeked over the side.

The desk jumped back, forcing the cat to drop onto all four paws. The chair cowered behind it.

"I don't think the desk likes your claws," Mary said.

"None of the furniture does," Yulik said in a voice that suggested he didn't much care.

"The desk does seem a little sensitive," Madame Z said. "Probably just tired. Fortunately, he can rest today."

Mary blinked, not quite following. "But I'm planning to copy the second quarter."

"It can wait," Madame Z said as one of the hands passed her a cup of rotten-leaf tea. "There's something I want to teach you, *devochka.*"

Mary sat up straighter in her seat. She had followed Koshchey's advice. She had worked hard on the cookbook, demonstrating her devotion to the task. She had even started to enjoy it. "Magic?"

But Madame Z just smiled. "I'll show you after breakfast."

Mary stuffed down her kasha, but Madame Z seemed to be eating even more slowly than usual. Breakfast dragged on and on. At last, Madame Z pushed away her bowl and stood up. "*Pora,*" she said, leading Mary back into the house. "Come."

As Mary followed her into the parlor, she noticed that the old loom had been threaded with the black wool yarn from Madame Z's dresser. She hoped this had nothing to do with what the witch wanted to teach her, but to her dismay, Madame Z led her straight to the loom.

"Did your mother ever teach you how to weave?" she asked.

Mary shook her head, trying not to appear disappointed. "Only sew. She was a seamstress."

"Sewing," Madame Z said with a dismissive wave of the hand. "Nothing to it. But weaving! What is life but warp and weft?"

"Warp and . . . ?" Mary repeated.

Madame Z pointed to the taut threads of yarn running lengthwise along the loom. "This is the warp," she said. "The weft is the yarn we weave across and between it."

She sat down on the bench and picked up an oblong wooden object that looked like a toy canoe. "This is called a shuttle," she said. "The weft yarn goes inside it." She popped it open. Inside was a bobbin like the type Mary remembered her mother winding thread from.

Producing another triangular cone of black yarn, Madame Z

wound it around the bobbin. Yulik slipped in to join them. He watched the dangling end of the yarn with unblinking interest; Mary imagined that only his dignity prevented him from pouncing on it.

"Now, watch carefully," Madame Z said as she popped the bobbin back into the shuttle. "There are two pedals for my feet, called treadles. I'll start with the right one." There was a *clack* as she pressed it down. "It pulls the warp yarn apart, creating a space called a shed. I pass the shuttle with my weft yarn through the shed and catch it with my other hand."

Madame Z tossed the shuttle from her right hand to her left with dexterity. "Then I take this reed and pull it in," she continued, grabbing onto a wooden bar and yanking it toward her with another clack, "to beat the warp and weft yarn together into cloth. Sometimes I beat it two or three times before continuing. Then it's back the opposite way."

Mary listened attentively, but once again nothing about the process seemed magical at all. If anything, it seemed repetitive and boring.

Madame Z stood up. "Your turn, *devochka*. Give it a try."

Mary reluctantly sat down on the bench. The wood was worn and slippery.

"Try the treadles first," Madame Z said.

Mary pressed down on the right treadle. The warp yarn only stretched an inch or two apart.

"Harder!" Madame Z said.

Mary pressed the treadle more. Pulling apart the coarse yarn was tougher than it looked.

"Good! Now pass the shuttle through."

Mary reached out with her left hand.

"No, use your right," Madame Z corrected.

Mary clumsily switched hands and passed the shuttle beneath the shed, sliding over on the bench to grab it with her left hand. Then she pulled back the reed to beat the yarn.

"Beat it again now," Madame Z said. "It needs to be tighter. Then switch feet."

Mary pressed down on the treadle with her left foot, passed the shuttle beneath the shed from her left hand to her right, and beat the yarn with the reed.

"Now switch! Open, pass, catch, beat!"

Click-clack went the loom as Mary haltingly managed another row.

"Very good, *devochka*," Madame Z said when Mary had finished. "Now all you have to do is weave until you're out of warp yarn."

Mary looked down at the tiny edge of cloth she had woven and the yards of warp yarn ahead. Weaving it all would take her weeks or even months. This wasn't what Madame Z had promised. "But what about teaching me magic?"

"Weaving is an ancient and important art," said Yulik.

"I told you, magic must be earned," Madame Z said. She gave Mary a sharp look. "Besides, what's the rush?"

"No rush," Mary said, picking up the shuttle. If Koshchey was right and Madame Z was testing her patience, it was best she do these tasks without complaint. But as she pressed the treadle down with her left foot and passed the shuttle beneath the shed, she wondered if Madame Z was just toying with her again, like Yulik with his mouse.

She wished she could discuss this with Jacob, but Madame Z and Yulik stayed home all morning. Even worse, the witch propped her feet up on the sofa and watched Mary, constantly calling out corrections—"Don't bounce the shuttle! Don't beat so hard! Keep moving! It's one motion! Don't stop!"

By noon, when the hands came bearing heaping bowls of cabbage soup and a loaf of black bread, Mary had woven barely four inches of cloth. Several spots were bumpy, and the edge was uneven. Her back ached and her fingers were stiff.

"You'll get the hang of it, *devochka*," Madame Z said over lunch. "Yulik and I need to go out, so you'll have the afternoon to practice on your own."

Mary was relieved to hear this, although she was beginning to wonder whether Madame Z kept leaving her on purpose, to see what she would do.

After lunch, Madame Z threw on her black shawl. Mary followed her and Yulik out to the porch, as if she just wanted to wave good-bye. But she really intended to watch which way they were going.

The afternoon was clear but cool. A breeze gently shook the trees. Mary shivered in her dress.

"We'll be back by dinnertime, *devochka*," Madame Z said.

Yulik pounced on a falling leaf. Then they turned and disappeared into the forest. At least they didn't seem to be headed toward Iris. As Mary stood there a moment longer to make sure they didn't reemerge, she thought about the Firebird. She had no doubt that Koshchey's claim that the bird was nearly impossible to catch was true. The Golden Bird from the *Household Tales* was just as elusive. But in that tale, an old fox had given the hero advice on how to capture it. Mary considered asking Yulik for help—he was, after all, a talking animal. But she feared he was too loyal to Madame Z to tell Mary anything. Koshchey had already discouraged her from pursuing the Firebird. Still, there had to be someone else who could help her.

Mary went back inside for her coat. Just as she was about to grab it from the rack, she stopped and stared at it. The answer was right in front of her.

TWENTY

"His name is Mr. Less," Mary said. "He runs the Magic and Curiosity Shop."

Jacob stood beside her outside the hotel, his eyes fixed on her coat. Mary had already filled him in on her talk with Koshchey, on her new weaving task, and on the story of "The Golden Bird" and how the hero had found a magical helper. Behind them, Mr. Kagan was packing up from his two o'clock show, stopping every so often to shoot an irritated glance at Jacob, presumably for not helping.

"You don't have to convince me," Jacob said. "Your coat has no seams."

Mary looked down. He was right. "When did you notice?"

"A while ago," Jacob admitted. "But I figured the seams were somehow cleverly hidden by a master tailor. And then once I knew who Madame Z really was, I figured she'd made it."

"No, it was Mr. Less. He never even measured me, just brought it out and it fit perfectly. Same with the boots. And you know what else?" Mary said, realizing it only as she spoke. "I've gained weight, and the coat still fits just as well."

"It must be growing with you," Jacob said.

"Madame Z took me to his shop. Since he knows her, will he help me?"

Jacob thought about this. "Koshchey risked helping you. Come on—it's worth a try."

A few minutes later, they opened the door to the Magic and Curiosity Shop. Just as Mary remembered from her earlier visits, objects cluttered the shelves, walls, floor, and ceiling— candelabras and crystals, carpets and headdresses, samurai swords and ostrich eggs, fishing nets and wands, and the enormous stuffed bear looming above the store on its hind legs. It reminded her of the bear she had seen briefly in the woods on the night of the mushroom hunt—the one she'd thought she imagined. Could there be some connection?

Mr. Less was sitting behind the counter, carefully wrapping up the set of antlers the swallow had landed on. A tall man was peeling bills from a thick roll. Mary and Jacob stood politely in line behind him.

"Glad to find something for myself," the man said. "The wife insisted I take her to Iris, but I'm not a believer in all this hocus-pocus. Much prefer to hunt. You a hunting man, Less?"

Mr. Less caught Mary's eye and winked. "No."

"A cool autumn morning. The quiet of the woods. A ten-point buck emerges from the mist. *Bang!*" The man shook his head. "I tell you, you're missing out."

"Will that be all?" Mr. Less asked as he handed the hunter his package, which seemed to have doubled in size during the wrapping.

"Yes," the man said as he took it with a grunt. "Heavier than you'd imagine."

Jacob ran over to hold open the door. The tall man staggered out with his package. Mary noticed that he didn't even bother to thank Jacob.

"What did you really give him?" Jacob asked after he had closed the door.

Mr. Less opened his green eyes wide, affecting an expression of innocence. "I just gave him what he wanted. Now, what can I do for you, Mary? A hat this time?"

"We need some magic," she said.

"You've come to the right place!" Mr. Less said, waving his hand around his shop. "I have it all. Wands, change bags, card decks, invisible thread, palming coins, dove decoys—"

"Real magic," Mary said. "Something to help us catch the Firebird."

Surprise flashed across Mr. Less's face before his eyes crinkled with mirth. "And what makes you think I can help?"

"You do real magic," Jacob said. "You made Mary's coat out of a single piece of fabric."

"And you turned that wood bird into a real one. Just like the one on Madame Z's door."

Mr. Less stepped out from behind the counter. This seemed like a good sign, but then he threw open his arms and laughed playfully. "Anything else?"

Mary glanced at Jacob, who was studying Mr. Less like a difficult trick.

"Your shoes are on backward," Jacob said.

Mary looked down at Mr. Less's feet. Jacob was right. This must have been what had seemed off before. The tips of the shopkeeper's boots were pointing the wrong way.

"Clever boy," Mr. Less said, stepping back behind the counter. "I have no shadow, either. Harder to see that in the shop, though."

"What are you?" Jacob asked.

But Mr. Less ignored him and, with a grin, turned to Mary. "So you are settling in with Madame Z?"

"She's adopted me and has promised to teach me magic," Mary said. "But I need to make sure she stays true to her word and doesn't eat me."

Mr. Less shook his head. "Do all orphans have such low standards for a parent?"

"She's no ordinary parent," Mary said with a stern glance. "You know how powerful she is."

"Parents always seem powerful to their children," Mr. Less declared.

"She *is* powerful, and you know it. We need your help. Please."

"A *leshy* doesn't help mortals."

"What's a *leshy*?" Jacob asked.

But the words were barely out of his mouth when the storekeeper vanished.

"Is he behind the counter?" Mary asked, leaning over it.

Jacob didn't even bother looking. "No. That was real vanishing. Not some trick."

"Mr. Less?" Mary called.

A low growl sounded from behind them.

Mary clutched Jacob's hand as they spun around. "What was that?"

"The bear!" he said.

The stuffed bear gave a roar as its enormous front paws, tipped with claws, hit the ground. Now on all fours, it lumbered past them, knocking over tribal masks, Chinese vases, Indian eagle carvings, and everything else in its path. It was so close that Mary could smell its musky fur and rank breath.

Jacob grabbed an African flute and brandished it between them and the bear.

"Wait!" Mary said, pulling it away. "I've seen that bear before. Mr. Less," she said as loudly as her shaking voice could manage, "I know what you're doing. Stop it!"

As if in answer, the bear began to shrink, its snout and tail growing longer and white. The bear-turned-wolf winked one yellow eye at her.

"He did this in the woods," Mary explained to Jacob. "Trying to get me lost."

This time, she wouldn't let him get away. Losing all fear, she chased the wolf, but with a burst of speed, it leaped over a knight's breastplate and a large stone gargoyle. As it raced toward the front of the shop, Mary thought she could corner it. But with a running jump, it sailed through the closed door like a ghost, flicking the OPEN sign to CLOSED with one paw.

Mary stopped just short of crashing into the solid wood. She gave the door a frustrated kick, then slumped against it. "Now what?"

But Jacob was looking intently around the shop. "Maybe there's something here we could use to catch the Firebird."

Mary looked at the overflowing shelves and covered walls. "Like what?"

Her eyes fell on the scuffed leather boot. She had forgotten all about it, and no wonder—it was no longer on top of the table where she had seen it before; now it was on the floor, next to a basket of Oriental fans. Her own boots stood next to it, just as she had suggested to Mr. Less.

"Jacob!" Mary whispered, beckoning him over.

She tiptoed to the boot, snatched it off the ground. The boot didn't resist, but Mary still held it tight just in case.

"The first time I was here I saw it move," she explained.

Jacob tapped on the sole and heel. "There are trick boots with compartments," he said. "But this one doesn't have any."

Then he stuck his hand inside. His eyes widened. "There's something in here! A doll? No, it feels . . . alive. Maybe a rabbit?"

Mary couldn't help smiling. "Aren't you supposed to yank a rabbit out of a hat, not a boot?"

Jacob's face twisted in confusion. "It doesn't feel like a rabbit. . . ."

He pulled out his hand. At the sight of what he was holding, Mary dropped the boot.

TWENTY-ONE

"BE CAREFUL WITH MY BOOT!" cried the creature. He was completely covered with white fur but had a face like a little old man's, with bristly eyebrows, a knobby nose, and a long white beard that blended in with his furry body.

"I'm . . . I'm sorry," Mary stammered.

The creature nodded, seeming to accept her apology, then squirmed around to look up at Jacob. Mary was impressed that Jacob managed to keep hold of him.

"I'm not a rabbit!" the creature said to him in a squeaky voice. "I'm a *domovoi*."

"Of course you are," said Mary. By this time she had collected herself. Although she had no idea what a *domovoi* was, she

figured it was some sort of elf. In the *Household Tales*, elves could be helpful—like the ones who made shoes during the night for the poor shoemaker—or they could be tricksters, stealing babies and inviting humans to revels that were supposed to last a single night and ended up lasting years. Either way, Mary knew it was important to be polite.

But Jacob stared at the *domovoi* with a fascination that bordered on rudeness. "What's a *domovoi*?"

"A house spirit." The creature did not seem the least bit offended by the question. Instead, he looked up at Jacob with interest. "I take it you don't have one?"

"I don't think so."

"Banging pots? Rattling dishes?"

Jacob shook his head.

"Are you Mr. Less's house spirit?" Mary asked.

The *domovoi* looked at Mary as if she was dim-witted. "What would a *leshy* need with a house spirit?"

"What is a *leshy*?"

"Just what you saw!" the *domovoi* said, not bothering to hide his irritation. He wiggled in Jacob's grasp, freeing a furry little hand, and began ticking off on his fingers. "Woodland spirit, protector of nature, shape-shifter who enjoys fooling travelers. If you were a bird or a beast, he might help, but a human trying to catch the Firebird, a creature of the forest? You're wasting your time!"

Jacob lifted the *domovoi* up to eye level. "Would we be wasting our time with you?"

"That depends."

"On what?" Mary asked.

The *domovoi* cleared his throat and assumed a serious expression. "I am looking for a home."

Mary almost laughed. If this was all the *domovoi* needed . . . "I could give you a home!"

"You?" the *domovoi* sputtered. "I can't be a *domovoi* for Baba Yaga! I need a human home. Besides, that nasty cat would chase me just for the fun of it."

Mary thought about defending Yulik but then, remembering the pleasure he'd taken in batting around the mouse, decided against it.

"Help us," Jacob said, "and you can live with me. I have only a single room, though."

The *domovoi* didn't seem to mind. His beard twitched as he fought a smile. Clearly, he had been hoping that Jacob might extend just such an invitation.

"Does it have a stove?" he asked.

"A small one," Jacob said.

"And pots and dishes?"

"A few."

The *domovoi* clapped his hands with glee. "I am not a big banger or rattler. You'll like me. Although, of course, you won't see me. Or let's hope you won't ever see me."

Jacob shook his head. "What do you mean?"

"Oh, you don't know the rules of house spirits," the *domovoi* said with far more good humor and patience than Mary felt he had exhibited with her. "Once I move into your home, we will no longer be able to speak to or see each other. The only time I am allowed to show myself is if you are in mortal danger."

Mary wished she could convince the *domovoi* that Yulik

wasn't so bad; she could really use a "mortal danger" alarm at Madame Z's. But it made her feel good to know that the *domovoi* was excited about his home, plus that he would be watching over Jacob.

"Understood," Jacob said. "Now, how can we catch the Firebird?"

The *domovoi* popped himself out of Jacob's grasp. Mary half-feared he was running away, but he merely hopped onto a table and began to rummage until at last he pulled out a small silver dagger. It had a colorful enamel hilt and a matching sheath decorated with images of foxes, pheasants, and other forest animals.

"Here it is!" he said emphatically.

Mary exchanged an alarmed glance with Jacob.

"We're not trying to kill the Firebird," Jacob said gently. "We're just trying to capture her."

"Of course! You can't kill her," the *domovoi* said. "She's immortal. But you can clip her wings so she can't fly! The dagger is magic. It will enable you do it without touching her."

"But if she can't fly away, then she can't be free," Mary said. "And we need to give her back her freedom after we capture her, in order to get our wishes."

The *domovoi*'s face fell. It was obvious he hadn't thought of this. He glanced at Jacob, blinking back tears.

"It's okay," Jacob said. "I'll still give you a home. And Mary could probably use a magic dagger."

Mary thought this was very gallant of Jacob.

"I will always be in your debt," the *domovoi* said, his voice trembling. With a loud sniff, he collected himself and handed the dagger to Mary.

"Thank you," she said. She admired the design on the sheath, trying to make the *domovoi* feel the gift was still appreciated. "How does it work?"

The *domovoi* perked up. "Start with something simple. Like that! Have the dagger spear it." He pointed to a red velvet pincushion on the table beside him, then clambered up onto Jacob's shoulder. Tugging on a lock of his hair, the *domovoi* added, "It would be wise for us to clear the area."

Jacob obediently took several steps away.

Mary held up the dagger, squinted one eye as she aimed—

"No, no, no!" said the *domovoi*, waving his furry little hands and jumping up and down. "Don't throw it! Speak to it!"

Mary lowered her hand and looked down at the dagger. "Hit the pincushion."

The dagger floated up out of her hands and lazily spun in the air.

"Amazing!" said Jacob. Mary guessed he was imagining a spinning-dagger act.

But the *domovoi* didn't seem the least bit impressed. "You need to be firm with it!" he shouted.

Mary grabbed the enamel hilt. "Hit the pincushion!" she barked.

Both Jacob and the *domovoi* ducked as the dagger whizzed over their heads and speared the wood counter.

The *domovoi* hopped up and down on Jacob's shoulder. "Your lack of manners nearly killed us! You must be firm but polite!"

Despite his brush with death, Jacob was laughing. "She *is* a beginner."

"I suppose you are right," replied the *domovoi*, who seemed to agree with anything Jacob said.

"Sorry," Mary said.

With great effort, she managed to pull the dagger out of the counter. "Hit the pincushion, please," she told it.

Up it sailed, out of her hands, and with a *thump*, it landed in the center of the pincushion.

Jacob applauded, and even the *domovoi* allowed her a nod of approval. "A few more times and I think you'll have it down."

On the *domovoi*'s orders, Mary practiced having the dagger cut out the appendix on the anatomical chart, trim a feather off a headdress, and attack the knight's breastplate. Jacob cheered for her each time. The *domovoi* sat cross-legged on his shoulder, offering an occasional tip, such as suggesting she praise the dagger when it did a good job, to keep up its self-esteem.

At last, Mary called the dagger back to her and slipped it into its sheath, then into her dress pocket. She knew it would be pointless to use against Madame Z—she imagined the witch knocking it off course as easily as she had tossed Koshchey up into the air. Still, it made Mary feel a little craftier and less vulnerable than before.

"Maybe you could give Jacob something magical, too," she said to the *domovoi*.

Jacob nodded. "Maybe something I can use in my father's act?"

The *domovoi* hopped off Jacob's shoulder and scurried across the floor until he reached the old boot, lying on its side where Mary had dropped it. Grabbing it by its laces, he dragged it over to Jacob.

"Here!" he said triumphantly.

Jacob smiled a little too hard as he picked up the boot. Mary could tell he was disappointed. After the dagger, it did seem like a rather second-rate magical object.

"What does it do?" he asked hopefully.

"It holds me," the *domovoi* said, puffing out his furry chest. "I must be in it if I am to be taken outside my home. Of course, I prefer never to leave my home, but if I must—"

"In the boot," Jacob said.

The *domovoi* nodded. "Exactly."

"Does the boot do anything else?" Mary asked.

The *domovoi* frowned at her. "What else would you demand of it?"

"It's perfect," Jacob said graciously. "I'll keep it by my bed."

After bowing to Jacob, the *domovoi* jumped into the boot. "Home!" he bellowed happily before pulling the tongue over his head.

Mary looked at a cuckoo clock hanging on the wall. "I need to get back soon," she said when the *domovoi* was out of sight. "But we still don't have a plan for how to catch the Firebird."

"Sure we do," Jacob said. "Look, we've already found three magical creatures hiding out in Iris—"

"All from Madame Z's world," she interrupted. "That's clearly where the magic is coming from."

He nodded. "And I'm betting there are more."

"So how do we find them?" she asked.

Jacob floated his top hat onto his head with a grin. "Simple. Next time you come to town, we watch some more acts, see who's doing real magic."

Mary nodded, but before she could say anything else, shouts rose up from outside. They ran to the window just in time to see an enormous stag leap off the porch of the hotel and race down the street toward the setting sun, string and wrapping paper tangled in its antlers.

TWENTY-TWO

BACK AT MADAME Z'S, Mary sat down in front of the loom, determined to make some progress. She wove a row but then hit the treadle on the same side twice instead of switching directions, unweaving what she had woven. Slamming her hand down on the bench, she tried again, but her anger made her pull the beater too hard, and the line of cloth became bumpy and bunched together.

It was clear she couldn't weave while angry. She took a deep breath. When she felt a little calmer, she started again, chanting out loud to herself as she worked. "Open, pass, catch, beat."

At first, she had to stop and think before each step. But gradually her hands fell into a rhythm, and as she tossed the shuttle back and forth between them, she found herself sliding from one side of the bench to the other. She could even feel the comforting groove in it that Madame Z must have worn before her.

As the afternoon lengthened, she still made mistakes and had to stop and start over. But there were also stretches where the *click-clack* of the loom started to sound even, like hoofbeats. She could smell the barnyard scent of the wool and even a hint of the forest in the loom's wooden frame. She let her hands do the work and her mind wander.

The door creaked open and, with a jerk, Mary stopped weaving and looked around the room. It had grown dark. But nearly two feet of woven cloth spilled over the side of the loom.

All three sets of hands flew out of the kitchen and into the foyer. Mary raced after them, watching as the hands took Madame Z's shawl and fussed around their mistress.

"And me?" Yulik said, waving his tail with mock outrage. "Not a pat on the head or a scratch beneath the chin?"

Mary knelt down to give him both a pat and a scratch.

"Such warm fingers," Yulik said, squinting his gooseberry-green eyes at her as he purred.

"Well, no one likes cold ones," Madame Z said, twisting her face as if at a bitter taste. She turned to the plumpest pair of hands. "What's for supper?"

But before the hands could motion, Madame Z waved away the question. "*Nyet*, wait! I have an idea. *Peekneek!*"

The hands burst into applause, but Mary didn't know whether to share their enthusiasm.

"What's *peekneek*?" she asked.

Madame Z smiled sweetly at her. "Let's see how your weaving is coming along first."

"Very well, hopefully. I'm famished," Yulik said, and began to lick his paws. Clearly, *peekneek* had something to do with food. But the mystery surrounding it made Mary nervous, especially as a former main ingredient.

"Then all of you, to the kitchen," Madame Z said, waving away the cat and hands. "Get ready while Mary shows me what she has done. Shall we, *devochka*?"

Mary hoped her weaving would satisfy Madame Z, especially since she'd spent several hours in Iris with Jacob when she was supposed to be at the loom. But whatever the witch thought of her work, Mary knew it was important to appear confident and unafraid. Luckily, acting this way was getting easier. "After you," she said, stepping aside with an unconcerned shrug.

Madame Z darted into the parlor, her gait swift and eager. Mary followed her to the loom.

"*Oomnichka!*" Madame Z exclaimed in delight. "Excellent work, *devochka*! You're making fewer mistakes."

Mary felt an unexpected burst of pride at this compliment. "Thank you."

"Motion conquers emotion," Madame Z continued, inspecting the cloth as if Mary's feelings had been woven into it. "That is why when I have a problem I always weave."

Mary wondered what kind of problems a witch like Madame Z might have, but she didn't dare ask. "What is *peekneek*?" she asked again instead.

But before Madame Z had a chance to answer, the hands burst out of the kitchen carrying white cloth bundles. Some of them clanked.

"You may proceed," the witch said to them.

They obediently flew off into the foyer. Yulik, who had been following them with his tail raised and an air of excitement, peeled off to twine himself through Mary's legs.

"You're going to love this," he said eagerly.

"Absolutely!" Madame Z said. Taking Mary's hand in her cold and bony one, she led Mary into the foyer. "*Pora!* Come. I'll show you."

The door with the flesh-eating lock was open. Mary craned her neck, but the door was propped open only a few inches, and it was too dark to see what was inside. The keyhole mouth of the lock gulped as if swallowing something, then smiled at her.

"Go on!" Madame Z said, nudging her toward the door. "It's the perfect time. The sun has set."

Time for what, Mary wondered? She remembered that one of the chimneys sat directly above the locked door, and wondered if it housed some special fireplace to roast children in. But this made no sense; Madame Z already had the *pech*. Besides, Mary had been working hard on Madame Z's tasks, and Madame Z seemed genuinely pleased with her efforts. Mary flung open the door the rest of the way.

Instead of the fireplace she had been imagining, Mary felt a cold draft from above. There was no hearth or kindling, either, only what looked to be a broomstick in the corner and a stone club leaning against an enormous gray bowl. The rim was as high as Mary's waist, and the bowl was deeper than a bathtub. The hands flew through the door and deposited the white bundles in the bottom of it, like a pile of dumplings.

Grabbing the club and broomstick, the witch jumped into the bowl. Yulik sprang up to the rim and began impatiently circling.

"Get in, *devochka*," Madame Z said, her voice merry.

Mary threw her leg over the rim and scrambled into the bowl. The stone was surprisingly warm and created a heated bubble so that the experience of sitting in it was not unlike a warm bath. Only the draft on her head was cold, and as Mary looked up, she realized why. She could see right up through the huge chimney into the sky. She could even see a few stars. They seemed to be falling toward her, and then, with a dizzying rush, she realized it was she who was rising toward them.

"The bowl—it's flying!" she exclaimed.

"It's a mortar," Yulik corrected. "A bowl used to crush ingredients."

Mary hoped she wasn't an ingredient about to be crushed. But it seemed unlikely, since Yulik and Madame Z were in the mortar with her. Her stomach lurched, and she gripped the sides as they shot up out of the chimney into the deepening blue night. Looking down, she could see the house tilt back as if to watch them, then turn around on its chicken legs. A moment later, the trees bent over to conceal it.

"And that," Yulik said, pointing with his tail to the club, which Madame Z had begun using as a rudder to steer them, "is a pestle. Normally, it's used to grind ingredients against the mortar."

To Mary's amazement, as they flew even higher, Yulik continued circling the rim of the mortar. Gradually, the fear of falling seemed to leave her as well, and she became less aware of the forest stretching into darkness below and more aware of the sky. It was a beautiful night, speckled with stars. Wisps of cloud blew past the mortar, and a rushing breeze tangled her hair.

"What do you think, *devochka*?" Madame Z asked.

"It's . . . unbelievable!" Mary said.

She reached out to grab a cloud, but it drifted through her fingers.

Madame Z stuck out her own bony hand and twined a wisp of cloud around it, then handed it to her. To Mary's delight, she found she could grasp it. It felt damp and soft.

Madame Z smiled. "You may be the only child who has ever held a cloud."

Mary stared at her. The witch sounded proud of her. Almost like a mother.

"What?" Madame Z demanded.

"Nothing," she said with a grin. "So this is *peekneek*?"

Yulik stopped circling the rim of the mortar. "Grabbing clouds with dreamy looks on our faces? Of course not!"

Madame Z's mouth twitched. "Yulik is right. We must set up, *devochka*."

She started singing to the white bundles. The first one opened, and a bottle of cloudy yellow liquid flew into the air, followed by a pair of goblets. Several plates and forks followed, hovering expectantly as the next bundle opened, releasing jars of pickled mushrooms, onions, and cabbage. From the third bundle emerged a loaf of rye bread, a platter of smoked pink fish, and a jellied meat dish. ("It's called *holodetz*, and it's made of pork and aspic," Yulik said.) The dishes and silverware rose in the air and arranged themselves as if on a table.

Mary burst into laughter. The *peekneek* she had been so nervous about was simply a picnic, one up in the clouds.

"What is it, *devochka*?" Madame Z asked, sounding worried.

Somehow this made Mary laugh harder. She clutched her stomach. Tears ran from her eyes. She hadn't laughed like this in years.

"I am not an expert on children," Yulik said, peering down to where Mary had collapsed against the side of the mortar, "but she appears to be giddy."

"*Peekneek!*" Mary managed to gasp.

"Perhaps she needs something to eat," Madame Z said.

But the witch's puzzled concern only tickled Mary more.

Yulik's tail twitched. "I'm starting to think I prefer children when they are terrified."

"She certainly doesn't smell very tasty," Madame Z agreed. She poured the bottle of cloudy liquid into the floating goblets and handed one to Mary. "*Na zdoroviya,*" she said, tipping her goblet toward Mary. "To your health."

As Mary caught her breath and gulped down the sweet, bubbly drink, she felt her laughter subside. Beside her, Madame Z caught wisps of cloud and molded them into horses and cats, then let them drift away on the wind. Yulik flicked his tail and ate a piece of smoked fish. There was no need to talk, only to enjoy the food and the night and one another's quiet company. Mary felt utterly contented. She plucked a pickled mushroom out of the air and then devoured a piece of rye bread with *holodetz*. It was slippery and savory. Below her, in the moonlight, the forest stretched endlessly toward the horizon.

"What's the broom for?" Mary asked. "Can you fly on it, too?"

"Of course not!" said Madame Z, as if the idea of a witch riding a broom were preposterous. "It's for sweeping."

Mary glanced at the mortar. There was a cobweb on one side, but otherwise it didn't seem dirty.

"No, not for the mortar, *devochka*," Madame Z said, shaking her head. "I'll show you."

With a yank on the pestle, she spun the mortar around. They sailed over the forest until Mary could see Madame Z's front yard and the skull gate. They whizzed over it.

"When I fly over your world," Madame Z said, "I must sweep away my traces." She said something to the pestle and released it. It continued to fly by itself. Then she picked up the broom, poked its bristly side over the rim of the mortar, and began sweeping the sky.

Iris came into view below. Mary leaned over the rim. The town was at its busiest now, in the early evening. Gas lamps flickered in the streets, and groups of tourists wandered in and out of the occult shops, their chatter rising up into the air. But not one of them looked up, oblivious to the real magic right above them. Mary wondered where Jacob was, whether he alone might notice a disturbance in the air or a shadow passing across the clouds.

"A ridiculous town," Madame Z said, peering down next to her. "But I'm fond of it."

"You certainly blend in," Yulik agreed. "And it seems unlikely anyone will drive us out."

Mary turned to look at the cat. "Has that happened before?"

"Of course not," Madame Z snapped. "We leave when I grow tired of the local cuisine."

Mary knew exactly what type of cuisine Madame Z was

referring to. But she also sensed that the witch was just trying to scare her. There was more power in being scary than unwanted.

"I like it here, too," Mary said. "With you."

Madame Z stopped sweeping, her hands frozen on the broomstick, and looked at her. "Strange child," she said. But a smile played on her lips, and Mary knew she didn't think her strange at all.

They left Iris and flew back over darkened fields and roads, above the silhouettes of trees. When they reached the skull gate, Madame Z put away the broom and spoke to the pestle. But instead of taking hold of it herself, she placed Mary's hand on top of it.

"Give it a try."

Mary's breath quickened. She looked down at the yard hundreds of feet below. "Are you sure?"

"It's simple. Just keep west, toward the night, and you'll stay over my kingdom."

Then Madame Z released her hand and Mary was propelling the mortar on her own. She kept the pestle exactly level. Madame Z was right—it wasn't hard at all. But after a minute or two, she became curious and tilted the pestle down. She nearly screamed as the mortar shot straight up into the sky. Feeling as if they would crash into the moon, she yanked the pestle up, and her stomach flip-flopped as they dropped nearly into the top of the trees. Yulik teetered on the rim.

"Sorry!" Mary said.

"Cats always land on their feet," said Yulik diplomatically.

Mary steadied the pestle, then flew the mortar in a wide

circle. The wind blew wildly through her hair, and she felt like shouting to the moon.

Madame Z watched her with a smile, but then suddenly, as if a cloud had passed over it, her face darkened. "Promise me one thing, *devochka*."

Mary slowed down, met her solemn gaze. "What?"

"Never take the mortar out without me."

Mary nodded, relieved that this was all Madame Z wanted. "I won't."

The witch clapped her on the back with a bony hand and took hold of the pestle. "It's time to head home. I think you're ready tomorrow for the next task."

"The next one?" Mary said. "But when do I learn magic?"

Madame Z's lips quivered as if fighting a smile. "Patience, *devochka*. This task is different."

TWENTY-THREE

THAT NIGHT, MARY COULD BARELY SLEEP. She wondered whether the new task had to do with magic—and Madame Z was going to teach her some at last—or whether the witch was just testing her again. She was so restless that Yulik finally jumped down from the bed and stalked off, muttering something about being considerate of one's animal bedmates.

In the morning, Mary was up before anyone except the hands, who were banging away as usual in the kitchen. She wove at the loom, then directed the sluggish desk and chair onto the porch, where she copied the cookbook. She paid attention now to the recipes, even enjoyed thinking about them. The most delicious ones, like borscht and *vareniki*, took patience, as the cook had to work through a number of steps. And then, just when Mary thought everything was about following the instructions, the recipe left it to the cook to "salt to taste" or "stir till done."

At last Madame Z emerged, followed by Yulik, who interrupted his own "good morning" with a loud yawn. It was clear he hadn't slept well without her.

"You are making progress," Madame Z commented, peering over her shoulder. "*Ochen horosho*, very good."

After breakfast, Madame Z called to the hands. One pair brought her shawl. The other held out Mary's coat and helped her put it on.

"Where are we going?" Mary asked.

"Into the woods, *devochka*."

"My task is out there?"

"Yes."

Mary eyed her suspiciously. The last time Madame Z had taken her into the woods was to lose her. If only she had her wish from the Firebird now just in case.

"Come," Madame Z said with a twinkle in her eye. *"Pora!"*

Mary followed Madame Z and Yulik into the forest. Behind her, she could hear the stairs folding themselves up and the house stomping around on its chicken legs. She hoped she would see it again.

Leaves crunched beneath their feet, and shafts of sunlight danced through the trees. Yulik scampered after them. But Madame Z didn't wander deep into the woods this time. Instead, she stopped in front of Sivka's paddock. At the sight of Madame Z, the large golden-brown horse snorted a smoky cloud and trotted over.

"What do you know about horses, *devochka*?" asked Madame Z, patting his flank.

Finally a task with more potential for learning magic than copying or weaving! Mary had always wanted a horse. Perhaps not a fire-breathing one, but Sivka seemed able to keep the flames under control. She jumped up on the paddock rail. "Do I get to ride him? Will you show me what else he can do?"

"Ride him?" Madame Z said with laugh. "No, *devochka*, I need you to take care of him. Fill his water, check his food, groom him."

"All very important, from an animal point of view," added Yulik.

Mary's vision of galloping on Sivka through the forest vanished, replaced by an image of her mucking out his stall. "But I thought Koshchey took care of him," she said, trying to hide her disappointment.

"He does," Madame Z said. "But he's happy for you to do the smaller tasks."

Yulik flicked his tail. "He's sloppy at them, too," he confided.

Mary could tell that the cat expected her to do better. Still, taking care of Sivka seemed no different from any of the other tasks Madame Z had given her. It was just as laborious and unmagical.

Madame Z produced the worn leather halter Mary had seen in her bedroom. "Sivka permits only me to ride him, and I don't always have time, so you'll also need to take him for a walk through the forest every day to give him exercise."

She slipped the halter over Sivka's head, then clipped a lead rope beneath his chin and handed the end of it to Mary. "Go ahead. Off you go."

Then, with Yulik at her heels, she headed back in the direction of the house.

Mary pulled the rope, leading Sivka to a gate in the paddock. He followed her, but his ears swiveled back and forth and his nostrils flared. She thought of the magic talking horse Falada from "The Goose-Girl," one of her favorite stories in the *Household Tales*. She had never heard Sivka talk, but even the ordinary workhorses that she and Caleb had always stopped to pet on the streets of Buffalo had seemed to enjoy being spoken to.

"There's nothing to be afraid of," Mary said as cheerily as she could. "I'm just going to take you for a walk. You'd like that, wouldn't you?"

Sivka's ears stopped swiveling and he lowered his head. Mary led him out through the gate and onto one of the forest paths. She could feel his hot breath on her shoulder and hear the swishing sound of his tail. Dappled light fell across them. Of all her chores, she decided this one might be the most pleasant, though she still wished she could ride Sivka. But just as she was thinking this, the giant horse stopped. She tugged at the rope, but he wouldn't budge.

"What's wrong?" Mary asked him.

Sivka raised his tail. There was a loud *bang* as a flame shot out of his rear end. It hit a pile of dry leaves, which burst into fire. With a frightened snort, the horse bolted, and the rope ripped out of Mary's hand.

She raced after him. "Sivka, stop!" she shouted. "Stop!"

She kept talking to him, and at last he slowed to a walk. Mary pounced on the end of the rope and scooped it up. Carefully steering clear of Sivka's rear, she pulled him to a stop. They were both breathing hard. A column of smoke rose behind them into the sky. Mary pulled out the magic dagger. "Fetch a pail, fill it with water, and put out that fire, please."

The dagger sailed off. She hoped it could find some water. Madame Z wouldn't be pleased with her if, on her first day of taking care of Sivka, Mary let him set the entire kingdom on fire. Caring for a magical horse—even in an ordinary way—was proving to be harder than she had expected.

Mary spoke softly to Sivka and patted his neck. The horse was still trembling. She wished she had a treat to calm him down. That's when she remembered the Great DeBosco's thumb.

"Here," she said, pulling the carrot out of her pocket and holding it out to Sivka. "Eat this."

Sivka nickered and gobbled it up. A minute later, the smoke thinned, then vanished, and the magic dagger came flying back to her. "Thank you," she said as she put it back in her pocket.

Sivka reached out his neck and gently touched Mary's shoulder with his hot muzzle.

"You're thirsty?" Mary guessed. "All right, let's go back and get you some water. And let's see what Koshchey is feeding you."

Sivka's stable had a dirt floor instead of a wooden one, which seemed wise, since instead of horse dung, the floor was covered with lumps of black coal. Mary raked away the still-smoking ones, then led Sivka inside. A water basin in the corner was empty. "No wonder you're thirsty," she said. "You've run out of water."

Mary took a bucket off a hook and went around back to a pump she had seen. She carried the sloshing bucket back inside and poured the water into the basin. The moment she moved away, Sivka dipped in his muzzle. Instantly, a cloud of steam filled the stable. Mary waved it away just in time to see the horse's tongue lap up the few remaining drops of water.

Mary refilled the bucket and tried again, but Sivka's hot mouth turned all but a few drops into steam.

"How many times does Koshchey do this?" Mary asked.

Sivka nodded a dozen times.

"And you're still thirsty, aren't you?" she asked him.

Sivka nickered.

There had to be a better solution. As Mary puzzled over Sivka's predicament, she took a look at his hay. Even before she approached the pile in his stall, she could smell the problem. The hay was damp, probably from the constant clouds of steam, and it had grown moldy. Between the moldy hay and the shortage of water, it was no wonder Sivka had such fiery gas.

To keep the hay dry and free of mold, Mary would have to stop the steam. But how would she do that when Sivka's mouth was so hot it instantly boiled away all his water? She thought about how Jacob had taught her to look at magic tricks in more than one way. Maybe the horse's breath wasn't too hot; maybe the water wasn't cold enough.

"That's it!" Mary exclaimed. She took out the magic dagger. "Get me a block of ice, please!"

The dagger flew off. While it was gone, Mary raked all the moldy hay out of Sivka's stall. Then she set to work on his tangled mane, which Koshchey had clearly neglected. The horse gratefully closed his eyes and lowered his head as she worked out the knots. She rubbed him behind the ears, then brushed him till he gleamed. At last the dagger returned, buried halfway to the hilt in a large block of ice. Mary clapped her hands. "Now drop it into the basin, please!"

The dagger wiggled, loosening itself from the ice, which fell into the basin with a crash.

Mary led Sivka over to it. "Go on," she said. "Drink."

Sivka bent down and poked the ice with his muzzle. Then he gave it a lick. It immediately started melting. But the growing pool of icy water was too cold for him to turn to steam. Mary listened to him slurping happily. Then she fetched fresh hay from a shed behind the stable. The horse knocked his dripping muzzle appreciatively against her shoulder and started eating.

"It's my lunchtime, too," Mary told him.

"Yes it is, *dochka*," said a voice behind her.

Mary swung around. Madame Z was standing in the doorway. She smiled sweetly, but Mary felt unsettled. *Dochka*. She had never heard Madame Z call her this word before. She was always *devochka*.

"What did you call me?" she asked.

"We'll discuss it when you've finished your tasks," Madame Z replied. "Now, *pora domoi*. Let's go home."

TWENTY-FOUR

AFTER LUNCH, Mary worked on her weaving again. But as soon as Madame Z and Yulik headed out, she threw down the shuttle, grabbed her coat, and slipped out the door.

When she reached Jacob's boardinghouse, she was relieved not to see the augur or the peregrine falcon. There was only Dobbin, drinking a mug of coffee on the stairs, with Fanny curled around his waist. The python still had a large bulge, though the meal had traveled a few feet farther along her body. Mary hoped it was still Socrates the counting dog and not the *domovoi*.

"Morning," Mary said. "Is Fanny still digesting . . . ?"

Dobbin nodded. "The neighbor's dog. It can take several weeks. But on the bright side, she is becoming less sleepy."

This didn't seem like such a positive development, but Mary smiled as if it were. Taking the long route around Fanny, she bounded up the stairs, dodging Harry the head-bump reader on the landing before he could pickpocket the dagger, then knocking on Jacob's door.

"It's Mary!" she called.

The door swung open.

"Glad you're back," said Jacob.

Behind him, Mary could see Mr. Kagan on his hands and knees in front of the stove.

"How is the *dom*—?" Mary whispered.

Jacob put a finger to his lips.

"Nothing looks loose," his father said, sitting upright. "But something is clearly broken."

"There's been some banging," Jacob explained with a meaningful glance.

"So all is . . . well?" Mary said.

"*Well?*" Mr. Kagan nearly shouted. "This is one of the worst rooms I've ever lived in! I'll talk to DeBosco, but I doubt it will do much good. He probably slipped in here and meddled with the stove. No doubt he wants us out even before next week!"

Staggering back to his feet, he grabbed his coat and stormed out past Mary. She could hear his muttered curses as he descended the stairs.

Mary looked at Jacob in alarm. It was already Tuesday. "You're definitely leaving next week?"

"Father's been in a bad mood about the banging. But nothing's definite. I'm going to try to persuade him to stay."

"Maybe you should tell him about the *domovoi*."

"He'd just think I was making the whole thing up. And it's not like I can show him the *domovoi* as proof. He comes out only when I'm in mortal peril."

Mary knew Jacob was right. "Well, I'm sorry that your magical creature is giving you trouble."

The stove rattled an indignant response.

"Actually," Jacob said, "I've been thinking he could be useful in a spirit act. All that banging."

"You'd have to bring the audience here, though," Mary said.

Jacob shook his head. "And there's hardly enough room even for us. But speaking of acts, I've drawn up a list of the ones we should try." He put his hand to his mouth and spit out a folded square of paper.

"It was in your hand the entire time," Mary said.

Jacob winked as he unfolded the paper, then handed it to her. "I wrote down all the acts in Iris. Then I circled the ones we know are real and crossed out the ones I'm sure are fake. Here are the ones we're left with."

Mary looked at the list of unmarked names:

Sybil von Hapsburg, Tarot Card Reader

The Voodoo Queen of New Orleans

Dr. Edgar Shepherd, Mind Reader

Rusalina, Medium

Theodosia Spring, Spiritualist

The Reverend Hezekiah, Healer

Aura the Eye, Psychic

"You can cross out Rusalina," she said, without looking up. "I've already visited her. She barely even does fake magic."

"So *she's* the one you gave the pennies to!" Jacob exclaimed.

"You knew they were gone?"

Jacob shrugged. "I checked your pockets."

"You're a pickpocket!" Mary said with a playful swat. But she secretly felt foolish that she hadn't told him earlier.

Jacob pretended to give a wounded look. "I like to think of myself as someone who *protects* your pockets. I thought maybe Harry took them, but he swore up and down. Anyway, we'll cross her off, but where should we go first?"

"How about Sybil von Hapsburg?" Mary said. "She claims to be from Europe, but maybe she's really from Madame Z's land."

"Sounds good to me," Jacob said. As the *domovoi* continued to bang away on the stove, Jacob grabbed his coat, folded up the list, and tucked the little square of paper into the band of his top hat. "Let's go," he said, flipping the hat onto his head.

On the way, Mary told Jacob about taking care of Sivka and how she had solved his water problem. "Clever," he said. "Madame Z must respect you for that."

"I still don't think she's going to teach me magic, though," Mary said. "She just keeps adding tasks."

"But you're doing them," Jacob said. "Why would she turn against you?"

"She's a witch," Mary said. "I'm a child. In every tale I've ever read, only one of us survives." But then she thought of the *peekneek* and Madame Z handing her the wisp of cloud. "I actually like living with her, though. Is that strange?"

Jacob shook his head. "Maybe she likes living with you, too. And anyway, real life is more complicated than fairy tales."

"But are real witches?" Mary asked.

"I don't know," he admitted. "But if you feel at home with her, keep doing the tasks. Especially if we can get you that Firebird wish just in case, sticking it out seems worth the risk."

"And we need that wish for you, too," Mary said. "You can't leave next week!"

By this time, they were standing in front of Sybil von Hapsburg's cottage, beneath the sign **TAROT TRUSTED BY THE KINGS OF EUROPE**.

"Don't worry," Jacob said. "Someone in Iris must be able to help us."

He pushed open the door, and Mary found herself in a fancy parlor with claw-foot chairs and red velvet curtains drawn back by braided gold sashes. A plump older woman with rouged cheeks and bright red lips sat behind a heavy oak table. She wore a fringed shawl and held a deck of tarot cards, her bejeweled fingers poised to lift the top card. A pretty young woman in silk and furs sat across from her, craning her neck expectantly. They were surrounded by a small group of rapt onlookers.

"I am a minor member of the Hapsburg family," Sybil von Hapsburg explained in a thick German accent. "Twenty-third in line for the throne. I still perform readings for several monarchs, which I send by post to their advisers, but I prefer that commoners benefit from my gift as well . . . like you, *fräulein.*"

With a nod at the young woman, she flipped over the first two cards and surveyed them with a deep frown. "The Fool upside down, and the Lovers! You will give your heart to a careless man."

The young woman's forehead creased with worry. She glanced at the man behind her, who rolled his eyes as if there were nothing to the tarot card reader's words. But one look at his monocle and foppish silk bow tie told Mary that Sybil von Hapsburg wasn't reading the cards.

Jacob caught Mary's eye and cocked his head toward the door. They started to tiptoe out, but Mary noticed the tarot card reader look up and appraise her elegant coat and new boots.

"I can tell that child will have an interesting effect on the cards," she said.

"We were just here to watch," Jacob said as he pulled Mary out the door.

As they ran down the stairs, Mary almost burst out laughing. "She's definitely not a Hapsburg."

"She's not even from Europe," Jacob said.

"Her accent slipped," Mary said. "On the word *effect*."

Jacob looked pleased. "You heard that Virginia drawl? You're getting good!"

Mary beamed, but it wasn't just the compliment that made her happy. Like in the old days with Caleb, she had a friend with whom to share adventures.

Next they tried the Reverend Hezekiah, who advertised Remedies for All Manners of Ailments from Gout to Grief. Inside his shop, a crowd of men solemnly watched him mix up a batch of his Miraculous Cure for Baldness. With a flourish, the reverend produced a vial of colorless liquid and poured it into a flask. The concoction instantly fizzed up, spilling over the side. "Behold the magical reaction that drives new hair up through the skull!" he declared.

"That wasn't magic," Jacob said with a laugh as they left the storefront. "Just baking soda and vinegar."

They found the Voodoo Queen of New Orleans in the back of her shop, which was cluttered with alligator heads, love potions, dolls, rosaries, masks, skeleton keys, and candles. She had gone into a trance for a crowd of tourists and was mumbling in what one old woman in an ostrich-plume hat knowingly explained to the others was the "spirit tongue." Mary thought it sounded an awful lot like pig Latin. Her hopes briefly rose when the Voodoo Queen levitated, but Jacob just shook his head. "She's turned her foot sideways in her shoe and covered it with her shawl so you can't see that she's actually standing on tiptoe."

The next afternoon, they met up again. It didn't take long for Jacob to see through the rest of the town's so-called magic. The otherworldly glow that filled the parlor of Theodosia Spring came from a bottle of sulfur match tips mixed with water. Dr. Edgar Shepherd, the Man Who Knows All, knew nothing more than what his pickpocket plant in the audience signaled to him. And even Mary could tell that Aura the Eye wasn't seeing the future so much as asking leading questions about the past.

"That's it," Mary said after they left Aura's parlor. "We have nowhere else to go."

Jacob pulled the list from the band of his top hat and looked it over.

"Are you sure about Rusalina?" he finally asked.

"There's nothing to be unsure about. She didn't do anything magical. She just told me to speak to the spirit in the room, but there was no one there but her."

Jacob's brow wrinkled. "What kind of act is that?"

"I know!" Mary said, feeling outraged by the memory. "It's no wonder she's all the way on the edge of town in that swampy little—"

She stopped, then grabbed his arm.

"Maybe she chose that watery spot on purpose. The night of the mushroom hunt, I heard a woman singing in the forest. I followed her voice to a stream."

"Was anyone there?"

"Not on land, but there was something—or *someone*—in the water, pulling at my fingers."

Jacob grinned. "Rusalina's act might not be so bad after all. Let's go see it."

TWENTY-FIVE

THEY OPENED THE DOOR and stepped into the small, clammy parlor. To Mary's surprise, Rusalina had a customer. A plump woman in a satin dress sat in one of the scalloped chairs. Tears streamed down her face. Across from her sat Rusalina, her pale hair falling down her back. Mary realized that it wasn't greasy so much as wet.

"Very unwise of him to go swimming at midnight," Rusalina said to the woman in the satin dress.

At this, the plump woman heaved a sob. "I don't understand what came over him."

"Water," Rusalina said drily. "But the spirit in the room promises he is well, and she will pass on your message."

The plump woman handed Rusalina some money, threw a mink coat over her shoulders, and shuffled out.

Rusalina's eyes passed over Mary and Jacob. Then she pulled one of the combs from her hair and began running it through her long locks. Mary noticed that Rusalina's hair seemed to glisten and bead with water as the teeth of the comb glided through it.

"Another message for your mother?" Rusalina asked.

"No," Mary said. "I'd just like to speak to the spirit in the room."

"She's here. Go ahead."

Mary sat down in the scalloped chair across from Rusalina.

"We want to catch the Firebird. We're asking the spirit to help us."

Rusalina gave a burbling laugh. "The spirit has no idea what you are talking about!"

At this, Jacob walked over and stood beside Rusalina. "But you're the spirit in the room."

Rusalina stopped combing her hair and stared suspiciously at him. "You're confused," she said. "I am only a guide, a medium."

Jacob pulled a coin from his pocket and threw it in the air. The coin hit the ceiling, and his right hand shot over Rusalina's head to catch it. Mary wasn't sure, but she thought she saw him reach out simultaneously with his left. "Want to bet?"

"You would lose," Rusalina said testily.

Mary shot him a warning glance. She didn't want Rusalina to vanish the way Mr. Less had. But she also sensed that Jacob was up to something.

"I don't think so," he said, slowly backing away. "Every time you comb your hair, it becomes wetter. Like this."

He opened his palm to reveal one of Rusalina's combs. At the sight of it, she jumped to her feet with a furious look, but Jacob was already running it through his hair, which was rapidly growing wet.

Rusalina fixed her eyes on him and began to sing in a high, girlish voice. Mary instantly recognized the familiar wordless tune from the forest, but it was louder, faster, angrier.

"Jacob!" she cried.

But she was too late. A torrent of water burst out of the comb, knocking him off his feet and pouring over his head. As he gasped and sputtered, the comb flew out of his hand. Rusalina caught it and gave Jacob a mean smile.

"It's very tempting to drown you," she said.

Water continued to gush out of the comb, flooding the parlor.

"Don't you dare!" Mary said, stepping between Jacob and Rusalina. She pulled the dagger out of her pocket and pointed it at Rusalina. But the surge of power she felt wasn't from the magical object, which she already realized might be useless against Rusalina. It came from knowing how she felt about Jacob. He had become the friend and confidant she thought she had lost forever when Caleb died. And she wasn't going to lose someone she cared about so much, not ever again.

Rusalina snickered. "Fearless! No wonder Baba Yaga has taken an interest in you." With a wave of her hand, the gushing water stopped. The flood receded, leaving damp floorboards and a new waterline on the wall. Rusalina tucked the comb back into her hair.

"You know about me?" Mary asked.

"There's been talk among us magical creatures that Baba Yaga adopted a child. I hardly believed it at first."

Jacob sputtered and caught his breath. "What are you?"

"A *rusalka*," Rusalina said, directing her answer to Mary. She was obviously still angry over his trick. "The undead spirit of a drowned girl."

"Can you really talk to the dead?" Mary asked.

Rusalina sat back down in her scalloped chair and, with a smirk, tossed her wet hair over her shoulder. "No. But being undead, I can menace the living. It's far more fun."

"That was you the night of the mushroom hunt, yanking my fingers in the stream, trying to pull me in," Mary said. "Are you always trying to drown people?"

"I wouldn't say always." Rusalina took the comb and began to run it through her hair. "I have other duties that occupy my time, especially when I'm in the human world. My hair must stay wet. If it dries out, I suffer the pain of my death all over again."

"How did you drown in the first place?" Jacob asked.

Rusalina fixed him with such a dark stare that Mary half-feared she might change her mind and drown him after all.

"If I knew, perhaps I could be at peace. But I don't remember."

"How can you not remember?" Mary asked.

Rusalina sighed deeply. "All I know is that I was once a girl with a home and family, and then, one night I woke up alone, a *rusalka* in Baba Yaga's kingdom."

Mary nodded sympathetically. She knew what it felt like to lose one's home and family and end up alone. But at least she knew how it had happened to her, even if she often wished she could forget. "Surely Baba Yaga must know how."

Rusalina shook her head. "You still don't realize who has taken you in, do you? Baba Yaga is no ordinary witch. She can control the moon, the wind, the forest, the seasons. She is as old as the earth, speaks only to her servants and a few old creatures. Do you think *I* am on casual terms with her? A mere *rusalka*?"

Mary swallowed hard. She was a mere girl. A witch as mighty as Madame Z could crush her in an instant. But Madame Z had also treated her in a way she had never treated any other child. She had given her a home and promised her magic.

Mary leaned over the table, stared Rusalina in the eye. "Maybe I do realize who she is. And I'm not afraid."

"Well, maybe you should be," Rusalina shot back.

Mary remembered how Madame Z had tossed Koshchey into the air. And despite her promise, Madame Z hadn't given her any magic—at least not yet. But Mary decided that she couldn't have these fears and doubts. This was her chance. There was no one else to help her and Jacob in Iris. She couldn't leave Rusalina's empty-handed.

"If she's so powerful, then help us! We need to catch the Firebird!"

Rusalina gave a dismissive sniff. "And cross Madame Z?"

"Can't you just give us one of your combs?" Jacob asked.

"Of course!" Mary exclaimed. "We could use it to put out the Firebird's flames."

Jacob turned to Rusalina. "You could just tell Madame Z we stole it."

Rusalina glared at him. "That part would be true. But there's nothing in it for me. How about this? I'll drown Mary if Baba Yaga turns against her."

"Not quite the help we were looking for," Jacob said.

"Better to drown than to be cooked in an oven," Rusalina said with a devilish grin.

"How do you know?" Mary shot back. "You don't even remember."

Rusalina winced. "I think you should go."

But Mary's own words had given her an idea. "Wait! You want to know how you drowned? I'll ask Baba Yaga myself. But if I find out for you, you must give us one of your combs."

Rusalina's hand flew up to her combs. Her pool-like eyes reflected her uncertainty.

"I may be just a girl, but she talks to me," Mary said.

"I suppose you are in a unique position," Rusalina admitted. "Baba Yaga occasionally will help a child, but as long as I've been a *rusalka*, she's never let one stay with her. Then again, I've never met a child crazy enough to want to."

"Well, now you've met me," Mary said. "Do we have a deal?"

Rusalina fingered her combs, then let out a deep sigh. "Yes. But if you want to extinguish the Firebird, I'll need to give you two combs."

TWENTY-SIX

WHEN MARY ARRIVED HOME THAT AFTERNOON, Madame Z still wasn't there. So she set to work on her tasks—copying a little more of the cookbook, weaving on the loom, and, finally, taking a carrot and another block of ice from Madame Z's icebox out to Sivka. The horse met her with a shake of his mane and a nicker. Mary noticed that there were a few new lumps of coal on the ground, but they weren't smoking. She raked them away as Sivka melted his ice block and devoured his carrot. Then Mary led him on a short walk through the forest, across a crunchy carpet of red and yellow leaves. Sivka's digestion seemed improved; this time, he didn't set anything on fire.

The shadows began to lengthen and the air to grow colder.

As Mary led Sivka back to his paddock, his ears pricked up. Koshchey was leaning against the paddock fence, watching them.

"Look at you!" he said cheerfully. "Taking care of Baba Yaga's horse."

"He needed some care," Mary said curtly, releasing Sivka into his paddock.

Koshchey lowered his head. "I deserve that, fair and square. But the daily care of this particular horse is not easy, as you know."

"It wasn't that hard for me," Mary said. "And I'm just a girl, not a wizard like you."

"I've kept him alive," Koshchey said.

"You're working to earn him, are you not?" Mary snapped.

Koshchey winced. "You sound just like Baba Yaga. Will you toss me up into the sky next and throw me around?"

"I wish I could," Mary said with a sigh.

"Ah!" Koshchey said, drawing closer. "But you're not as powerless as you think. Madame Z has let you take care of her horse. Don't you realize what this means? It's just as we suspected. She truly likes you."

Mary's heart leaped before she realized that Koshchey was probably just trying to flatter her. "She's still not teaching me magic."

"She's just testing you," Koshchey said.

"Why should I believe that?" Mary asked.

She thought her remark might offend Koshchey, but he just smiled. "I understand completely. I am the same way—not easily trusting. You need more evidence."

"That's right," Mary said. "I need to be sure."

"Wise girl. I wouldn't want to be wrong about this, either. But is there any other evidence? Has she treated you any differently?"

Mary started to shake her head, but then she remembered the word Madame Z had called her. "What does *dochka* mean?"

Koshchey's pale blue eyes lit up. "She called you that?"

Mary hesitated, taken aback by Koshchey's wild gaze.

"Did she?" he repeated. "Are you sure? Not *devochka*?"

"Yes," Mary admitted.

Koshchey did a little dance. "*Devochka* just means *girl*. It's what she called all the others. But *dochka*—it means *daughter!*"

Mary looked up at him in surprise. Madame Z was nobody's mother—she had said so herself. But she had kept Mary alive, taken care of her, given her the key to her house and a ride in her mortar. True, she hadn't honored her promise to teach Mary magic yet, but she had taught her skills—cooking, weaving, animal care—that a mother might. Was it possible that Madame Z's affection for Mary not only was real but also had grown over their past weeks together into something larger—into love? Mary hadn't asked for a mother, but she realized how deeply she wanted one, even one who was a witch.

"Don't you see?" Koshchey said. "She'd never harm you, not in a thousand years. She loves you!"

Back at the house, Mary wove faster than ever as she waited for Madame Z. The steady *click-clack* of the loom matched her racing thoughts. She was somebody's daughter! But she still needed to catch the Firebird—just in case she was wrong and Madame Z didn't think of her as a daughter at all. She also didn't quite trust Koshchey's enthusiasm. He seemed so eager for her to believe she was safe. She wondered once again what was in it for him.

The door opened. *"Dochka,"* Madame Z called. "I'm home!"

"Daughter," Mary whispered. The word felt so good, like the coat that fit perfectly. She ran to the foyer and kissed Madame Z on her wrinkled cheek.

Madame Z drew back with a grin. "What was that for?"

Mary shrugged, not wishing to explain. She would wait until after Madame Z taught her magic.

Still, she felt happier that night than she had since her mother and Caleb were alive, and the rest of Madame Z's household seemed to share her mood. The hands served a wonderful dinner—buckwheat cakes, pickled mushrooms, and roasted quail. After they had eaten their fill, Madame Z produced what she called a *gusli* but what Mary thought looked like a small harp. The old woman whispered something into its strings, and the *gusli* struck up lively songs. At Madame Z's encouragement, Mary even got up and danced.

"Bravo!" said Yulik, purring loudly.

After the food and music, Madame Z suggested Mary read aloud from the *Household Tales*. While Madame Z stretched out on the couch, Mary sat by the fire with Yulik snoozing on her lap and read "Frau Holle." The hands turned the pages. Madame Z liked the tale about a magical old woman with sharp teeth who rewards a hardworking girl, much like Mary, for doing her household tasks.

When Mary was done reading, they sat quietly together, the

way she used to do with her mother and Caleb after a good story. Mary gazed at the witch. She was clever, playful, passionate, generous, full of surprises—someone who took pleasure in nature, music, stories. Just like Madame Z, Mary knew what it was like to feel unlovable and unwanted. But she also knew that she didn't feel that way with Madame Z.

Mary longed to be right about Madame Z's affection for her. But it would be foolish to abandon her fallback plan based on a longing. Plus, Jacob needed to get his wish from the Firebird before his father moved him away. It was time to ask Madame Z about Rusalina. They would never be able to extinguish the Firebird and keep her from bursting back into flame without Rusalina's combs.

As the fire crackled in the hearth, she turned to Madame Z and said casually, "When I was in town a while back, I met a *rusalka*. She works as a spirit guide."

Madame Z didn't seem surprised. "Several of the creatures from my realm like to moonlight in Iris. They enjoy tricking humans."

"An ancient pastime," Yulik added.

Mary debated how to proceed before deciding that a direct question was best. "I was wondering: Do you know how she died?"

Madame Z fixed her with her keen gray eyes. "You went to see her. Why?"

"I thought she could summon my mother," Mary admitted.

Madame Z made a *tsk* sound, but her voice was kind. "The dead are gone, *dochka*."

Mary nodded. She had always known this, deep in her heart. But having Madame Z call her *dochka* helped blunt the sting. "But not the undead."

"Yes, *rusalka*s," Madame Z agreed, "such an ill-tempered bunch. But I suppose it's because they died before their time."

"What happened to this one?" Mary pressed. "Rusalina?"

Madame Z's lined face darkened. She propped herself up. "Yes, that one. Happened about a century ago. She was engaged to be married, changed her mind. The young man she jilted chased her, and she ran into my kingdom. I saw it all from the mortar one night. She tried to cross a river and drowned."

Mary was relieved that Madame Z had given her the answer she needed. But she shuddered at the *rusalka*'s fate. "Why didn't you save her?"

Madame Z looked away and shrugged. "I have been on this earth a very long time. People live, people die. I am part of nature, and nature rarely takes a side."

"You helped me," Mary said.

"Yes, *dochka*, but that's not my usual instinct with children."

Mary stifled a shiver, but not before Yulik noticed.

"You're different," he said, rubbing his cheek against Mary's fingers. "Brave and kind."

But his words did little to console her. Even if she was safe and loved, Mary didn't want a mother who ate children. With a rising sense of dread, she thought of Jacob. She needed him to stay, but he had to be safe in Iris, too. She locked eyes on Madame Z.

"Why do you eat them?"

"Why do you eat a sweet?"

Mary knew the answer—sweets tasted good—but she didn't like thinking of herself or any other child as a bonbon. "So you don't *need* to eat children?"

Madame Z smiled. "Are you asking me to stop?"

"Yes."

"She hasn't eaten a single one since you arrived," Yulik said. "Remarkable self-control. I can barely go a week without a mouse."

"Then, you *can* stop," Mary said to Madame Z.

The witch stroked her bristly chin thoughtfully. "For you, *dochka*, I will try."

TWENTY-SEVEN

THE NEXT MORNING, after Madame Z and Yulik left, Mary raced to Iris. It was an overcast day, with the smell of chimney smoke and a hint of snow in the air. The red and orange leaves were in sharp relief against the dull pewter sky. Cassandra the augur sat on the steps of the boardinghouse, squinting up at the clouds from beneath her nest of frizzy black hair.

"Second time I've seen a peregrine falcon above you," she said to Mary. "Bad luck, deceit."

Mary looked up. The falcon was circling overhead, just like last time. She wondered if the falcon was Mr. Less in yet another animal form. But most likely Cassandra had seen the bird over the boardinghouse a bunch of times and was just trying to get Mary to pay her something for the prediction.

"You don't really believe that," she scolded the augur. Still, she felt a slight apprehension.

"Mary!" shouted a voice from above.

Mary looked up. Jacob's head was hanging out the attic window.

"Did you find out?"

"Yes!" she shouted back. Forgetting all about the falcon, Mary rushed inside. Halfway up the stairs, she and Jacob nearly crashed into each other.

"Madame Z started calling me her daughter!" she said.

"I'm not surprised," Jacob said with a gentle smile. But there was a sadness in his dark eyes.

"What is it?" Mary asked.

"The *domovoi* is driving my father half mad. He's threatening to meet with DeBosco to see if he'll refund the rest of the week's rent. He wants to leave town tomorrow."

"No," Mary said firmly. "We've got to get to Rusalina's—fast!"

As they ran to the forlorn little shop at the edge of town, Jacob turned to Mary.

"Once we get the combs, how are we going to find the Firebird?"

"We could go to her shop, but she'll probably fly up the chimney the moment she sees us."

"She's not going to make this easy," Jacob agreed. "Even if we douse her flames, she could still fly out of reach."

Mary took a deep breath, trying not to feel discouraged. "Let's get the combs first, and I'll think about it."

Rusalina was alone when they entered, combing her hair with a faraway look on her face. Mary wondered whether she was wondering about her family and home. But the moment Rusalina saw Mary and Jacob, the soft look on her face vanished, replaced by a hard glare.

"Back so soon?" she asked.

"I talked to Baba Yaga," Mary said.

Rusalina stopped combing her hair and blinked her large blue-green eyes. "And did she tell you what happened to me?"

"Yes. Are you ready to hear it?"

Rusalina nodded. "Sit," she ordered, and began combing her hair again, fast and carelessly. Water dripped to the floor.

Mary sat on the scalloped chair in front of the *rusalka*, and Jacob took his place beside Mary. As Mary told the story she had learned from Madame Z, Rusalina's comb slowed to a stop, her hand frozen beside her wet hair. Tears pooled in her eyes and rolled down her cheeks. Jacob offered her a handkerchief, and she wordlessly took it, dabbing her eyes.

"I remember now," Rusalina said after Mary had finished. "He was young and very handsome, a visitor to the village where I lived many years ago. He did clever little tricks." She sniffed into Jacob's handkerchief and looked accusingly at him. "Like you."

"Was he an illusionist?" Jacob asked.

"He certainly wasn't what he seemed," Rusalina said. "After I agreed to marry him, he stopped being so charming. He told me to leave my home and family and go away with him. When I refused, he chased me. I ran into the woods—I didn't know they were Baba Yaga's. I thought if I crossed the river . . ."

Rusalina's voice trailed off and she gave a little sob.

"Stop crying," Mary said. "You're drying yourself out."

But this just seemed to make Rusalina cry harder. "It's not

my death. It's my family. I miss them. But they must have died long ago. Now I'm alone."

"No, you're not," Mary said softly. She reached out and touched Rusalina's hand. Her fingers were damp and cold. They curled around Mary's but didn't pull at her, as they had in the stream.

After a moment, Rusalina took a deep breath and let go of Mary's hand. "The only way for a *rusalka* to be truly at peace is for her death to be avenged. But that scoundrel is long dead." Then she pulled two of the combs out of her hair. "Here," she said, handing one to Mary and, more reluctantly, one to Jacob.

"How do they work?" Mary asked.

"You need to hum this tune." Rusalina quietly hummed the familiar yet eerie melody she had sung before. "Try it."

Mary and Jacob held out their combs and hummed softly. Water trickled from the teeth, forming two small puddles at their feet.

"Louder now," Rusalina instructed.

Mary and Jacob hummed louder. Water sprayed forcefully out of the combs onto the floor. They jumped back to avoid getting wet. Rusalina let out a burbling laugh.

"That should extinguish the Firebird! Then you can grab her."

"Without burning ourselves," Mary said. "Thank you!"

Rusalina's expression grew more serious. "There is one other thing the combs can do if you're having trouble putting out her fire. But I wouldn't advise doing it lightly. If you push them together, they will make a sea."

"An entire sea?" Mary said, amazed that the combs had such power.

"I don't think that'll be necessary," Jacob said. "Besides, we don't want to drown the Firebird. Or ourselves."

"Are you sure?" Rusalina said. She winked mischievously at Mary. "*Rusalkas* are sociable creatures. We could share the same stream. Sing duets in the moonlight. Drown a few nice boys—"

"Very tempting," Mary said. "But I need to catch the Firebird and keep this particular boy safe." She realized it was the type of thing Madame Z might say—playful, yet with a serious edge.

"I appreciate that," Jacob said under his breath.

"I hope we can be friends, though, even if I'm not a *rusalka*," Mary added.

Rusalina considered this for a moment, then shook her head. "My instinct is to drown humans."

Mary thought of Madame Z and how it was her instinct to eat children. "Just because we have certain instincts doesn't mean we have to act on them. We could be friends. Remember that. And thank you for the combs."

"You did it!" Jacob said as they raced down the steps of the cottage.

"*We* did it," Mary corrected. "I never would have realized the combs were magic if you hadn't swiped one."

Jacob took a small bow. "*We*, then."

"And anyway," Mary said, "we still have to catch the Firebird."

"Any ideas?" Jacob asked.

She shook her head.

"If only we could fly after her," he said.

Mary stopped short. The mortar! She knew how fast it could fly—fast enough to catch the Firebird. But she had promised

Madame Z that she would never take it out without her. She also remembered how angry the witch had been when Koshchey disobeyed her.

"What is it?" Jacob asked.

Madame Z would be furious if she caught them. She had no special feelings for Jacob. He was just an ordinary child, the type she might be tempted to gobble up. But she had promised not to eat any more children, or at least to try. And if Mary did nothing, tomorrow Jacob's father would take him away; he wouldn't have a home, and she wouldn't have a friend. They needed the Firebird's wishes so Jacob could stay in Iris and she could—

But at that moment, Mary realized that her wish had changed. She no longer wanted the power to protect herself from Madame Z; she wanted the power to protect Jacob, to keep him safe. She looked at him. He was leaning in close, eager to hear her plan.

"I think I have an idea," Mary said. "Can you be at your window at three tonight?"

TWENTY-EIGHT

ALL AFTERNOON AND EVENING, Mary diligently worked on her tasks—taking care of Sivka, weaving, copying the cookbook. Before she headed up to bed, Madame Z complimented her on the quality of the cloth she had woven and the carefulness of her penmanship. "You are learning, *dochka*."

Mary was relieved to hear her praise. Considering what she was about to do, it was important for Madame Z to be pleased with her.

At two thirty, Mary slipped out of bed. Yulik, who was curled into his usual ball at her feet, opened one eye.

"Can't sleep?"

"I'm hungry," Mary lied.

"So wake up a child and chase it," he muttered sleepily.

"It's me!" Mary said. "I don't eat children."

But Yulik's eye had shut, and his ears twitched as if he were dreaming. Mary gathered up the dagger, comb, and feather, then quietly closed the door behind her. Madame Z's bedroom door was closed, the house still. At the bottom of the stairs, Mary held out the feather, flooding the foyer with soft orange light. Mary gave the door beside the stairs a tug, but as expected, it was locked. Thinking of her nipped finger, she knew she could never coax it to open on an empty stomach. She pulled the dagger out of its sheath. "Go to the kitchen," she ordered it, "and bring me some *vareniki*, please. Take care not to wake the hands, though."

The dagger flew out of her hand and toward the kitchen. A moment later it returned, four dumplings speared on its blade. Mary pulled one off and pressed it against the keyhole, but it was too thick to fit inside. She was about to ask the dagger to slice it when the keyhole widened and devoured the dumpling whole. Mary yanked back her fingers just in time from being swallowed along with the food. The keyhole chewed voraciously, then opened wide, waiting for more.

"I figured you might be hungry," Mary said drily.

She held out the next dumpling with the tips of her fingers, pulling back before the keyhole mouth mistook them for part of the meal. After the keyhole had polished off the rest, Mary sent the dagger back to the kitchen for seconds. In between bites, she stuck the edge of the comb inside the keyhole, hummed Rusalina's song softly, and heard loud gulps as it drank. Several times, it belched loudly. By the last dumpling, it chewed slowly and did not even try to nip Mary's fingers when she wiped its messy keyhole mouth with the bottom of her nightgown. But the door remained locked, and when she commanded it to open, the keyhole yawned rudely in her face.

"Ungrateful thing," Mary scolded. But then she realized that it wasn't ungrateful so much as tired. Belly full, it was fighting sleep. But perhaps if it fell asleep, it would open.

Mary tucked the feather into her sleeve, and the foyer grew dark. But the keyhole only made a grumbling sound, as if to remind Mary it was still awake. She wished she could cast a spell over it, but Madame Z hadn't taught her any. When she couldn't sleep, her mother or Caleb used to read to her. The soft lull of their voices, the fairy-tale worlds—stories were their own kind of magic.

Mary ran into the parlor and fetched the *Household Tales*. As she carried the book back to the foyer, it occurred to her that she no longer took it up to her room at night or slept with it, as she had at the orphanage. She mostly just read it with Yulik and Madame Z.

She returned to find the keyhole puckering its mouth, defiantly awake. Pulling the tip of the feather out of her sleeve, she cast just enough light over the book to read. She chose "The Girl Without Hands," which seemed like it might appeal to the keyhole's finger-nipping tastes and was also long and repetitive. As soon as she began, the keyhole stopped making faces. Halfway through the story, the keyhole yawned. After several more minutes, a snore erupted from the keyhole and, with a click, the door popped open.

Mary returned the book to the parlor, then slipped into the chilly closet. After closing the door behind her, she picked up the pestle and the broom and climbed inside the mortar.

As she stood in Madame Z's spot, she felt a pang of guilt. Madame Z had never broken a promise to her. Mary knew from the *Household Tales* the importance of keeping promises. In "The Frog King," when the princess broke her promise to the frog, her father, the king, warned, "What you have promised, you must keep." But then Mary imagined Jacob grinning as he tapped money out of his ear to cheer her up, or praising her when she figured out a trick. She couldn't bear the thought that he would have to leave Iris and she would never see him again.

"Go!" she whispered to the mortar.

It shot up the chimney. As Mary's stomach dropped, she wondered whether she could control the mortar without Madame Z. But as she pushed on the pestle, the mortar burst out into the night and sailed obediently away from the house.

Her decision made, Mary felt a rush of exhilaration. The clouds had blown away, and the sky was filled with swarms of twinkling stars. She steered the pestle east, toward Iris. As the little town came into sight, she grabbed the broom in her other hand and swept away her tracks so that no one could see her. At the crisscross of buildings, she flew the mortar lower, swooping down over the boardinghouse. She lowered the mortar until it hovered beside Jacob's window, and then she tapped lightly on the glass.

Jacob quietly opened the window and leaned out. His eyes widened. He studied the mortar and shook his head a few times as if he couldn't quite believe it was really there.

"It's real," Mary said.

"I know," Jacob whispered. "Nothing's holding it up. It's amazing!"

His eyes, Mary noticed, had dark shadows beneath them.

"Is everything all right?" she asked.

"Of course," he said quickly.

She reached out her hand. "Climb in, then!"

Jacob peered back into the room behind him.

"Don't worry," Mary said. "We'll be back by dawn. Your father won't even know you're gone."

Jacob turned back to her and nodded, but his brow was furrowed and he still seemed preoccupied. "I'm just going to throw on my coat."

"You don't need it," Mary said. "The mortar will keep you warm."

"If we're going to catch the Firebird, it could come in handy," Jacob whispered. He pulled on his coat, took her hand, and climbed out the window and into the mortar.

"Incredible how it stays warm," he said, pressing his palm against the stone in wonder.

Mary pulled back on the pestle, and the mortar sailed back up over Iris. Jacob held on to the sides, wide-eyed but grinning as he peered at the boardinghouse, now far below, then up into the sky. "The stars seem so close!" he cried.

Mary wondered if Madame Z had felt the same pleasure watching her during her first trip in the mortar as she now felt watching Jacob.

"I'm afraid I have to put you to work now," Mary said, handing him the broom. "We need to sweep away our tracks so we're invisible."

He took the broom and swept the sky after them as Mary steered the mortar away from Iris and back toward Madame Z's kingdom.

"Time to start looking for an orange light dancing above the trees," Mary said.

Both of them peered out over the forest, looking for a flicker or flash of light. But all Mary could see was the dark silhouettes of endless trees. As she steered the mortar in big, gentle loops, she hoped Madame Z was fast asleep and not peering up at the sky.

"Look! Over there!" Jacob said.

He pointed at a tiny orange light in the distance. At first Mary wasn't sure it was the Firebird, but then the light moved, drifting over the forest.

"That's her!"

Mary turned the pestle, steering the mortar toward the Firebird. But as they drew closer, the Firebird picked up speed, flapping her flaming wings. Mary pushed the pestle hard as they whizzed over the forest after her.

"Hang on!" Mary shouted.

With a squawk, the Firebird darted up into the starry sky, soaring across it like a comet. But Mary just pushed the pestle down and the mortar zoomed straight up.

Jacob gripped the side of the mortar, his hair flying in the wind. "There's something I need to tell you," he said.

"What?"

The bird was flying faster than Mary thought possible. It was hard to focus on anything other than not losing sight of her.

"I saw the *domovoi* tonight."

In an instant, Mary understood why he'd seemed so anxious when she picked him up. Why he'd kept looking back into the dark room. She had assumed he was thinking of his father, but there was another occupant she had forgotten about, one who appeared only to warn of mortal peril.

"This really has put you in danger!" she cried. What a foolish risk she had taken! Even if Madame Z intended to keep her promise not to eat any more children, Mary had broken her own promise not to take the mortar. What were the chances that Madame Z would still keep her side of the bargain?

Mary pushed the mortar hard. They had to catch the Firebird as quickly as possible. Mary desperately needed her wish. She had to protect Jacob.

The mortar began to shake, and Mary feared it might crack apart as they hurtled through the sky. But little by little they were gaining on the Firebird. The creature began flying now in panicked zigzags. Mary yanked the pestle from side to side, zigzagging along with her.

"A little faster!" Jacob shouted.

They were in reach of the bird's magnificent fiery tail, but they needed to get a little closer to douse the rest of her. Mary nudged the pestle, bringing them alongside the Firebird.

"Now!" she cried.

They took out their combs, aimed them at the bird, and began to hum. A stream of water hit the bird. There was a sizzling sound as her wings began smoking. But the rest of her was still on fire.

"Louder!" Mary shouted.

They sang again, pointing their combs at the bird. A torrent of water poured over the Firebird. There was a loud hiss.

Jacob's hand touched hers, grabbing the pestle. Mary flung

herself against the side of the mortar, stretched out her arms, and grabbed the still-smoking bird. She flapped her wings and clawed with her feet, struggling to get free. Mary tried to keep hold of the Firebird, but she was losing her grasp. Worse, the bird was growing warmer as her feathers dried. Mary hadn't expected that to happen.

"She's going to catch fire again!" Mary cried.

Jacob let go of the pestle and pulled at the sleeve of his coat. A wire birdcage appeared between his hands. She realized at once what he had done—it was the collapsible birdcage trick in reverse! But the cage looked much bigger. Jacob had clearly modified it to fit the Firebird.

"Hang on!" he shouted. The mortar sailed wildly up and down. Mary struggled to stay on her feet and keep hold of the blistering-hot bird as she opened one side of the cage.

Mary shoved the Firebird inside and slammed the door. Then she lurched for the pestle and steadied the mortar as Jacob held the cage. Inside it, the Firebird flapped once, then gave up her struggle.

Jacob grinned at Mary, his eyes shining. "We did it!"

"Thanks to you," she said. "I couldn't have held on to the Firebird if you hadn't pulled that birdcage out of your sleeve. Go ahead, you first."

Mary had never noticed Jacob's hands shake, even during the hardest tricks. But they trembled now as he opened the door to the cage.

The Firebird flew out and flapped in place in front of him. "What is your wish?"

He didn't hesitate. "I want Iris to be my home, one that my father will never make us leave."

"And you?" the Firebird said, turning to Mary.

Mary took a deep breath. She needed to protect Jacob, but she knew from the *Household Tales* that there was an art to making a wish. Request something you couldn't handle (like to become God in "The Fisherman and His Wife") and you were sure to find yourself damned by it. Request something too basic and immediate (like a string of sausages in "The Three Wishes") and you were sure to discover you had wasted your wish. It was important to choose her words carefully.

"You can save your wish," the Firebird said, interrupting Mary's thoughts. "When you are ready to use it, just call my name, *Jhar-ptitsa*, which means *Firebird* in Russian, three times and I will appear."

"No," Mary said. "I'm ready."

But before she could speak, a loud whinny filled the air. With a frightened squawk, the Firebird burst into flames and flew away.

"No!" Mary shouted. "Don't go!"

But it was too late. Sivka was galloping across the sky toward them, flames spurting from his mouth. On top of him, her bristly mouth set in a hard frown, was Madame Z, with Yulik perched on her shoulder.

TWENTY-NINE

As Sivka pulled alongside them, he nickered softly at Mary, but he was under Madame Z's control. Mary threw herself in front of Jacob. "Please don't harm him!"

Madame Z laughed harshly. "You take *my* mortar, breaking your promise, and this is how you apologize?"

"I'm sorry," Mary said. "I shouldn't have. We just needed a wish—"

"*I* needed it," Jacob said. Mary glanced back at him. With his wide, nervous eyes, he looked terrified. But he was still trying to protect her, even as he faced down a witch. Madame Z looked particularly fearsome with her flashing eyes and her coarse gray hair blowing wildly around her face.

She ignored Jacob and glared at Mary. "I told you I would teach you magic. But instead of being patient, you take *my* mortar and go chasing after the Firebird. And for what? A wish! Don't you know wishes always backfire unless you make them come true yourself?"

"I'm sorry," Mary pleaded. It was all her fault for taking the mortar. She had put Jacob in mortal danger. She had to get him out of it. "Please, just let me take him home."

"You?" Madame Z said with a sharp laugh. "Yulik, accompany Mary back to the house in the mortar and make sure she stays there till I return! I will take the boy home myself on Sivka."

"No!" Mary said. She yanked the pestle, and the mortar lurched forward. But Madame Z waved her hand and it jerked to a stop. No matter how hard Mary tried, she couldn't get the mortar to budge. They were helpless, hanging in the air.

"Don't be a fool," Madame Z snapped. "I am taking him back to his home. I won't eat him, as delicious as he might smell at the moment."

"It's okay, Mary," a voice whispered in her ear.

Mary turned around and faced Jacob. His face was pale, but his voice was calm. "I'll be fine."

She threw her arms around him. But he had barely just done the same when, with a single, swift motion, Madame Z grabbed the collar of Jacob's coat and pulled him up onto Sivka. Yulik jumped down into the mortar. Then, before Mary even had a chance to shout good-bye, Madame Z gave a loud shriek. The horse galloped off, with Jacob hanging on behind, and disappeared into a bank of dark clouds that had appeared out of nowhere.

Yulik grabbed the pestle with his tail. "You have behaved abysmally."

He continued to scold her in wounded feline tones, but Mary barely listened. What had she done? She had to save Jacob.

"*Jhar-petitsa, Jhar-petitsa*—" Mary started to call.

"I wouldn't waste your breath," Yulik interrupted. "No bird is going to show up while I'm around, especially the type that comes already roasted."

He licked his paw at the thought. Mary realized he was probably right. The Firebird had certainly taken off quickly at the sight of him and Madame Z.

"Not to mention that you'd be wasting your wish," he added. "Which is usually what humans do, but still . . ."

Mary looked at Yulik hopefully. He had never lied to her. "Madame Z won't eat him?"

"You asked her not to eat children, remember?" Yulik said in his peevish voice. "Besides, the boy was brave—certainly braver than you! He did not panic when Madame Z took him."

Mary tried to calm herself. Yulik was right. Brave children were less appetizing to Madame Z. And she had said she wouldn't eat him. But Mary had broken her own word—she just hoped she could trust Madame Z's.

"He'll be fine!" Yulik said as he steered the mortar back toward the chimney. "But will Baba Yaga?"

"What do you mean?"

"Did you even think about all the worry you caused her?" Yulik said with a sniff.

Madame Z had been worried? Of course this made sense. Mothers worried about their daughters. "I didn't realize."

"Children," Yulik grumbled. "So unaware."

As he steered the mortar back down toward the chimney,

the house tilted up to look at them, then stomped its chicken feet with vigor. Mary had the impression it was angry with her, too. Back inside, she didn't have to guess at the mood of the hands. They floated into the foyer, each one shaking a finger at her.

Mary was exhausted, but she knew she wouldn't be able to sleep till Madame Z returned home. So she sat at the loom and began to weave, her fingers absently going through the motions. The minutes ticked by as Yulik sat curled in front of the crackling fire, his chin resting on his paws. Mary closed her eyes.

She awoke with a start. Sunlight flooded through the window. She jerked upright to find Madame Z sitting beside her. Her gray eyes were fixed on Mary as she sipped from a cup of rotten-leaf tea.

"Is he home?" Mary asked.

Madame Z pointed a twisted yellow nail at her. "You shouldn't have taken my mortar."

Mary felt a burst of panic. "I'm sorry! But you need to tell me if he's home."

Madame Z sighed. "Safe and sound, *dochka*, just as I promised."

She was still *dochka*. This was a good sign. But Mary couldn't help searching Madame Z's face for a hint of dishonesty.

"You don't believe me?" Madame Z asked.

"No, it's not that. It's just—"

Madame Z scowled. "I did not harm the boy. How could I? You have ruined the pleasure of eating children for me! You see, *dochka* . . ." She hesitated, shook her head as if at the craziness of it. "As delicious as a child might smell, the thought of taking a bite now turns my stomach. I think of you."

I can't eat other children because they remind me of you: it was the strangest declaration of love that Mary had ever heard. But it seemed entirely genuine coming from Madame Z. Mary longed to grasp her hand, to say she knew what *dochka* meant and that she loved her, too. But she couldn't until she had proof that Jacob was safe.

Madame Z's gray eyes bored into hers. "I can see you continue to distrust me, so go. Go see the boy yourself!"

Mary looked at her in surprise. "Right now?"

"I should punish you for taking my mortar. I should keep you inside for a few days. But if this is the only way to convince you, *dochka* . . ."

She shook her head but did not continue.

A smile spread across Mary's face. If Madame Z had harmed Jacob, she wouldn't send her into Iris to see him. She grasped Madame Z's bony old hand and gave it a squeeze. "Thank you. I won't be long. And then I promise I'll come back home. I'm almost done with the cookbook and the cloth. Then you'll teach me magic?"

Madame Z smiled. "Perhaps I already have."

Mary shook her head. "I don't understand."

"You will in time. Go!" Madame Z waved her away.

Mary ran to the foyer for her coat.

"Good-bye, *dochka*," Madame Z called after her.

"Good-bye," Mary called back.

She almost added *Mama* but stopped herself. It was a powerful word. She feared that once said, she could never take it back.

THIRTY

THERE WAS FROST ON THE GROUND, but the sun was shining, promising a warmer day ahead. As Mary raced to Iris, she imagined her happy reunion with Jacob, how he would open the door or run down the stairs, throwing his arms around her. He might pull a coin or a flower from her ear, or simply flash the easy, open smile that made her feel as though nothing could be so bad as long as he was around. Mary grinned up at the cloudless blue sky as she thought about how they would celebrate his new home.

But as she reached town, a dark smudge caught her eye. It was the peregrine falcon, circling high above her. As its shadow traveled over her, her hopeful mood flickered. She scolded herself—the falcon wasn't some dark omen or sign of treachery, just a bird. Still, she ran faster now, a stab of fear driving her toward the boardinghouse.

Despite the nice weather, no one was outside, not even Dobbin and Fanny. This seemed strange, but then she remembered that Dobbin didn't like the falcon. Perhaps he was just keeping Fanny inside.

She took the stairs two at a time, hoping with each step that Jacob would hear her and come running down. But no one appeared. Breathless, she reached the attic landing. Before she could even rap on the door, it swung open.

"Jacob!" she started to say.

But the person facing her was Mr. Kagan. His face fell at the sight of her, as if he had expected someone else.

Mary looked past him, into the room. But there was no sign of Jacob.

"Is Jacob here?" she managed to choke out.

His father shook his head. "I woke up this morning and he was gone. You're his friend, aren't you? You haven't seen him?"

Mary leaned against the door, tried to breathe. Madame Z had been the last one to see Jacob. She realized that Mr. Kagan was staring at her, waiting for an answer.

"No," she lied. How could she explain what had happened? Mr. Kagan would never believe in child-eating witches and flying mortars.

Mr. Kagan shook his head as if he didn't understand the trick Jacob had pulled. "I'd told him the other day that it was time for us to move, but he didn't want to go. Perhaps he's hiding? A few others in the house have offered to look for him while I stay in case he returns. The people here aren't so bad, really," he added gruffly.

"I'll find him," Mary said.

Then with a quick wave, she ran back down the stairs and out to the street. She had to save Jacob—if it wasn't too late. She ran around to the side of the boardinghouse, where no one could see her.

"Jhar-petitsa, Jhar-petitsa, Jhar-petitsa!" she said.

She waited, but nothing happened. There was no cat to frighten away the bird—where was she? Mary tried again.

"Jhar-petitsa, Jhar-petitsa, Jhar-petitsa!"

Once again, nothing happened. Her chest tightened and her fingers felt numb. She wondered if Madame Z had done something to the Firebird so that she couldn't give Mary her wish.

There was only one way to find out what had happened. She raced out of Iris, toward Madame Z's. As she ran, she berated herself. She never should have taken Jacob out in the mortar. She should have made her wish faster. Most of all, she never should have trusted a witch, especially one whose instinct was to eat children. Instincts were too powerful to change.

But words were powerful, too. Madame Z had called her *daughter*. Her love had seemed genuine. Others had believed it, as well—Yulik, Koshchey, even Jacob. No mother would harm her child's friend. And when Mary really thought about it, it made no sense for Madame Z to send her to Iris to prove Jacob was home safe if he wasn't. Something wasn't adding up.

Mary reached the gate of skulls and opened it. But as she

stepped back into Madame Z's realm, Koshchey sprang from behind a grove of trees.

"Mary! There you are!" he said with a cheerful grin.

Mary drew back, wondering why Koshchey was there and why he seemed so happy. His pale blue eyes gleamed with pleasure.

"What are you doing here?" she asked.

"Looking for you, actually."

Mary took a step back, trying to size him up. With his unblinking stare and wolfish grin, he didn't seem so friendly anymore. She thought of "Fitcher's Bird," a story from the *Household Tales* about a powerful sorcerer who appears as a poor, weak beggar so he can steal village girls.

Mary's breath caught in her throat. It had never made sense that Koshchey had helped her. Or that he'd enslaved himself to Madame Z only to neglect the horse he was supposedly working to earn. What if Koshchey, not Madame Z, was the mortal danger the *domovoi* had foreseen?

There was only one way to find out.

Mary squared her shoulders, took a deep breath, and looked him in the eye. "Did you take Jacob?"

Still smiling, Koshchey put one long, skeletal hand on her shoulder. Then he hunched over her, bringing his sharp nose and scraggly beard right up to her face. "Let's take a walk."

The warmth drained out of Mary's fingers. She lurched away and tried to squirm out of his grasp, but his nails dug into her skin. As she winced, she realized they weren't nails at all, but long brown talons.

"You were the falcon circling over Iris!"

Koshchey began dragging her toward the house. "The whirlwind isn't my only other form. And I had to keep an eye on you."

To think she had suspected Madame Z! Mary felt a wave of revulsion at her own mistake. She thrashed and struggled, but he held her tight, as a falcon holds its prey. "What have you done with Jacob?"

Koshchey gave a cold laugh. "The very first time I saw you, I had a feeling you were the perfect child for Baba Yaga. So brave and spirited! And now everyone has passed the final test!"

Mary felt a sickening dread. "What test?"

"When you told me Baba Yaga called you *dochka*, I thought she loved you. But I had to be completely sure. And then your silly chase for the Firebird gave me the perfect opportunity. I told Baba Yaga what you were up to. And she returned the boy without harming him! That was the proof I needed. As for the boy, I took him right after that. He seemed useful to me just in case you tried anything foolish."

Mary stopped struggling. The trap had already been set. "Why have you done all this? To get Sivka?"

Koshchey gave a snort as he dragged her across the yard. "You should know by now that the horse is hardly important to me. I've always wanted more than that. But first Baba Yaga needs to let me into the house, where she must do something only a mother can."

The devilish look in his eyes made Mary frantic. "What? What are you going to do to her?"

But Koshchey just shoved Mary in front of him. "Baba Yaga, come out, you old hag," he shouted. "We need to talk!"

The door of the house opened, and Madame Z stood in the

threshold. Her jaw jutted forward. "What are you doing, Koshchey Bessmertny? Let her go. You know what I am capable of."

Koshchey's hair darkened from gray to brown, his beard faded, and his face grew fuller as the lines on it vanished. "Don't forget what *I* am capable of," said a young and handsome Koshchey, with a smug grin. "But this child is different, isn't she, Baba Yaga? You wouldn't want me to chase *her* into a river. You'd give anything to keep her alive."

"It was you who chased Rusalina!" Mary shouted.

Madame Z raised her hand, but just as swiftly Koshchey pressed one of his talons against Mary's cheek, piercing her skin. She yelped as a trickle of warm blood dripped down it.

"Stop!" Koshchey shouted. "Or I'll kill her!"

Madame Z lowered her hand. "What do you want?" she asked in a softer voice.

"I want it all," Koshchey said. "Your entire kingdom."

Madame Z bristled. "The forest and those who live in it will suffer under you."

"Not if they obey me," Koshchey snapped. "Now, enough stalling, old hag. You know what you must do to give up the kingdom. Let me in, and I'll allow the girl to live."

Mary wanted to cry out, "No, don't do it!" but Koshchey's talon was pressing against her cheek.

"How do I know you'll keep your promise?" Madame Z asked Koshchey.

"I would be lonely living here by myself," he said. "Besides, the girl is no threat to me without you around. She's powerless."

Madame Z's gray eyes locked onto Mary's. "I suppose there

is no other way to save her." But her calm, steady gaze seemed at odds with her words. Mary returned the look. Madame Z had to have some trick up her sleeve. She was cunning, crafty—a witch, as old and wise as the earth.

Koshchey sneered. "Your love for the girl has made you weak."

"Perhaps you are right," Madame Z said.

"So we have a deal?"

Madame Z waved Koshchey up the stairs. "Yes, Koshchey Bessmertny. Come in."

With an eager grin, Koshchey dragged Mary up the stairs by the shoulder. Mary could hardly believe what was happening. She hoped that Madame Z's resignation was some sort of act, that the witch was just trying to get Koshchey close enough to . . . Mary didn't know what. But as Koshchey barreled toward the door, Madame Z made no move to stop him. She just stared at Mary.

Mary reached into the pocket of her coat and yanked out the dagger.

Madame Z shook her head in warning, but Mary ignored her. "Please, attack him!" she cried.

The dagger flew out of her hand and sank into Koshchey's chest with a *thump*. For a moment his stare looked vacant, but then he smiled, his eyes sharp. In a single fluid motion, he plucked the dagger out of his chest. Mary looked at his gray shirt; although it was torn, there was no wound and not even a drop of blood. Koshchey tossed the dagger so that it landed at her feet with a clatter.

"Don't waste your energy. You can't kill me without my soul.

That's why they call me Koshchey Bessmertny—Koshchey the Deathless."

Still holding tight to Mary, he grabbed Madame Z roughly by the shoulder and shoved her into the house. But she wrenched around to face Mary.

"Remember what I taught you, *dochka*."

"No!" Mary screamed.

She fought to shove her way inside, but Koshchey released his talons from her shoulder and slammed the door in her face.

THIRTY-ONE

MARY PUSHED AT THE DOOR, but it wouldn't open. She rammed her entire body into it—still it didn't budge. She pressed her palm against the carved bird. Seconds turned into minutes. Minutes ticked by. The wood remained cold. It had never taken this long for the bird to come to life. Mary pressed down more vigorously. "Please," she whispered to it. But though her own heart raced, the bird had no heartbeat at all.

Mary pounded on the door with her fists.

"Let me in!" she shouted.

"*Jhar-petitsa, Jhar-petitsa, Jhar-petitsa!*" she said, but the Firebird didn't come. Mary was certain now that Koshchey must have done something to her.

Mary picked up the dagger from the porch floor.

"Please open the door!" she begged it.

The dagger tried to wedge open the door, but it wouldn't budge. The door's magic was too strong. Madame Z had made sure that no one, no matter how powerful, could open it. Only Mary. But now Koshchey had taken away this power, and her home with it.

She had to save Madame Z, Yulik, and the busy hands. She ran around the porch to each of the windows, tried to open them, break them. But they were as impenetrable as the door. She tried to see in, but the panes were steamed up. What was Koshchey doing?

She ran back to the front of the house. As she pounded on the door, she thought about Jacob. Koshchey could have already done any number of terrible things to him as well, from killing him outright to hiding him away where he'd never be found, like the wizard's own soul.

Shoving the door with all her might, she gave a piercing, desperate scream.

At just this moment, it swung open, and she toppled into the house, landing on all fours. As she scrambled to her feet, the door banged shut behind her. The foyer was dark. The air was warm and close.

"May-a-ree," called a singsong voice from the parlor.

Mary rushed into the room. Koshchey sat on the bench, his muddy boots resting on top of Mary's weaving, which sagged under their weight. A fire raged in the hearth, and the air was so hot that his face was mottled red. An enormous birdcage hung on a chain from the ceiling, but instead of a bird, its prisoners were the three pairs of helping hands, which wedged their fingers through the bars as they reached for her in desperation, and Yulik. Mary imagined the cat had many words to describe such an indignity, but at the sight of her, all he seemed able to do was yowl piteously. Koshchey must have taken away his voice. The writing desk trembled in the corner, the recipe book still on top of it.

"I do not care for talking animals," Koshchey remarked, smacking the cage so it swung back and forth, nearly toppling Yulik onto the hands.

"Stop that!" Mary said. "Where's Madame Z?"

"You see, Mary," Koshchey said patiently, as if teaching a lesson, "when we love, we make ourselves vulnerable. You should have seen how willingly she crawled inside. All I had to do was remind her of my promise not to hurt you."

But Mary could only think about three words: *she crawled inside*. The thick, heavy heat, Yulik's plaintive cries—it all made horrible sense. The way to kill a witch in the *Household Tales* was to burn her. Madame Z was inside the *pech*. Mary staggered toward the kitchen.

"Go if you like," Koshchey said with a dismissive wave. "She's nothing but ashes now."

Mary opened the kitchen door, releasing a blast of air so hot that she was forced to stumble backward. She slid to the floor. In "Hansel and Gretel," Gretel had tricked the wicked witch into crawling into her own oven. But Madame Z had crawled into her own oven, giving up her life and kingdom willingly, to save Mary. This is what Koshchey had bet on from the beginning. A mother always protected her child, even with her own life. Tears flowed down Mary's burning cheeks as she rested her head on her knees and sobbed. Once again, she had failed to save someone who loved her.

"You're not a sentimental child," Koshchey said sternly. "It does not suit you. You want a home, same as I do. You will have one here with me."

"I don't want one with *you!*" Mary managed to spit out. "Where's Jacob?"

She was afraid of the answer, but she had to know.

"Locked away in the woods."

Mary let out her breath. At least he was still alive.

"But everything has worked out now," Koshchey continued. "Baba Yaga is dead and her kingdom is mine. The boy could cause trouble if I keep him alive." Koshchey's pale blue eyes glinted. "Besides, I'm not like Baba Yaga. Your feelings for him mean nothing to me."

Mary sprang to her feet. "Promise me you won't hurt him, and I'll stay with you."

"You're just like Baba Yaga," Koshchey said with a trace of amusement. "But in your case, you have nothing to bargain with. You're already staying. I have enchanted the house so the doors will not open to let you out—including the one to the mortar. I am off now."

"Wait!" Mary cried, but he was already transforming. As he shrank, his nose grew longer and beaky, his hair turned into feathers, his arms into wings, his nails into talons. He flew into the foyer as she chased after him. The door creaked open just wide enough for him to fly through before it slammed shut. Mary yanked at it with all her might, but the door wouldn't open.

Koshchey's enchantment was too strong. She was a prisoner now in her own home. Worst of all, she was just as powerless to save Jacob as she had been to save Madame Z.

Remember what I taught you. That's what Madame Z had said. But all she'd taught her was how to cook and weave and take care of a horse, when what she needed was powerful magic. But Madame Z wouldn't have just left her to Koshchey. There had to be a message in her final words, a way out.

"*Dochka*," she said out loud.

She was a witch's daughter. She wasn't going to give up yet.

Mary ran back to the birdcage hanging in the parlor. Yulik yowled loudly at the sight of her, and the hands clasped one another, pleading. Perhaps they could help her understand what Madame Z had been trying to tell her. But first she needed to get them out.

"Hold on!" she shouted.

Mary pulled the dagger out of her pocket. "Please, release Yulik and the hands," she said.

The dagger flew swiftly into the air and cut the chain that attached the birdcage to the ceiling. It crashed to the ground and split in half. Yulik leaped out and jumped into Mary's arms, purring loudly, as the hands flew into the air and applauded. But the sound of the doorknob rattling in the foyer interrupted their celebration.

"Koshchey!" Mary whispered.

Had the wizard come back to punish Mary for breaking the birdcage and freeing the others?

A loud rap sounded on the window behind them. Mary swung around as one of the hands frantically wiped away the steam.

THIRTY-TWO

JACOB'S FACE APPEARED IN THE WINDOW.

Mary froze, wondering if he was an illusion. But at the sight of her, he broke into a grin.

"Can you hear me, Mary?" he asked through the glass.

"Yes!" she cried. "Yes! But how did you—? I thought Koshchey—?"

As the hands worked to clear off more of the steam, Mary could see the *domovoi* perched on Jacob's shoulder. "*You* helped him!"

"Of course I did," the *domovoi* said through the glass, with an imperious sniff.

"Right before Koshchey came, he jumped in his boot and told me to put it on," Jacob said.

"Fortunately, young Jacob does not have very large feet," the *domovoi* remarked.

"Koshchey locked me in a cage deep in the woods, but this morning, after he finally left, the *domovoi* slipped through the bars and freed me. Then he led me here."

"Madame Z is dead," Mary blurted out. "She . . ."

She tried to say what Madame Z had done to save her, but her eyes filled with tears. She blinked them back. "There's no way for me to get out of the house or get you in. You need to leave—now! Koshchey's headed back to kill you. As soon as he discovers you've escaped—"

"Mary, it's okay," Jacob said. "There was another prisoner there with us. The Firebird! Koshchey had locked her up so she couldn't come to you."

"I couldn't do much to help you catch her," the *domovoi* said, with an apologetic shrug. "So I figured it was the least I could do."

Jacob burst into a grin. "He freed her! You can make your wish now!"

Mary didn't even have to think. She knew what her wish was. She wanted Madame Z back. She loved her. And Madame Z was the only one who could save them all from Koshchey.

"*Jhar-petitsa, Jhar-petitsa, Jhar-petitsa!*" she called.

There was a loud clap and a burst of light. Jacob jumped back as the Firebird took his place in front of the window. She hovered on the other side of the glass from Mary, her flaming feathers turning orange, gold, and even blue where the fire seemed hottest. "You have summoned me," she said in Madame Petitsa's silvery voice.

"I know my wish," Mary said. "Bring Madame Z back to life!"

The hands clasped each other, and Yulik butted his head against her. Mary knew if he could talk, he'd be saying "Thank you."

But the Firebird said nothing. She flapped her fiery wings softly. "If only I had such powers," she said sadly.

"You can't bring her back?" Mary burst out.

The Firebird shook her delicate head. "No."

Mary bit her lip, trying not to cry, but the tears were spilling down her cheeks. Madame Z had told her that the dead were gone. Some wishes were impossible.

"You can," the Firebird said.

Mary's breath caught in her throat. She blinked back her tears. There was still hope. "How?"

The moment the word escaped her lips, Mary realized she had used up her wish. Still, she didn't regret it.

"By using the magic Baba Yaga taught you," the Firebird said.

"She didn't teach Mary any magic," Jacob said from behind the Firebird.

Mary remembered what Madame Z had told her that very morning: *Perhaps I already have.* "Wait! She hinted this morning that she *had* taught me magic. The last thing she said was to remember what she'd taught me. But she only taught me—"

She swung around to face the writing desk, still trembling in the corner. "The cookbook!" she nearly shouted. "Recipes are like spells!"

"Koshchey is on his way," the *domovoi* said, sniffing the air.

"Hurry, Mary!" Jacob said through the window. "Maybe there's a recipe to bring back Madame Z."

"Come here!" Mary said to the desk.

The desk scampered over to her. She flipped to the end of the cookbook—she had copied all the recipes except for the ones on the last few pages. But they had been torn out. Mary wondered now if they had been recipes for children. Only the very last page remained, and it was blank.

She would have to write it herself, then. She grabbed the quill and dipped it in ink:

RECIPE FOR MADAME Z

A WITCH'S ASHES

She paused, the quill raised, trying to think of what should come next. Just then something caught her eye. Black ink was soaking into the paper. Beneath "a witch's ashes" letters appeared and formed into words.

A CHILD'S TEARS
A WIND EGG'S SHELL
A HORSE'S HAIRS
A PINCH OF SALT
A SPRINKLING OF FLOUR
A FIREBIRD'S FEATHER
A *DOCHKA*'S POWER

COMBINE INGREDIENTS. BAKE IN A COLD OVEN UNTIL DONE.

THIRTY-THREE

"Look!" Mary said, holding up the cookbook to the window to show Jacob, the *domovoi*, and the Firebird. "But what's a wind egg?"

"An egg without a yolk," the Firebird said.

"Wait—Koshchey told me his soul was in an egg!" Mary said.

"And didn't you say he can turn into a wind?" Jacob asked.

Inside the house, Yulik yowled and butted his head against Mary's shins.

"That must be the egg we're looking for!" Mary said. "But where is it?"

"All I know is that it looks exactly like an ordinary chicken egg," the Firebird said. "But I don't know where Koshchey hides it."

Mary turned to the others trapped in the house with her. The hands turned palms up and rose a few inches in the air. Yulik shook his head and flopped onto the floor in despair.

Outside, Jacob and the *domovoi* looked just as perplexed.

"Koshchey could have hidden it anywhere!" the *domovoi* shouted through the window. He hopped up and down on Jacob's shoulder, casting anxious glances behind him. "You could spend years on a problem like that, and we have only a few minutes!"

"A problem," Mary repeated softly. *When I have a problem, I always weave,* Madame Z had said. Mary ran over to the loom, sat down on the bench, and began to weave, just as Madame Z had taught her.

"This is no time for handicrafts!" she could hear the *domovoi* shout over the *click-clack* of the loom, followed by Jacob's voice: "No, don't you see! There's got to be magic in that weaving! Just like the cookbook."

Where is Koshchey's soul? Mary thought to herself as she pumped the treadle and threw the shuttle back and forth and beat with the reed. Outside, she could hear the wind picking up. Koshchey would catch Jacob and the *domovoi* first. There was nothing she could do to protect them. But the regular rhythm of her hands and feet kept her calm, even as the *domovoi* continued to panic.

"We're wasting time!" he shouted at Jacob. "We need to run back to Iris and hide!"

"No!" Jacob said. "I'm not leaving Mary."

Twigs, snapped off by the wind, hit the windows. Yulik began to race around the room meowing.

"He's coming!" shouted the *domovoi*. "He's really coming!"

Mary stopped as one pair of hands yanked her sleeve. The others, each balancing on two fingers, ran across the floor in every direction.

"But how can we run away?" she asked them. She was locked inside; Jacob was locked out. The hands pointed in every direction—up at the ceiling, at the walls, at the ground.

"Wait!" Mary said. "The house! The house can run!"

She ran to the window. "Jacob, grab onto the railing and hold on tight!" Then she shouted, "*Izba!* Run deep into the forest. Hide among the trees!"

Outside, the stairs folded up with a loud clack. Then the whole house rumbled and swayed. Mary stumbled and barely managed to grab onto the windowsill. The house took off, its chicken legs thumping the ground with surprising speed. Mary could see Jacob gripping the porch railing, his feet flying in the air, the *domovoi* clinging to his coat. The Firebird flew swiftly alongside them, lighting the way. Trees jumped out of the house's path as it barreled through the forest. At last, it stopped in a clearing. But it remained a clearing for less than a moment—tall oaks moved in and clustered around it. Their limbs bent in protective arcs, concealing the house beneath them. The stairs clattered back down.

Jacob let go of the railing and ran to the window. "Quick, Mary, finish weaving!"

"You've bought us a little more time," admitted the *domovoi*,

his fur ruffled by the ride. "But Koshchey will find us soon enough, and the house can't run forever."

Mary raced back to the loom. The warp thread was almost done. Where is Koshchey's soul? she thought again. As she wove the last row, the cloth shimmered, then turned from black to silver to blue.

"Something's happening!" she shouted.

She rolled out the cloth. In the center of it, an oval appeared and turned brown, save for a large green tree. The word BUYAN appeared below it. The blue section of cloth began to undulate like waves.

Mary turned to Yulik. "Is there an island named Buyan in Madame Z's kingdom? Meow once for yes!"

Yulik meowed once.

Mary ran to the window. "Koshchey's soul is on an island called Buyan."

"Could the house take us there?" Jacob asked.

The hands flew over, shaking their fingers.

"Chickens can't fly long distances," the Firebird said.

"I need to get out," Mary said.

"I've been thinking about that," Jacob said. "The doors and windows are under Koshchey's spell, but how about the walls?"

"How are you going to break through the wall?" Mary asked. "You'd need—"

"Stone and speed."

Mary understood at once. "The mortar! Then we'll use it to fly to Buyan."

"If I could get up to the chimney and climb down it—"

"You'll do no such thing!" the *domovoi* interrupted. "You could fall. This is a job for a house spirit, not a boy."

"You'll do it, then?" Mary asked.

The *domovoi* sighed in an exaggerated manner. "What choice do I have? If I'm ever going to get home again . . ."

"We'll get you home," Jacob promised him. "And not just you. All of us." Then he turned to Mary. "I'm going to help him up, as much as I can. I'll be back in a few minutes."

Mary turned to the Firebird. "I know I've used up my wish, but, please, do this out of the goodness of your heart. Tell the other magical creatures what Koshchey has done and that we're going to Buyan to try to stop him."

"I shall," the Firebird replied in her musical voice. "Madame Z had faith in you, and I do, too."

Before Mary could thank her, the Firebird flew away.

Mary waited anxiously as the minutes ticked by. The sky was growing darker, and clouds gathered above. At last, she heard the crack of tree limbs, followed by shouts. She ran to the window just in time to see the *domovoi* in the mortar, crashing through branches. He clung to the pestle as he struggled to steer.

"I'm sorry," Mary whispered, patting the wall of the house. "But we need to break you to save you."

The house shuddered but did not run. She felt it understood.

"Mary, get away from the wall!" Jacob shouted.

Mary ran to the other side of the parlor, followed by the hands and Yulik.

There was a loud crash as the mortar broke through the wall, skidded into the loom, and cracked in half. The *domovoi* went flying through the air and would have landed in the fireplace were it not for a pair of the helping hands, which caught him just in time.

Jacob ran in through the gaping hole.

"Is everyone all right?"

"Everyone but the house," Mary said. "Poor *izba!*"

"How about poor *domovoi?*" said the *domovoi* from where the hands were fussing over him. "Just so you know, that was above and beyond the usual house-spirit duty!"

"You did a great job," Jacob said. "I'm proud you're my *domovoi.*"

The *domovoi* said nothing but puffed out his chest.

"But the mortar is broken." Mary stared at the cracked pieces. "What are we going to do now?"

A gust of cold air blew in through the hole. The fire flickered in the hearth. Outside, leaves flew off the trees, a fierce wind stripping them bare.

The *domovoi* slumped over. "And Koshchey's almost here! We'll never outrun him!"

Mary looked at the *domovoi*. "But maybe we can outride him!"

"Madame Z's horse!" Jacob said.

"Taking care of him was my third task!" Mary said. "He knows me."

She pulled out the magic dagger. "Find Sivka, please! Free him if Koshchey's tied him up, and lead him here, fast!"

THIRTY-FOUR

MARY RAN OUT TO THE PORCH and scanned the sky. Dark clouds were rolling in from every direction. Jacob, Yulik, and the hands—still carrying the *domovoi*—crowded around her.

"Even if Sivka comes, will he let you ride him?" the *domovoi* asked.

"That's why Madame Z had me take care of him," Mary said. "Love is taking care of someone, doing those simple everyday tasks. He trusts me."

"Will he trust the dagger, though?" Jacob asked, looking up.

"He knows it's mine," Mary said. "I used the dagger to get him the ice."

"Well, he'd better get here fast," the *domovoi* said.

Overhead, the corona of blue sky was growing smaller and smaller. Just as the circle of blue was about to vanish completely, there was a flash of silver. The dagger flew through the shrinking hole in the clouds, and the enormous golden-brown horse dove after it, flames spurting from his mouth.

"Sivka!" Mary cried.

The horse circled down roughly on the gusty drafts of wind, then landed, kicking up dirt as he hit the ground at a full gallop. He circled the house once, then stopped in front of Mary, tossing his mane and nickering. A little piece of lead rope dangled from his halter. The dagger, which had clearly slashed off the rest of the rope to free him, flew back into the sheath in Mary's pocket.

"Good boy," Mary said, patting the froth of smoky-smelling sweat on Sivka's neck. She hummed softly to give him a drink from Rusalina's comb, then climbed up the railing. There was no time for nerves. The horse trusted her—now she had to trust him. With a deep breath, she threw her leg over his bare back and hoisted herself up. Sivka stood perfectly still, his ears upright, his head tilted warily up at the sky. Mary grabbed his mane tight. Although she had never ridden a horse, the feeling of his curved, slippery back reminded her of the weaving bench. She felt determined but not afraid.

Jacob took off his boot to allow the *domovoi* to scramble inside, wedged it back on, and then clambered up behind Mary and wrapped his arms around her waist. The clouds swirled overhead.

"He's coming!" the *domovoi* said, sticking his head out the top of Jacob's boot.

In the center of a particularly black cloud, Mary could just make out a funnel beginning to form. "Stay here to protect what's left of our home," she said to the hands and Yulik. But the cat, who had been balancing on the porch railing, leaped onto Sivka's rump and from there up onto Mary's shoulder with a defiant meow. Sivka seemed to take this as a sign to move. He jumped into the air.

"Hold on tight!" Mary shouted. As his hooves left the ground, she could feel her stomach drop and Jacob's arms clutching her waist. But she swayed along with Sivka's rhythmic strides, just as she had learned to sway along with the loom.

The horse rose, fighting the wind as he flew toward the edge of the great mass of clouds. Looking down on the forest, Mary noticed that the red and yellow leaves were gone. As far as she could see, the trees were spindly and naked, the ground brown and lifeless. Flakes of snow drifted down through the cold air. Koshchey had turned the kingdom to winter. The birds and animals had to be confused—probably hungry and cold as well.

But her thoughts were interrupted by the shouts of the *domovoi*, who was ramming the boot against Sivka's side to spur him on. "Behind us!" he squeaked. "Koshchey is coming!"

Mary looked over her shoulder at the narrow funnel descending from the clouds. It looked small, almost harmless, until one of Koshchey's pale blue eyes appeared in its center. A thunderous peal of laughter shook the sky. Then the twister whirled after them. As fast as Sivka could fly, it gained on them, sucking them in. Mary clung to the horse's neck. Jacob's arms tightened around her waist. Yulik's claws dug painfully into her shoulder, but she didn't blame him—how else could he hold on? As the wind increased, Mary felt one of Yulik's paws pull away, then the other. There was a loud yowl. Mary reached up, nearly losing her balance, as she tried to save the cat, but he was already gone.

"Yulik!" Mary cried.

"The *domovoi*!" Jacob shouted over the wind.

Mary glanced at Jacob's boot. The *domovoi* had been blown out of it and was holding on to the end of a lace with one hand. Before they could reach down, he too was sucked away.

They had time only to exchange a horrified look as the funnel began to pull them in. Sivka whinnied loudly and struggled to fly away, but tendrils of wind yanked them back. Mary peered down at the forest, far below. They'd never survive the fall.

Then the sight of the brown, leafless trees gave her an idea.

"Mr. Less!" Mary shouted. "Look at what Koshchey has done to the forest, freezing the animals. Save us so we can help protect them and your home!"

The wind blew harder, whistling loudly over her words. But just as Sivka was about to be dragged into the gray, swirling walls of the funnel, hundreds of thousands of swallows burst out of the trees below. Black and thick as a cloud, they swarmed around the whirlwind.

"A distraction!" said Jacob. The fierce wind died down enough for Sivka to pull away.

"Go!" Mary shouted.

Sivka took off across the sky at a gallop. A group of the swallows flew around him like a magician's cape, hiding the horse and his riders from view.

"We're searching for an island!" Mary said. "Look in every direction!"

"There's nothing but trees," Jacob said.

Mary glanced behind them. The swallows continued to swarm around the whirlwind, but Koshchey was sucking some of them into his funnel, blowing others away with big gusts. She spurred Sivka on.

"There's no sign of a sea down there, and without a sea, we're never going to find an island," Jacob said.

"You're right," Mary started to say. But the word *sea* stopped her. "That's it!" Mary dug into her pocket. "If we can't find the sea, we'll make it ourselves."

"The combs!" Jacob pulled out his at the same time Mary pulled out hers. They pushed the teeth together until they seemed to lock, then let go. Sivka circled as they watched the intertwined combs fall, tumbling toward the earth. The combs dropped through the trees and disappeared from view.

Mary waited. She knew from Madame Z to be patient with magic, but she also knew they didn't have much time. The swallows wouldn't be able to hold back Koshchey for much longer.

"Maybe the combs broke apart," she said.

But the words were barely out of her mouth when there was a rumble below, and a crack split the forest in two. It grew wider and wider, pushing the land away until it had become an enormous sand-colored basin. Within seconds, the bottom had turned a shimmering blue.

"It's working!" Jacob said.

The water rose swiftly until the basin had become a sea that spread out for miles in every direction. Mary could see the shadows of clouds moving across the water, the wind whipping up whitecaps, even a school of fish leaping out of the waves.

"Is there an island?" Mary said.

Sivka circled above the sea.

"I don't see one," Jacob said.

"Me neither."

The wind was picking up, and the light was changing behind them, the sun fading.

"Anything else you know about it?" Jacob asked.

Mary shrugged. "Just Buyan, its name."

"But why would the map give you its name?"

Mary thought of the *izba*. A magic house responded to its name; why not a magic island? There was power in names— *Jhar-petitsa, Sivka, dochka.*

"Buyan!" she shouted. "If you are there, show yourself!"

The water below churned and bubbled. The top of an oak tree pierced the waves, and its leafy branches rose from the water. The trunk emerged, and an island rumbled up out of the sea with it. It was no larger than the town of Iris. There was a sandy white beach and a hillside covered with shrubs. Perched on the grassy headland, just like on the woven map on the loom, stood the oak tree.

"Go, Sivka!" Mary cried. "Take us there!"

As the sky darkened, the horse raced over the waves toward Buyan. They were still over the water when the funnel smacked into them. The force knocked Sivka upside down. Mary grabbed Jacob's hand as they tumbled off.

"I can't swim!" he cried.

But the water was coming up too fast for her to answer.

THIRTY-FIVE

MARY TRIED TO HOLD ON TO JACOB'S HAND, but as they splashed down, the force of the water yanked them apart. She sank into the cold sea. She could barely swim herself, but all she could think about was trying to grab hold of Jacob again. She couldn't lose him. She reached up and kicked her feet until she surfaced.

"Jacob!" she shouted frantically. But there was no sight of him—no head bobbing in the water, no cries for help. She flailed, and with each shout, she felt her strength weaken. She could see the shore of Buyan a hundred feet away, but it might as well have been a hundred miles. She'd never make it. Her head bobbed under and she kicked, fighting to stay above water.

"Relax," a voice said behind her. "I've got him."

Mary lurched around. Rusalina had an arm around Jacob,

holding his head and shoulders above the surface as he coughed. The *rusalka* floated calmly and without effort, her pale, wet locks spread out around her.

"He'll be okay," Rusalina said. "Grab on."

Mary gratefully hung on to the *rusalka's* back. "You don't want us to drown?" she asked when she'd caught her breath.

With her free arm, Rusalina quickly swam a sidestroke toward the shore. "You wouldn't want to be my friend if I did, would you?"

"Probably not. But I want to be now."

Rusalina looked back at Mary, her large blue-green eyes serious. "The Firebird told me what happened. I can't do much to help you on land, but I can at least get you there."

"Koshchey's the one who chased you into the river," Mary quickly explained. "He can shape-shift into a young man. He threatened to chase me into a river, too."

Rusalina faltered for only a second before her stroke quickened.

"Then you must defeat him. But not just for me—for all of us."

Mary thought of all the magical creatures who had helped her—and who had been hurt by Koshchey.

"We will," Mary promised solemnly.

They neared the shore, and she felt sandy bottom beneath her. Jacob stumbled to his feet.

"Thank you," he said to Rusalina. "You saved my life."

Rusalina shook her head. "Not what a *rusalka* wants to hear." She turned to Mary. "Your hair looks nice like that, though."

"Like what?" Mary asked. As she touched her hair, her fingers ran over ivory and pearls.

"The combs!" Jacob said. "You gave them back."

"They're yours now." Rusalina gave an impish smile, dove into the water, and vanished.

Mary grabbed Jacob's hand and helped him to shore. The sky had cleared, and the late-afternoon sun reassured Mary, though they were wet and shivering.

"Maybe Koshchey thinks we drowned?"

"He'll want to be sure," Jacob said, looking nervously up at the sky.

"Which doesn't leave us much time," Mary agreed. "We need to head to that oak tree. It had to be on the map for a reason. Where else could the egg be?"

She ran up the beach to the shrub line. A narrow, sandy trail wound around the hill through the shrubs. But just as she was about to turn back to tell Jacob, she heard him whisper loudly, "Mary, get down!"

She dove into the shrubs as a loud whinny filled the air. She peeked out through the branches. Sivka was flying toward the island, bucking and breathing fire as he tried to throw off his rider. But Koshchey had dug his talons into the horse's withers and was kicking him hard.

Jacob didn't run. He stood on the beach, waiting for the wizard.

"Where's the girl?" Koshchey shouted as he forced Sivka to land.

Mary wasn't going to let Jacob sacrifice himself. But before she could jump up, she heard his voice.

"You're too late," Jacob said calmly.

Mary froze, crouched behind the bushes. She knew Koshchey couldn't see her, but she could see him, blinking in confusion. She felt the same way. What was Jacob doing?

He took a step toward Koshchey and opened his palm. In it was a chicken egg. Mary stared at it in wonder. Where had Jacob gotten it? There hadn't been time to find the real egg. But from the horrified look on his face, Koshchey didn't know that.

"Careful with that!" he hissed.

"With what?" Jacob said, closing his fist. When he opened it, the egg was gone.

"What have you done with it?" Koshchey shouted, leaping off Sivka.

"Stay where you are!" Jacob said in a commanding voice.

Koshchey stopped short. His face was red and his eyes flickered with fear. He watched intently as Jacob pulled the egg from behind his ear.

"You wouldn't want to startle me so I drop it!" Jacob said. He pretended to lose hold of the egg. Koshchey gasped loudly. Jacob caught it.

Mary understood at once what he was doing. As Jacob made the egg disappear, reappear, and nearly drop again, she backed out of the bush and crawled, low to the ground, up the trail.

When the trail rounded the hill and she was certain she was out of sight, she jumped to her feet and ran straight up the hillside. The shrubs scratched her legs, and once she tripped and nearly fell, loosening a small slide of rocks that made her freeze for fear Koshchey had heard it. But the only sound besides the falling rocks was Jacob's patter as he continued his act. As she neared the top of the hill, she could still hear him. Peering over the rise, she saw the oak tree, its gnarled roots spread out around it, anchoring it to the ground. The headland was visible from the beach below; if she raced around searching for the egg, Koshchey might look up and see her. She also knew she didn't have much time. Jacob was the best illusionist in Iris, but how long could he fool a real wizard?

"Dagger," she said, pulling it out of her pocket, "please find Koshchey's soul, fast!"

The dagger flew out of her hands and sank into the trunk of the oak tree with a thump. Koshchey might see her, but there was no other way to get the egg. Mary ran over and gave the dagger a tug. As she did, a small door in the trunk opened.

An angry roar rose up from the beach. "Mary!"

She'd been spotted! Mary frantically reached inside the hollow and pulled out an iron chest shaped like a falcon.

"You may have my soul," Koshchey shouted, "but I'll have the boy's!"

Mary turned around just as the wizard lunged for him. But before Koshchey could grab Jacob, Sivka charged between them, puffs of smoke snorting up from his nostrils. Mary flung open the lid of the chest.

"Meddlesome beast!" With a wave of his hand, Koshchey conjured a burst of wind so powerful that it lifted Sivka into the air and spun him out to sea.

Mary grabbed the egg, nearly identical to the one in Jacob's hand, and held it over her head. "Don't move!" she shouted.

Koshchey froze.

His stricken face made her hesitate. She had never killed anyone before. She was a witch's daughter—but not a witch.

"What are you waiting for?" Koshchey called up to her. "Baba Yaga would have killed me already. Perhaps you're feeling sorry for old Koshchey? After all, I'm the one who really helped you find this home of yours."

His words flooded her with anger. "You used me!" she said. "And you destroyed my family!"

"Baba Yaga is dead," Koshchey admitted. "That cannot be undone. But *I* can still give you a home."

Mary shook her head. "You have nothing to give. A home without love isn't a home."

"I can give you power, then!" Koshchey shouted. "Love won't give you that!"

"I have power." She and Jacob had tricked a cunning wizard using their friends' magic and their own wits. Now she held his life in her hands.

"You think you do," Koshchey said with a smirk. "But the ones you love will always make you vulnerable."

"You're wrong, Koshchey Bessmertny," Mary said, her voice as firm and commanding as Madame Z's.

Love hadn't weakened Madame Z. The clever old witch had outsmarted Koshchey after all. She hadn't put her life in his hands. She had put it in Mary's.

"Is that so?" Koshchey asked, his face twisting into a smug grin.

Faster than Mary thought was possible, he transformed into a whirlwind, sucking Jacob into the funnel. Spidery fingers with long talons began to reach out for Jacob's throat. Mary dashed the egg against the ground.

The moment it cracked, splattering against the roots of the tree, Koshchey staggered back with a rattling gasp, his pale blue eyes blank and lifeless. Jacob, released from the wind's pull, fell against the sand.

"Jacob!" Mary shouted, but he didn't answer.

His eyes were closed, and a trickle of blood dripped down his neck.

Koshchey tumbled back beside him. But the moment he hit the ground, his body turned into tendrils of wind and blew away.

Mary raced down the hill, barely bothering to notice the branches scraping her legs. Her heart pounded as she threw herself to the ground beside Jacob and took his hand. She was relieved to see the rise and fall of his chest. Pulling the comb out of her hair, she hummed softly so a trickle of water washed the blood from his skin.

His eyes opened. "Mary," he said with a smile.

She studied the small punctures on his neck. "He just managed to prick you. But he's gone forever now."

Jacob sat up. Only as he took her hand did Mary realize she was shaking. Koshchey hadn't been entirely wrong about love, either. There was always the terrible risk that the people you loved would die, like her mother and Caleb. Like Madame Z and—very nearly—Jacob.

"I think I just fainted," Jacob said. "I'm okay now."

"Where did you get the egg?" she asked.

"Where else?" Jacob said with a mischievous smile. "The

house. While the *domovoi* was getting the mortar, I crawled underneath and asked the house to lay one for me. You said Koshchey's soul was in an egg, so I thought it might be useful."

"Jacob, you're brilliant!"

A whinny made them both look out over the sea. Sivka was flying toward them. The dark clouds had blown away, and behind him the sun was setting, leaving pink and orange streaks across the sky. Mary smiled and helped Jacob back to his feet. The enormous horse landed on the beach in front of them. He shook his mane and stamped his hooves impatiently.

"I think he wants to go home," Mary said.

But at the word *home*, her voice wavered.

Jacob squeezed her hand. "Let's gather the eggshells."

Sivka flew them back up to the headland, where they collected the smashed shells of Koshchey's wind egg.

The most important task, and the most magical, was yet to come. Mary pictured the *pech* and took a deep, determined breath. "I'm going to bring her back."

THIRTY-SIX

NIGHT WAS FALLING when Sivka landed in front of the *izba*. Mary and Jacob hopped off. The house tottered toward them on its chicken feet. The hands flew out of the gaping hole like bats from a cave.

"We're okay," Mary said as the *izba* trembled and the hands swarmed around them. She looked for Yulik and the *domovoi*, but there was no sign of them. She had been hoping to find them back at the house, safe after Koshchey's death. She could tell Jacob had been hoping the same thing, because he glanced sadly at his boot.

"First, Madame Z," she said. "Then maybe we can find the others."

"We need her help," Jacob agreed.

Mary recited the recipe list: "A witch's ashes, a child's

tears—I have no shortage of those right now," she remarked. "A wind egg's shells, a horse's hairs."

Mary petted Sivka's flank. "Baba Yaga needs your help," she said. Then she pulled out the dagger. "Cut a few strands of Sivka's mane, please."

Sivka lowered his head and stood still to let the dagger do its job. Mary held the golden hairs, then fished in her pocket for the Firebird's feather, which lit up the growing darkness.

"A pinch of salt, a sprinkling of flour—"

The hands stuck their thumbs up at these basic ingredients.

"A Firebird's feather, a *dochka*'s power." She looked at Jacob. "*Dochka* means *daughter*. I'm not exactly sure about the last one, but we have everything else."

"Maybe she just means all the magic she taught you?" Jacob asked.

"Perhaps," Mary said. "Anyway, it's time to try."

They ran up the stairs to the porch and through the hole in the *izba*'s wall. The fire in the hearth had gone out, and the parlor was dark. The Firebird feather's glow revealed a grim picture: the loom smashed and Mary's cloth torn, the mortar cracked in half, chunks of broken amber scattered across the room. Cold winter air blew through the parlor. The hands, which had followed them inside, rubbed themselves together for warmth.

Mary and Jacob picked their way through the debris to the kitchen door. Mary pushed it open. The air inside was no longer hot, but an acrid smell made her draw back. Breathing only through her mouth to avoid the odor, Mary forced herself to step into the kitchen and over to the enormous oven.

She touched the front of it as the helping hands dropped two small satchels of flour and salt into her pocket.

"It's cold," she said to Jacob.

"The recipe does say bake in a cold oven," he said.

Mary checked her other pocket for the wind egg's shells and the horse's hairs. "A good thing, too, because I'm going to have to crawl inside. It's the only way to mix everything together."

"Are you sure?" Jacob said. "I can crawl in with you."

Mary shook her head. "I have a feeling I need to do this myself."

"I'll be right here, then," he said.

Mary squeezed his hand, thinking of how he had stood by her every step of the way. But she never had been as alone as she had thought. Yulik, the *domovoi*, and even the house itself had tried to protect her; Madame Z had made the ultimate sacrifice to save her. At the thought of Madame Z, Mary's eyes grew wet with tears. But she didn't want to shed them too soon. Holding the Firebird feather up in front of her, she opened the door of the *pech*. Then she took a deep breath and crawled inside, closing the door behind her.

The orange glow of the feather flickered off the blackened sides of the oven, creating the illusion of flames. The smoky carbon smell made her want to gag. For a moment, she felt as if she were back at the Buffalo Asylum for Young Ladies, wedged into the chimney. But this time, she wasn't trying to escape. She imagined Madame Z calling her *dochka*, and crawled forward.

Mary was surprised at how deep the oven was. As she crawled farther, she steeled herself to find Madame Z's remains.

But Koshchey was right. When she finally reached the curved back wall of the oven, all she found was a small pile of ashes. She was afraid to touch it, afraid the ashes would disintegrate in her hands. They were all that was left of Madame Z. Mary imagined that the authors of the *Household Tales* would find it fitting that a witch had died in her own oven. But what would they make of a witch dying for a child, and a child willingly crawling into an oven to bring her back to life?

Love. That's what Mary made of it. She remembered her mother calling her and Caleb *my heart, my soul*; Caleb letting her lean against his shoulder as he read her the *Household Tales*; her first night at Madame Z's, when Yulik had slept in her bed; the afternoon with Sivka when Madame Z had first called her *dochka*. As these loving memories flashed through her head, the tears she had been holding back began to flow. They fell down her cheeks and onto the brick, mingling with the ashes. Mary quickly added the wind egg's shells and Sivka's hairs, then opened the satchels and added a pinch of salt and a sprinkling of flour.

She looked at the feather in her hand. The Firebird regularly burst into flame, and yet she didn't die. Mary remembered the bird's glow on her first night at Madame Z's, the hope she'd felt when she saw it. She touched the tip of the feather to the pile of other ingredients.

An orange spark shot out from the end. Then the ashes glimmered and began swirling around the bottom of the oven.

"Please come back, Madame Z!" she cried.

But no sooner had she said this than the glimmer faded and the ashes floated back to the ground, gray and lifeless. She remembered what she had learned from copying the cook-book—how each ingredient had a role. Miss one and the dish was incomplete. She was missing a *dochka*'s power.

"What's my power?" Mary asked aloud.

But the only answer was her voice echoing against the oven walls.

Mary curled into a ball and lay down beside the pile of ingredients. Madame Z had put her life in Mary's hands. She had depended on her. Now Mary was failing her.

Their tale couldn't end like this. Mary had to find the words to change it.

She sat up, blinked back tears. Words were powerful. And so was a daughter's love.

Touching the tip of the feather to the ingredients again, she spoke in the same firm voice she remembered Madame Z using to command the clouds and the stars.

"I want my mother."

The feather sparked, and the ashes glittered and swirled around her. But this time, they didn't fade or fall. They grew brighter, forming ribbons of light. The ribbons wove themselves together into the shape of a woman, and then there was a flash. Mary covered her eyes.

Arms embraced her, bony yet strong. But it was the voice in her ear that was unmistakable.

"*Dochka.*"

THIRTY-SEVEN

MARY OPENED HER EYES. At the sight of the ancient face gazing tenderly down at her, she threw her arms around Madame Z. The witch sniffed. But Mary knew that Madame Z wasn't smelling her. She was trying not to cry.

"It's okay," Mary said. "You're home and so am I."

Madame Z cleared her throat, blinked the tears from her gray eyes. "Koshchey Bessmertny was right. A child takes everything from a parent. And yet in doing so, you have saved me. It's you who are powerful, *dochka*. You always have been."

Mary shook her head, but she couldn't help smiling. "We are a match, is all."

A knock made them both turn. Then the door of the *pech*

opened, and Jacob peered in as the hands burst into applause.

"They were getting impatient," he said with a grin. "Plus I thought I heard voices."

"I think we have cooked long enough," Madame Z declared.

Mary laughed. "Definitely done!" she said, scrambling out.

"You are absolutely the last child ever to occupy my oven," Madame Z remarked as she followed Mary.

"A relief to hear," Jacob said to one of the hands.

"The experience of being baked has eternally soured me on that particular dish," Madame Z said. Then she turned to face the kitchen door and sniffed. "But here comes someone who will never give up the hunt."

There was a scratching sound at the door.

"Yulik!" Mary cried, yanking it open.

The cat trotted in, carrying the *domovoi* in his mouth.

"You can drop me already!" the *domovoi* said. "It's a bit of an indignity to arrive this way, you know."

Yulik opened his mouth, and the *domovoi* dropped out onto the floor and ran to Jacob, who scooped him up and nestled him to his cheek.

"You didn't complain when I carried you halfway across the forest," Yulik said with a swat of his tail. "Truly, he's lucky I didn't chase him home. There is something mouselike about him."

The *domovoi*, however, only seemed to hear one word as he gently patted Jacob's cheek. "Can we go *home* now?"

"Our home," Jacob said firmly. "Yes."

"Put me back in my boot, then," the *domovoi* ordered. "You're out of danger now, so you can't see me anymore."

"But, Yulik, you fell from all the way—" Mary said.

"I told you I always land on my feet," the cat said proudly. Then he twined himself around his mistress. "Hello, Baba Yaga."

Madame Z scratched him under the chin. "Hello, rascal."

"I wasn't worried at all," he said.

"Why was that?" Madame Z asked.

"I knew Mary would save you."

Madame Z laughed. "Always trying to take credit, eh? You liked her from the start, saw she was special?"

"Of course," the cat said, continuing to twine through her legs. "But I also always thought you had it in you to be a *mamachka*."

Madame Z looked genuinely surprised, but Yulik just lay down and began cleaning his fur as if he hadn't said anything memorable at all.

"Mamachka," Mary repeated. It was the perfect word.

THIRTY-EIGHT

MARY PEEKED OUT FROM BEHIND THE CURTAIN. As usual, the rows of seats were packed. Every day, just before four, tourists flocked to the former boardinghouse. It was standing room only, and on many days not even that.

Mr. Kagan had been so overjoyed at Jacob's safe return that he decided to stop running from his grief and give his son a home. However, he still wanted to leave the boardinghouse, until Jacob explained to him about the *domovoi* and the real magic in Iris. At first Mr. Kagan didn't believe him, but then Jacob asked the boot to do a few tricks that even the old illusionist couldn't explain.

Within a few weeks, the show they put together—with Mr. Kagan as master of ceremonies—had become the hottest act in Iris. They were even able to buy the building from the Great DeBosco, who was short on cash and happy to sell, since his own act couldn't compete. Both Kagans had insisted that all the tenants remain. Together, they had converted the first floor into a theater.

Mary watched Dobbin warm up the crowd by charming Fanny out of a basket with a flute serenade. She could see Cassandra, the augur, selling tickets near the entrance. (After complaints of pickpockets, Professor Horatio St. John the head-bump reader, aka Harry, had been politely asked to work lights instead.)

The audience applauded as Dobbin wrapped Fanny around his shoulders and took several bows. As soon as he left the stage, the lights dimmed. The audience grew quiet with anticipation. A spotlight turned on, revealing the Illusionist Kagan, standing at center stage in front of the curtain.

"Ladies and gentlemen!" he announced. "You have come from far and wide to see a show the likes of which you can't even begin to imagine. Tonight, the impossible will be possible! Magic, my friends, truly exists here in Iris. And now, without further ado, I present—the Illusionists Jacob Kagan and Mary Hayes!"

The spotlight vanished as the curtain rose. Mary counted to three in the darkness, then pulled the Firebird feather out of her sleeve. The theater filled with an orange glow to oohs and aahs from the audience.

"Anyone thirsty?" Mary asked with a wave of her arm.

Jacob held up one of Rusalina's combs and began to hum loudly. Water spurted from its teeth onto the floor. Several tourists jumped to their feet at this extraordinary sight while others shouted for them to sit down.

During the commotion, Mary sent the dagger out into the audience, where it lifted the hat off the head of a man blocking the view and brought it to Jacob. The audience murmured in amazement.

"Why, thank you," Jacob said. He reached his hand inside the hat. "But what's this?"

He pulled out the old boot and set it on the ground. The boot impatiently tapped its toe.

"You want to dance?" Jacob asked it.

The boot did a jig and Jacob joined in. Mary took out the comb and hummed, creating puddles for them to splash in as they danced.

At last, Mary threw the Firebird feather up into the air. As it floated down, she clapped loudly. The audience gasped as a cage appeared in Jacob's hands and the feather fell into it. Mary threw a black cloth over it. As the lights came on, she pulled the cloth away. The feather was gone, but a yellow finch chirped inside.

The audience jumped to their feet, applauding loudly. "Bravo!" they cried.

Jacob and Mary bowed.

"I think Mr. Less is here," Jacob whispered.

Mary scanned the crowd until she spotted a man with a bushy beard standing off to the side, his shoes on backward. He was clapping as loudly as the rest of the audience. She flashed him a smile.

After several more standing ovations, they left the stage.

As usual, Jacob walked Mary to the theater's back door, where he helped her put on her coat and slipped the Firebird feather into her hand. "Are you sure you don't want to stay for supper?"

"Thanks," Mary said, "but my mother's waiting for me."

As many times now as she'd said these words, they still gave her a thrill.

"See you tomorrow, then?" Jacob said, with a tip of his top hat.

Mary smiled. "And all the days after."

It was their regular parting.

Snow was falling outside as Mary ran past Mr. Yu's Tea Shop, the Magic and Curiosity Shop, and the Voodoo Queen of New Orleans. She stopped to give a tap on Rusalina's window and a quick wave. The *rusalka's* business had boomed now that she was at peace and was no longer drowning her customers. She and Mary had become close friends. But today Mary was eager to get home, and after Rusalina waved back, she headed west out of town.

Winter had come to Iris, as it did every year in the human world, and with it the sun set early. But as the sky darkened, Mary felt no fear, only exhilaration for the long night ahead. She never knew what Madame Z had planned—a *peekneek* in the new, more spacious mortar; a ride around the earth on Sivka; or simply a quiet evening at home, reading to each other from the *Household Tales* after supper.

In the early-January twilight, Mary reached the gate. As she opened it and crossed through to the other side, the snow stopped falling. The trees were once again covered with red and orange leaves, the air crisp but not cold. After Koshchey's death and Madame Z's rebirth, she had restored the kingdom's eternal autumn—or, as she called it, the season of borders and in-betweens. It was the two-faced season she liked best.

The house, of course, was nowhere in sight. But Mary wasn't worried. This home always came back to her.

"Izba!" she shouted. "Turn your back to the forest and your face to me!"

The trees stretched their limbs like children waking up from a long night of sleep, revealing the house. It spun around excitedly on its chicken legs before stopping to face her. Madame Z had repaired the hole in its wall, using magic so strong that the seams of the repair weren't even visible. The stairs clacked down. Mary ran up them and placed her palm against the wooden bird, feeling its heartbeat against her hand as the door opened.

"Mamachka, I'm home!"

THE END/*KONETZ*

ACKNOWLEDGMENTS

MANY THANKS TO my editor, Rotem Moscovich, who helped me perform the magic of revision. Thanks as well to everyone at Disney, including Stephanie Lurie, copy editor Barbara Bakowski, and designer Marci Senders. I'm also grateful to Abby Ranger, who recognized the potential of this story. There is simply no better agent than Alex Glass.

I'd also like to express my gratitude to those who helped me with the research for this book. Weaver Victoria Armentrout shared her extensive knowledge of this ancient art. Russian speakers Alina Lisyanskaya and Danara Oldeeva helped check my Russian and English translations. Julia Ioffe also helped, and for those interested in learning more about Russian *pech* cooking, I highly recommend her *New Yorker* article "The Borscht Belt." Andreas Johns's book *Baba Yaga: The Ambiguous Mother and Witch of the Russian Folktale* served as an invaluable scholarly resource, one I recommend to those wishing to learn more about this fascinating folkloric figure.

I am particularly indebted to Lyda Phillips, my critique partner, and Julian E. Barnes, my husband, for their immense support and guidance during the writing of this book. Caitlin Ruthman and her family—Jared, Walter, and May—generously provided a weeklong writer's retreat in Maine, aided by Donna Barnes and her partner, Bob Griffith. Richard Barnes also generously gave his support. Thanks to Caroline Hickey, Erica Envall, Amie Hsia, and Ben Harder for their friendship, and my father, Ken Marsh, for his encouragement. I am also grateful to my mother, Elaine Milosh Marsh, for her generosity to me and my family as I wrote this book, and my late grandmother Natalia Milosh, for first introducing me to Russian cooking in her kitchen. Thanks to my son, Sasha, for his sharp insights as a six-year-old critic, and my daughter, Natalia, for inspiring Mary's fiercely loving spirit. Finally, a nod—or a rub under the chin—to my cat, Egg, the original Yulik.

ABOUT THE AUTHOR

KATHERINE MARSH is the Edgar Award–winning author of *The Night Tourist*; *The Twilight Prisoner*; and *Jepp, Who Defied the Stars*. She grew up in New York with her Russian grandmother, who lovingly prepared many of the dishes in this book. Katherine currently lives in Brussels, Belgium, with her husband and two children. Visit her online at www.katherinemarsh.com.